TAKEN by WEREWOLVES

THE LOST PRINCESS OF HOWLING SKY BOOK 1

KESTRA PINGREE

Living in Fantasy

Claim the princess, rule the world.

CHAPTER 1

SORISSA

*I*T WAS really happening. For the first time in my life, I was going to see the world outside of the woods. This was the best present Babaga could have given me for my eighteenth birthday. This meant everything. For years, I had been asking for this. This meant I was old enough to handle it. This meant she trusted me.

Babaga stayed a few paces behind me as I sped up. My boots touched the cold earth below with gentle taps as my lightweight tunic swished against my pants. The new blades of soft grass and fresh dirt absorbed the sound of my footfalls. The deciduous trees were emerging from their dormant state to welcome the first day of spring with a myriad of greens. I darted around small flowers offering splashes of color, and I smiled as the first warm breeze of the season wafted past me.

It wasn't long after that when the woods began to thin. I could see the rays of morning sunlight rise from my back and trickle through the canopy overhead. The trickle grew, morphing into wide rays. The lake was the only place inside of the woods where I could feel the sun like this without trees to obstruct it. I knew we were getting close to the edge.

Through the thin trunks of young trees and the gnarled trunks of old trees, I caught my first glimpse of the world outside. All my life, I wished for this. All my life, I envisioned what it would be like. Everything I thought I'd see was fueled by the fairytales Babaga read to me and taught me to read as she raised me. I imagined something beautiful. I imagined seeing a pack of werewolves, my own kind, for the first time and becoming the first werea to reach alpha. I imagined catching and befriending a vampire in the night to challenge their belief that they ruled it. I imagined humans working in the sun, farming the vegetables and fruits they lived off of while singing jovially.

The world I had imagined fractured as I neared the end of the woods. My face fell, but I didn't slow my pace. I sped up because this couldn't be true. I cleared the last of the trees and came to a dead stop.

This was not the world I wanted.

Everything was ashen and flat aside from bare mounds of earth and mountains in the distance. My boots left imprints in ground that was solid but coated with a thick layer of gray powder. Each step I took created a dust cloud that made me cough and gummed up my mouth. The sun was harsh as it continued to rise higher in the sky, highlighting nothing but a wasteland. There was nothing.

Suddenly, I wanted to flee. I wanted to go back to the woods. Why hadn't Babaga told me? Why did she let me believe those fairytales were real? It was obvious they were nothing but stories. I was the last werewolf. She was the last witch. Us and the animals in the woods. That was the world. Everything outside was hell.

"Babaga!" I pleaded as I turned to face my caregiver with tears in my eyes.

She raised a speckled, knobby finger and pointed past me as a harsh gust of wind stole away strands of her silver hair out from under the hood of her cloak.

I reluctantly looked behind me again, more toward my left to decipher what she could possibly be pointing at. Then I saw it, color beyond the ash. I squinted, trying to make out more, but a big cloud of dust was billowing toward us. I considered delving into my low reserves of moonlight to heighten my eyesight, but Babaga came up behind me and grabbed my arm, hard. I flinched at the pinching sensation.

"What's going on?" I asked.

"It's time for you to leave," she replied, "to live your destiny, perhaps, my sweet Sorissa. No. Princess Sorissa va Lupin of Howling Sky."

"W-what?" I balked. "What are you talking about, Babaga? Princess? Va Lupin? Howling Sky?"

I tried to pull out of Babaga's grasp, but she held fast. I'd break her hand if I struggled too much. She was old and frail. I was young and strong. I glanced at the large dust cloud rolling toward us. There was a horrible roaring sound accompanying it.

"We need to get back inside of the woods," I urged. "Whatever beast is inside of that cloud is dangerous."

"That beast is your escort."

"No," I growled, and anger consumed me. I didn't know what was going on. I didn't like how calm Babaga was acting because it made me wonder if we were in danger at all, but I was going to get an explanation from *inside* of the woods. I would carry Babaga back. I went to grab her, but she shied away from me, releasing my arm at the same time.

"Don't fight me," she warned. "I don't want to force you."

"What is that noise?!" I demanded as I covered my throbbing ears, squinted, and looked back at the dust storm. It was almost right in front of us now. It was moving so fast, about to consume us. Then the sound stopped. The dust cloud puffed out angrily and dissipated into the air. I blinked the burning sensation away from my eyes and saw a metal monster with four rectangular glowing eyes. It was still, sitting on top of fat blackish wheels that distantly resembled the wheels on Babaga's wooden wagon back at the cottage. It had glass fitted all around it similar to the windows back at the cottage too, but they were tinted, hard to see through. Maybe it wasn't alive at all…

I gasped and jumped back when three doors at its sides flung open. Babaga took my arm again. I thought it was to steady me, but I soon realized she did it to hold me in place. Three figures hopped out of the metal beast. They were big, intimidating. Though I had never seen a male of my own species, or anyone other than myself, I recognized them as just that; there was a subtle tingling in my nose that told me so. The only males I knew anything about were the animals in the woods—and the werewolves, vampires, and humans illustrated in the books Babaga had. At least I had that, but I ended up gawking at the strangers, overcome with curiosity rather than fear. Then it turned to nervousness. They were much older than me. Their skin was worn but not wrinkled. They were wearing strange clothes, crisp uniforms made of steel-gray material. They had only a small pop of yellow coming from an insignia on their right breasts; it depicted a paw.

"Babaga," I hissed, "I think I deserve some sort of explanation."

Her reply was to push me forward. I wasn't expecting this kind of strength from her withered form, but it wasn't physical strength. She used her magic to shove me like a powerful burst of wind. My dark curly hair fanned around me and into my face as I stumbled toward the males. The werewolf in front of the others caught my arm and grabbed my chin with his other hand. His skin was coarse. My jaw clenched when he forced my head from side to side, examining me. I tried to examine him in turn. It was hard to get a good look at him; however, I took note of his dark brown skin and the angry pink scar on his right cheek.

"Here she is," Babaga said, "as promised."

"I won't ask what the fuck she's wearing. It makes her look male," the werewolf holding me replied. "But she looks like she's in good shape."

The grit in his voice sent a shiver down my spine. His tone was so deep, like nothing I'd ever heard before. And he sounded hostile. I wanted to bare my teeth, but I couldn't muster the strength. My head was spinning. Babaga promised to give me to them?

My captor pressed his nose to my neck, and I yelped as his hot breath on my skin mingled with the scratchy sensation of his facial hair. I had enough. I squirmed and tried to bite him, but he was ready for me. He took a fistful of my long hair and jerked my head back so hard it burned. Stars burst in my vision, bright and white-hot.

"Put her in the roader," he said gruffly as he shoved me toward the other two werewolves.

"Wait," Babaga commanded. Her voice was deadly calm, quiet even, but these werewolves knew to obey. I desperately hoped she had changed her mind about sending me off with these males. I was dependent on her because I was too stupid to ration my moonlight reserves from the last full moon. I was almost drained at a time when I actually *needed* my power. I cursed Babaga for doing this to me. Yes, I was careless to use it without restraint, but I had never needed to care. I had never suspected she would betray me like this.

Betrayal. This was my first taste of it, the thread that would unravel my naivety.

The werewolves hesitated. They didn't let me go, but they didn't force me into their beast, this *roader*. They stood still as Babaga hobbled over to me. Her hands disappeared inside of her plain black cloak and surfaced again with a parcel. It was rectangular, covered in brown paper and tied with twine.

"This is for you, Princess Sorissa," Babaga murmured as she took my hands and placed the parcel in them. It felt like the weight of a book. A damn fairytale.

Tears collected in my eyes, and I tried to blink them away. "Let me stay," I begged. "Whatever I did wrong, I'll fix it. Please, Babaga. Please."

She knew she could overpower me if she didn't want me in her woods. She also knew I lacked the moonlight needed to get away from these males. I had already figured out that their base physical strength was greater than mine. I was outnumbered, unarmed. Babaga had taken my hunting knife. She did it on purpose so I would use up my moonlight. She knew I would rely on it more than ever. She did this to me on purpose. All of it was planned, and it stung like salt rubbed into a gaping wound.

I was too distressed to attempt slipping away. I might have been able to manage it. I knew how to fight. But where would I go? I didn't know this world. Would I be better off on my own, or would I be better off with the werewolves who wanted me for reasons I didn't understand?

I thought Babaga loved me.

"I'm sorry," Babaga said in barely a whisper. "This is out of my control. The deal was struck when I first took you in. You no longer have a place in these woods. You never belonged to me. I have fulfilled my end of the bargain, and the deed is done."

"What are you talking about?" I sobbed and clutched the little brown parcel, pressing it into my chest. I had still been hoping she would change her mind, but that hope was shattered with the finality of her words. Then she turned her back on me. No more words. No pity. I no longer existed to her.

"No!" I roared and dug into the small amount of moonlight I did have left. Blue lights exploded around me in angry moving tendrils. It was enough to power me up for a couple minutes or to maybe shift once for one minute. I didn't care. I just knew, right then, that I didn't want to go with these males.

My boots dug into the earth as the muscles in my legs coiled in preparation for a powerful leap. I expected to be soaring through the air, but I was grounded instead. Two of the males were on me, pressing me into the ashy earth and sending up a cloud of throat-tickling dust. I coughed and quickly let my moonlight settle into dormancy deep within me again. The werewolves on top of me were glowing brightly, different hues of blues dancing around them on full blast. They had much more moonlight to spare than I did. At that moment, I knew I wouldn't escape if I acted rashly. I would have to bide my time and wait. There was no powering my way out of this situation. That handicap was something I wasn't accustomed to, but I never lacked in determination.

I quieted down, allowing the males to pull me upright just to shove me into their metal beast. I was still holding on to that parcel Babaga gave me, tighter with each passing moment, almost melding it to my chest as I squished it against my breasts to avoid being touched. I couldn't move. The two werewolves slid in and sat at either side of me. They locked me into this firm leather seat, moonlight coming off them like flames licking at my skin, biting and burning. I shrunk further inside of myself, trying to escape the sensation. I had never known moonlight to be virulent, but I had never experienced anyone, aside from myself, wielding it. Moonlight was neutral when presented by the moon.

"Let's get the fuck out of here before the witch changes her mind," the male to my left barked. He was completely bald, no eyebrows or eyelashes either. His eyes were impossibly light, a bit unnerving. I wondered if his moonlight form was as naked and white as he appeared to be.

"Don't tell me what to do if you want to keep breathing, Den," the scarred one threatened as he sat in a seat located in front of me and to the left. He had a wheel at his hands and a key he stuck inside of the beast and turned. The roader roared to life, and I instinctively covered my ears just to hear my heart pounding inside of them like a hammer smashing rocks. This roar was metallic, not a breathing beast. A roader wasn't a living thing after all. It was technocraft. Babaga went off on a wild rant about that "unholy magic" once before when I was pestering her about leaving the woods. Did I ever regret that now.

"Seatbelts," the scarred one announced.

A small gasp escaped my lips as the dark-skinned male to my right snapped a restrictive bind around me and the roader began to move. At first, it was slow, rickety, as the scarred male turned the wheel in his hands and the roader looped around. He turned the wheel back, pressed his foot down hard, and the roader squealed ferociously as gray surrounded us, blocking out the world outside of the tinted windows. There was no coughing this time since the roader effectively kept all the dust outside, but I was glued to my seat as it picked up speed, escaping the cloud while leaving a swirling storm behind in its wake. Technocraft truly was monstrous.

I glanced at the werewolf to my right. He was staring out the window. His dark hair was shaved down to his scalp, and he had a solemn face. My captors mostly looked alike because of their similar age, uniforms, and in the way they were shaped. Flat chests, big arms, hard and chiseled faces. They looked a lot like the males in those fairytale illustrations. They looked like me too, but my arms were sticks in comparison. I was smaller, smoother, my face soft.

I looked past him to watch the world zooming by through a window. We were leaving gray behind and approaching color. That had to be a good thing, at least.

"Where are we going?" I asked.

"Paws Peak," the scarred male in front replied, "back to your own kind." His eyes were focused on the world in front of him. It seemed he was in complete control of the roader, using his hands and feet in tandem.

"I can't believe you were in those godsforsaken woods with that witch for eighteen years," Den, the bald one to my left, commented. "I wonder if crazy is catching." He was staring at me with his unsettlingly pale eyes. There was a strange heat in them for a moment. Then they widened impossibly, and he shimmied as far away from me as he could get, his back against the door.

"Den!" the scarred male growled. "Treat the Lost Princess with some fucking respect. She'll be your queen one day."

"I'm not a princess," I retorted. "And I wasn't lost until you males came and stole me away from my woods."

The scarred male laughed boisterously, and the dark-skinned male to my right cracked a sinister grin.

The scarred one quieted down a moment later and cleared his throat.

"Do you know anything at all, Princess Sorissa?" he asked. His tone was condescending.

I slumped into my seat and brushed my fingers across the parcel Babaga gave me. I wasn't sure if it was reassuring or if it made everything happening feel more real, more irrevocable.

"At least she doesn't speak in a witch tongue," Den said.

"Last warning," the scarred one stated. Then he glanced at me through a mirror dangling front and center inside of the roader. "Everything will make sense when we get you back to Paws Peak, Princess. I sure as hell ain't gonna waste my breath on an explanation."

I bit my lower lip as I tried to keep my emotions under control. I was seething with anger. I didn't like these males one bit. Babaga didn't want me. This world was not the one I pictured or the one depicted in those books of fairytales. I was on my own for the first time in my life. I had only myself to count on and no better plan than to go along quietly until the next full moon appeared in three nights so I could recharge. Then these males would know exactly what I was capable of.

CHAPTER 2

RODRICK

*T*HE BADLANDS made my skin crawl. They weren't places any sane creature would tread. We were four guys protected inside of a roader, but it didn't ease the tension. Tension was more or less the constant state of Phantom Fangs, so it wasn't all because of the badlands; however, the stretch of gray nothing that spanned miles and miles was a grim reminder of how Prime was almost destroyed one hundred and fifty-six years ago. The Hellfire Strike was the reason why the world was the way it was now. It was a dark point in rebel history, but it did make the playing field more even—at the cost of the last human kingdom: Glory Valley.

The world was basically a mess, whittled down to

almost nothing, and yet the Prime War, war since the beginning of time, continued. It would keep going until one of three—humans, werewolves, or vampires—finally ruled all. It looked like werewolves were winning. Werewolves and vampires thought humans were out of the running, but they were wrong. Glory Valley had fallen, but a branch of survivors, rebels, founded Freedom. It was small, hidden and unknown by most, but the three main parties of this war continued to be *major* players, even if the rebels were only pulling strings from the shadows and the vampires were currently in hiding. The playing field would change again very soon.

Sooty particles bloomed around our roader when Todd brought the vehicle to a stop just outside of the Witch Woods. An involuntary shiver racked my body as the dust cleared enough to reveal the small and large trees coming out of their dormant winter state. They were traces of green, life, right on the border of death.

As foreboding as the badlands were, the Witch Woods were worse. They were an outright taboo, the one place that survived the fallout of the Hellfire Strike even though it was well within the strike zone. The woods should have been obliterated like everything else around them. Messing with ghosts and/or witches was not my thing. They were a whole other beast, outliers of the Prime War because they were hardly of Prime in the first place. Anyone who entered those woods would be cursed. I wondered if the same rules applied to the Lost Princess of Howling Sky or if she was exempt.

"Don't everyone get out at once," Caspian commented when none of us made a move to leave the roader. The space wasn't cramped exactly, but since we couldn't stand each other, we usually deserted the thing as soon as possible.

"Scared?" he asked when he turned his head back from the front passenger seat to look at me and Aerre with his almost black dark brown eyes. It wasn't like Caspian to tease on a mission. He became the no-nonsense type. Clearly, he was the one who was "scared."

"I don't see the Paws Peak scouts," Aerre said, his blue eyes scanning the area in one quick sweep.

"Because we're late. We probably lost the Lost Princess," I replied sardonically as I scratched at my short beard.

Todd, the pasty runt always wearing a black beanie, scowled from the driver's seat and kicked open his door. He hesitated a moment before taking the first step into the badlands.

"No one's blaming you, Todd," Caspian called after him. "I should have accounted for delays. We should have left earlier."

"So our roader broke down on the biggest mission

since Phantom Fangs was formed. No big deal," I said. Then I kicked open the door to my left and joined Todd on ashy earth. A puff of dust escaped the impact of my boots, and I resisted the urge to cough. Gods, there was a lot of powder. Good thing there was solid ground somewhere underneath it all. Walk out here for long, and we'd turn the same color as the rest of the badlands. My boots were the first casualty.

"Shut up, Rodrick," Aerre growled at me as he emerged on the other side of the roader. Hey, at least he called me by my name instead of saying asshole or something. That was a big step up for him. Then again, he had been unusually quiet instead of heckling me this whole trip.

The Lost Princess of Howling Sky fucked up our dynamics because she meant a change, the biggest change since the Hellfire Strike—if the legend was true. Would she mend the world or obliterate it? Once she became common knowledge, everyone would want their hands on her. Paws Peak would have had her all to themselves right now if we hadn't listened in on a private conversation about the Lost Princess herself. Everyone thought she was *lost*. But the Witch of Witch Woods had her all along. She kept her for eighteen years, hidden from the rest of the world, until she decided to hand her over to Paws Peak. Why Paws Peak?

Caspian was the last to leave the roader. I ignored everyone and started investigating the area. I was looking for tracks. With the way the wind acted up around here, blowing one way and then the other, creating little dust devils every now and then, I wasn't holding out much hope for clues.

I looked back at the tracks our roader left behind. It was a heavy metal vehicle with deep treads on the tires. Unlike my footprints, the roader seemed to dig down into hard yet moldable clay, way past the ever-changing ashy top. It left an indent that dust wasn't quick to hide.

"Interesting," I muttered to myself.

Then I walked up to the edge of the woods. I stayed on the dusty gray ground because I wasn't interested in getting cursed. There was a blatant line that separated the badlands from the Witch Woods. If I took one step, I could have stood in soft blades of new grass. They didn't have a touch of gray on them. Here was a witchcraft barrier that worked like a glass case to keep the tainted badlands out of the woods. That was the best I could come up with anyway. I didn't know a damn thing about witchcraft, and I didn't care to.

I walked away from the woods and scanned the expanse of gray. The Paws Peak scouts hadn't passed through Wolf Bridge to get here, so they must have taken the old bridge in the Glory Valley ruins, not the safest idea, but really their only option. Todd had kept that in mind when he drove us here, so I didn't think we'd be too far away from where they had arrived; the runt was good with shit like that. With that in mind, I gathered my bearings and walked south. The sun was rising higher into the sky, and it burned against my brown skin. This place was like a desert. I didn't usually have issues with the sun, unlike Todd, but the badlands made everything harsher.

Then I saw them: roader tracks. The dust had tried to cover them up, but they were imprinted on the earth just like our own.

"Here's our confirmation!" I shouted at the others. There were even remnants of tracks left by several pairs of shoes. Three males and two females from the look of it. It seemed there had been a bit of a scuffle.

As the rest of Phantom Fangs gathered around, Caspian sighed and said, "We missed her."

"I guess she's real," Acrre murmured.

"I doubt we're too far behind," I informed.

"To Paws Peak then. We can still get her before she's sealed by the Mate Claim," Caspian concluded and led the way back to our roader. Todd didn't waste any time starting up the engine and getting us rolling.

"Are we going to be able to sneak inside of Paws Peak?" Caspian asked.

"Yes," Todd replied. "I'm tuned to their wavelength.

I'll hack the spires and bring down their security system. Should get in and out without detection, but I haven't tested it."

"Good enough. It isn't ideal, but the king wants us to retrieve the Lost Princess no matter the cost. Since we're already behind, we're not going to get there before they do. That means stealth. We're going to sneak in and sneak out with the Lost Princess. Got it?" He looked right at me. "No engaging the enemy. We can't afford to alert Paws Peak."

"Maybe we should head back through Wolf Bridge and call on your father's army then," I suggested. "Claim the Lost Princess and Paws Peak in one trip."

"Maybe we should just leave this asshole behind," Aerre joined in. Now he was starting to sound more like himself.

"It makes the most sense," I said simply. "Doing this in two trips now is a waste of time. The King of Wolf Bridge would agree with me. So what if she's sealed by the Mate Claim? You'll just have to kill the werewolf who made the claim."

"We're not doing that," Caspian stated. "Either of those things." He glanced at Aerre. "We're not going back to Wolf Bridge, and we're bringing Rodrick. I don't want to make the princess stay with those maneaters any longer than she has to. We're going to get her before she's sealed by the Mate Claim. We're going to pass through the Glory Valley ruins, and we're going to rescue her."

Rescue. Only an oddball werewolf like Caspian would say that word and mean it. I knew Caspian had no love for the maneaters in Paws Peak, but he was also at odds with the shields in Wolf Bridge. He more closely aligned himself as a shield, "protector of humans and peacekeeper," but he marched to the beat of his own drum. If werewolves weren't the enemy, I might have tried to get him to join the rebels. But a werewolf was a werewolf just like a tethered was a tethered. Though I was more werewolf than human now, I would always be human first.

"We'll be quiet. Sneak in, get the princess, and sneak out," I reiterated. And I meant it. Brawling was my specialty, but she was my top priority. Causing trouble wouldn't benefit the rebels. I needed to get the Lost Princess out of Paws Peak and safely back to Wolf Bridge, where I'd have a much easier time handing her off. With her, humans, rebels and complacents alike, would have a priceless set piece.

Like I said, big changes were ahead.

But my path was clear black or white because there was no point floundering in muddled grays. Floundering was what made this team and Aerre, a fellow tethered, black, my enemy. It was simple—as was my decision to become tethered to the Phantom Prince and therefore Phantom Fangs. Luckily for me, Caspian was very trusting and gave me, "a no-good agitator" in Aerre's words, the opportunity. Thanks to that, the alpha-omega sort of bond I shared with the Phantom Prince hadn't really gotten in my way yet—much to Aerre's chagrin.

I glanced to my right to see Aerre glaring at me with those lake-blue eyes of his. I wondered how many ladies he had won with his pretty-boy looks, those eyes and that long blond hair meticulously braided back against his skull, before he became tethered to Caspian. His personality really could have used some work, though. He was my only problem, my only obstacle. Caspian and Todd didn't pay me any mind, but it was Aerre's mission in life to expose me. He didn't know what I was doing. He didn't have proof that I was still in contact with rebels, but he was suspicious as hell and ironically right. I grinned back at him just to make him sneer.

I couldn't ignore him any longer. If Aerre kept on like this, I would be forced to put him down quietly.

CHAPTER 3

SORISSA

*T*HE WORLD close to me blurred by while the grass fields, winding river, and tall mountains in the distance moved by slowly. I was used to the blur because the speeds I attained while running in my moonlight form created the same effect, but I wasn't used to seeing things so far away. The trees were so dense in the woods I never saw outside of them. I never saw a hint of lifeless gray before today.

Aside from the constant growl emanating from the roader, it was silent. I would have had my face plastered to a window if I had not been seated in between two of the male werewolves who took me away from my home. Not one of us had spoken since the scarred one in front told me he would give me no explanations, that I'd understand everything I needed to once we reached "Paws Peak." I decided I wasn't going to beg these louts for anything. That left silence.

Silence wasn't so bad. We had left the hellish landscape of gray behind in a hurry, which I was grateful for, and started following an overgrown path in a grassy field with budding flowers of every color imaginable. Even though the windows were closed and I was shut inside of this beast created by technocraft, I swore I could feel a difference in the quality of air. It became easier to breathe. Blue skies spanned as far as I could see with puffy clouds floating by at random intervals. *This* place was beautiful. This was much closer to the world I had imagined. I still didn't enjoy my company, but this gave me some hope. Babaga hadn't completely forsaken me. Maybe she hadn't forsaken me at all. This was sort of what I had asked for, wasn't it? Why didn't it feel like a victory then?

I ran my hands along the brown paper of that parcel Babaga had given me. I considered opening it, but I wasn't sure I wanted to see what was inside. I had a hunch it was one of the many fairytales we read together. Those books were the only reason I knew anything outside of the woods, the only reason I knew what a mountain was called. I wondered what kind of a shoddy education it would turn out to be. Babaga was intent on teaching me many things, including reading and writing, but there were also many things she was intent on hiding. Babaga made me feel smart. Being outside of my woods made me feel dumb.

I was allowed a moment to stretch my legs in the field when the alpha of the trio called for a break. It wasn't a long one, maybe five minutes, and we had to fill up our stomachs with meat during that time limit as well. Then I was rounded up and forced into that middle seat of the roader again. I wondered how far away Paws Peak was. We had already covered miles worth of distance.

I continued to watch the world from the window. The river got bigger and bigger as we neared it, angry white foam frothing in the wild current. I hadn't realized before we got close enough, but the water was actually deep inside of a gulch. It was so wild it was constantly splashing above its container. I had never seen anything like it. The lake back in the woods was always still and calm. Not even the storms could do much to disrupt it because the trees around it always stood guard, blocking raging winds and downpours.

Along with river rapids, I started seeing chunks of rock and old ruins that were likely buildings of some sort at one point in time. They were overgrown with grass, broken down and brittle.

"What is this place?" I asked. I was tired of silence, and I was just putting the question out there. I figured maybe one of them would feel up to chatting. If not, I only wasted a breath.

"I told you I wasn't going to answer any questions, Princess," the werewolf in front droned.

"Because silence is so interesting," I deadpanned. "Maybe you could tell me your names, because I only know one."

The dark-skinned werewolf to my right snickered and Den, the pale, hairless one to my left, laughed nervously.

"Truth be told, talking to you, being anywhere near you, is a bit fucking difficult," the scarred one said.

"What does that mean?" I asked.

The two beside me laughed again, one full of confidence, the other one a jittery mess of nerves.

My heart rate sped up as we neared a bridge. It was in the same crumbling state as the rest of the buildings around here, and it led to a land of rubble. This was a place some species lived once—werewolves, vampires, or humans—and it had been demolished. There was a literal mountain of it across the bridge. It must have been a kingdom—if the half-truths I learned from Babaga really meant anything out here. Castles, towers, houses all built closely together within nearly impenetrable walls. I saw illustrations of kingdoms standing, not falling.

"What I mean," the scarred one said calmly, "is that wereas are rare and every werewolf aches for one to claim."

I didn't say any more on the topic. I was too worried about the upcoming bridge. "We're not going over that," I said.

"We are," he replied and sent power to his leg, smashing a pedal that made the roader roar louder as it sped up.

I screamed and held fast to Babaga's parcel when we hit the bridge because the middle section was missing. I was sure we were going to fall into the gulch and get swept away by the rushing water. But the roader jumped over the gap. It landed with a hard thud that made us all bounce up and down. It was then I realized the importance of the "seatbelt" they strapped around me. I would have hit my head on the metal above if I hadn't been strapped in.

My chest was bobbing up and down with latent shock, but I took deep breaths and calmed myself when I could look behind me and see the bridge shrinking down a ripped-up cobblestone road. We survived.

I caught Den staring at my chest and reflexively covered myself with Babaga's parcel. I wondered what could have possibly been so interesting that he would stare at my chest like that. Did he want to rip into me and carve out my heart? His colorless eyes made me think so. Maybe these werewolves were cannibals.

"What do you think her breasts would look like if she wasn't wearing that baggy tunic?" he asked.

"Shut. Up," the scarred one bellowed. "I will stop this roader and rip out your fucking throat, Den. Get a grip."

"I think you're the one who needs to get a grip."

"Den," the dark-skinned werewolf warned. "What happened to her being cursed by a witch and catching?"

"Human females aren't enough." Den panted. "I can't take it anymore. I only want to touch her."

I curled into myself, trying to make myself smaller. I would have leaned away from Den's lasciviously wiggling fingers, but there was another werewolf right beside me. I didn't know what he was planning to do, but it made me think about running again—even if my chances were low. If I had been fully charged with moonlight, none of this would have been an issue. Because I wasn't, I had to play this waiting game, search for an opportunity, and take it when the time was right. But what would I have to withstand until then?

An ear-piercing squeal filled the air, and I was thrown back into my seat. It knocked the air out of my lungs, and I hit my head on the leather headrest. It wouldn't have been a big deal if I had been prepared, but the suddenness was jarring. When I looked up, Den was dragged out of the roader by his alpha, who immediately started pummeling him into the grass among the rubble. My jaw dropped open as I watched. I had never seen blatant violence like this. I hunted for food. I challenged bears in the forest to brawls, but I never killed unless I had to. The scarred werewolf looked like he was going to kill Den, and Den was his subordinate, his pack, friend, or family. Wasn't he? The thing that bothered me the most was the fact that Den was not fighting back. It all felt… wrong.

"Stupid bastard," the werewolf still seated beside me muttered.

"Why?" I whispered.

"Because he can't talk about you that way. You're his princess." It seemed the least chatty of the three was willing to talk to me now. I wondered if it was to distract me from the horrible bone-cracking sounds to my left. I turned my eyes away because the sight of so much blood was unsettling. I didn't know if the anger in my chest meant I wanted to jump in and stop it, or if it was just anger over my own confusion.

"What was your alpha talking about before?" I asked.

"Wereas are rare, our females, you. The number of cubs born male vastly outweigh those born female."

"So?"

"So most of us don't have mates." He smirked, and I decided I didn't like the way he was looking at me either. "I won't touch you though. I'm not stupid. You're a werea way out of my league. Messing with you would just get me killed." He glanced at Den as if to restate what he just said.

I thought about mates and how mates led to cubs. A werewolf claimed a werea and then they were mates. I didn't know what claiming entailed, but I knew what made a cub: sex. I knew the general mechanics of it because of the animals I saw in the woods, but I hadn't ever given it much thought. It appeared Den was either thinking about claiming me or sex and that was what brought on his punishment.

"Why am I here?" I asked.

"Because King George ve Paz of Paws Peak sent for you."

I was exasperated. "But what does that *mean*?"

"Enough talking," the scarred one growled as he shoved Den all bloody, black, and blue into the seat next to his at the front of the roader. "Nash, don't let her jump out of the side. Keep her in the middle."

"You got it," the werewolf next to me replied as the roader roared to life and moved again.

Nash. I finally learned another name. By the time we got to Paws Peak, I might know their alpha's name too.

Not that it mattered. I didn't plan on remembering them for long.

CHAPTER 4

SORISSA

S ILENCE ENSUED. Most of the day was spent in the roader with breaks here and there. Just like we werewolves needed meat, the roader had to be fed gasoline, which they kept in canisters tied to its back. There wasn't a peep out of Den even though it was obvious he was in intense pain. I was certain he had at least one broken bone on top of all his cuts and bruises. I wondered why he didn't use moonlight to heal himself. It was possible he didn't have much to spare, or maybe it was because his alpha wouldn't have been pleased.

If I had found an animal in his state back in the woods, I would have killed it out of mercy and out of my own need for sustenance. I didn't know what I would have done if *he* had been the one I found in the forest.

Would I have killed him out of mercy or tried to heal him? Did it make a difference because he was the same species as me? As it was, knowing what I knew about Den, I would have opted for that mercy killing. I didn't like him, but his suffering seemed unfair.

We passed fields and trees, a vast nature scenery, as the roader climbed mountains. There were still a few spots of snow on top of the higher peaks, but most of the mountains looked like the valley we had come from: green grass and colorful, blooming flowers. The trees, however, resembled my woods. The thought made my chest ache. The sun was beginning to set, casting long shadows with all the mountains cutting through its light. I had almost been away from the woods for an entire day. I wondered if I would ever see them again.

The dirt trail the roader followed continued to wind up the mountains. The sun would duck behind cliffs and reemerge as we climbed higher and trees became thicker. It felt like a race: reach the highest peak before the sun sets.

We rounded another mountain, and I saw a big stone wall. It was the first sign of a kingdom, a standing kingdom. We headed right for the meshed iron gate. I deduced that we had, at last, arrived at Paws Peak. I squeezed Babaga's parcel, feeling the brown paper about to tear under the pressure. I relaxed my anxious fingers, not ready to see its contents. I twisted my fingers in the twine to distract myself from the anxiety moving into my chest. We were going inside of fortified walls. It would be a lot harder to escape from inside. Did I really want to wait this out? Or did I want to do everything I could to escape even without moonlight to assist me? And where would I go? I didn't have a home anymore. I could survive in the wild. I knew how to find food, but that wasn't what I wanted either. I didn't want to be alone.

The roader stopped in front of the gate that slowly began lifting off the ground. There were werewolves in armor on top of parapets, staring down at us. I had to crane my neck and shift toward the window near the empty seat to my left to see them because the walls were so tall. Each stone used to build the wall was as gray as the land outside of my woods. I didn't like that. When the path was clear, the roader moved forward again.

It was just like those fairytales. Inside of the walls was a town: brick houses bundled together, stone-paved streets crisscrossing, and, of course, the denizens of the kingdom. They were bustling about. Some were carrying baskets. Others were lighting lamps. Then I realized something. These individuals didn't move like the three werewolves with me. They weren't as big. There was something about the way they were built. Maybe their eyes weren't as intense. I couldn't pinpoint what it was, but my eyes knew the difference. These people were humans. I didn't know werewolves and humans lived together. Now that I thought about it, the fairytales I read back in the woods never showed the three species mingling. That seemed strange because why wouldn't werewolves, humans, and vampires all be seen in the same place if they lived in the same world?

I flinched when bright lights exploded into the darkness. They were coming from tall poles in the distance. It wasn't the same quality of light as the gas lamps in the area. They were much brighter.

"What are those?" I asked. "And why are there so many humans here?"

The scarred alpha grunted. "No questions, Princess. Not part of my job to answer your damn questions." He was in a worse mood ever since he laid into Den, so I fell silent.

Was it more technocraft? That was the only explanation I had. They did have this monstrous metal beast called a roader. Why couldn't they have magical lights too?

I spotted more werewolves in steel-gray uniforms as the roader took us forward. These ones were gathering around a woman, a female human who was skin and bones. One yanked a weaved basket from her arms, spilling some vegetables onto the ground. I could hear him bellow through the growl of the roader. "Equal portions! No more and no less unless you've been picked by the king to fatten up! Laborers don't need fat!"

I frowned. Did this werewolf, this soldier, view this human as his prey? That would have been like me thinking of Babaga as my prey—which I couldn't. We were too alike. She was practically my mother. She didn't have a moonlight form, so we were technically different, but there was much more that was the same. Thinking of her as something other than someone I loved made my stomach churn. I didn't like this exchange. I didn't like Paws Peak or the werewolves that brought me here.

This wasn't the world I wanted. Everything I thought I knew about the world outside was skewed. It was like Babaga only wanted me to know the good things about this world, the kind things. But what good and kind things? I hadn't seen a trace of them. Fairytales were nothing but fairytales after all.

I flinched when one of the uniformed werewolves took out his whip and slashed the woman hard across the back. The roader drove by without any compassion, and the woman's screams rang in my ears as we neared the largest building I had seen yet: the castle. It had multiple towers all built in semi-reflective stones that almost looked more like metal. There were millions of windows, and it glowed in the oncoming night. The bright lights cast by the tall poles created abstract shapes across its surface as it reflected their lights as well as the last reds and oranges of the dying sun. It was spectacular. I would have called it beautiful if it hadn't looked like the maw of hell.

As we got closer to the castle, the scarred alpha directed the roader to what sort of resembled a stable. It was blocked off with a big gate that seemed to open magically, revealing a shelter with a wide smooth floor. There were other roaders sleeping quietly inside. When our roader rolled up next to one of the others and its roaring died, the scarred alpha spoke, "Everybody out."

I waited to get out until Nash got out. I didn't want to risk any conflict—not yet.

"If you don't want any strong-arming, behave yourself," the alpha told me when I got out.

I hadn't caused any trouble since we were just outside of Babaga's woods. I thought I was doing well at avoiding suspicion. Maybe that wasn't the case, or maybe he simply didn't want to deal with any more shenanigans and felt a warning was in order. Whatever it was, I nodded submissively to play along. I continued to hold Babaga's parcel in my hands, my one belonging, my only piece of home—aside from my clothes.

"Keep up, Princess." The scarred alpha commanded. Every bone in my body wanted to rebel, but I needed to be patient. I kept reminding myself of that fact.

Nash shoved me forward and stayed behind me as the alpha led the way. Den walked with us, but he stood apart, the visible outcast in the group. He limped with each step he took as we made our way out of the shelter, but he kept up and didn't complain.

The shelter was close to the castle, so it didn't take us long to get to a small side-door entrance. A couple of soldiers were marching around the perimeter and stared at me as we entered. It was hunger. The way everyone looked at me so far was with hunger. Was I their prey too? Had I walked willingly to my death? I might have thought that if they hadn't kept calling me "Princess" and praising my "rarity." I was highly valued, and that had to be somehow in my favor.

I thought the kingdom was magnificent in a terrifying kind of way, but the castle was isolated in its own category of wonder. As soon as I stepped foot inside, I spotted several objects similar to gas lamps. One was close to me. It was attached to the wall and emitted the same kind of light I saw from those tall poles outside. I wondered if it would burn me if I touched it, but it wasn't flickering like any fire I had ever seen. It had a constant glow that stayed the same intensity no matter how long I stared at it. I looked away when it started to hurt my eyes.

"C'mon," Nash growled, nudging me forward with

his elbow. "It's a fucking lightbulb."

"Lightbulb?" I asked.

He nudged me again, and I had to remind myself of the word I was really starting to hate: patience.

I stared at the floor that was polished to the point it reflected my face like a metal mirror as we passed through long and brightly lit corridors. There was a little variation from the constant gray in the form of a light-colored pearly material. It lined windows and was pieced together to create murals of the moon on the floor near those same windows. It was harsh and angry due to the red sunset. It looked like it would reflect any color cast on it, but the red was fitting. This castle was the most jarring thing I had encountered yet. It outdid the ash land outside of the woods too. It gave me a bad gut feeling, and I had a habit of trusting my gut.

"In here," a soldier said, gesturing to a gray metal door as the alpha leading my group stopped abruptly. "The king wants her washed up and made presentable before he and Prince Charles meet her. A maid is in there waiting."

"Understood."

Nash nudged me again. This time I couldn't help it, I whipped around and bared my teeth at him. "Stop pushing me. I've done everything you've told me to."

"Except stay quiet," the scarred alpha said with a

snarl. He grabbed my arm and pulled me inside of the room. His fingers felt like they were digging into my flesh, and he nearly ripped my arm from its socket. It hurt, but I didn't yelp. I refused to show this brute any weakness. Then he pushed me into a wall, breathing hot air on my neck as he leaned down. My skin crawled and goosebumps rose to the surface as he pressed his hard body against mine and placed his mouth on my ear.

"Bitches shouldn't speak," he said. "They should only do as they're told. Princess or not. The only reason I don't put you in your place right here and now is because you are Princess Sorissa va Lupin of Howling Sky, the Moonlight Child blessed by Lureine. Soon you will become the only princess Paws Peak has, and you have my respect, the entire kingdom's respect, but it'd be fucking wise of you to remember that our king and his favorite son will not be so lenient when it comes to your insolence."

He moved away after that, releasing me from the wall. I watched him, unblinking. I was prepared for whatever he might do next, but all he did was turn around and usher Den and Nash outside as he slammed the door behind them.

"What about that parcel the witch gave her? It could be dangerous," Nash said from outside.

"Fuck that! I can't take another second near her or I'm going to lose my mind. It's fine. The parcel is fine.

Now, move your ass!"

"You'd probably get cursed if you took it anyway. Right, Den?"

I held the parcel close to my chest, anticipating their return, but their footsteps faded away from the door. I let out a pent-up breath and inspected the room. A human female stood previously unnoticed by a wall, wide-eyed and pale. Her trembling hands were clasped in front of her dingy dress and her black hair was mostly hidden by a bonnet.

"Hello," I said.

Her lips trembled, and she gave a jerky nod of her head. She turned to a large closet she could walk inside and returned with a dress the same bright yellow as the paw-print insignia the soldiers wore on their uniforms. She laid it out on a utilitarian bed which I might have appreciated if it hadn't looked so metallic. The woman held out her hand to me after that. Her shaking seemed to have subsided some.

"We need to get you cleaned," she said.

"I'm not dirty," I protested. "I took a bath last night."

She looked me up and down, frowning. "The king insists."

"I don't care if the king insists."

She started shaking again. "Please, Princess."

"What's your name?"

"Please, Princess," she repeated.

I thought about the woman getting whipped by a werewolf soldier in the town outside of the castle. I didn't want the same to happen to this woman because of my stubbornness. She wasn't trying to harm me. Besides, patience was in order. My worst enemy.

"As you wish," I said.

This was what the woman wanted to hear. The words were like a cure for her shaking. She took me into another large room attached to this one. There was a bath in the center, gray and metal like some sort of trophy or centerpiece. She moved to a metal pole with a bulbous head that pointed into the bath and turned a handle. Water sprayed out of the head as if it were a metal raincloud. It was mesmerizing.

The woman touched the water and said, "The temperature is good. It's all set for you. We must hurry. The king wants to see you as quickly as possible."

"I'll be back," I said and turned tail before she could stop me.

I searched in the big main room for a place to hide my parcel. I didn't want it to be seen by the king after what I heard outside between the werewolves that brought me here. I picked a place haphazardly because I didn't trust anyone else to know where the parcel was being kept, certainly not this timid woman. There was a space in between the bed and the nightstand where my parcel slipped in perfectly. It worked, but if someone was looking, they'd find it easily enough. I just hoped no one would be looking and that it'd be forgotten about. Out of sight, out of mind. I also hoped I'd be returning to this room so I could retrieve it later.

"Princess?" the woman poked her head into the bedroom as I sat on the edge of the bed and pulled off my boots, pretending that was what I had intended all along. "No need for that. I'll take your clothes. Come into the bathroom so you can jump right in. We don't want you to catch a cold."

That worked out well enough, but I knew this woman had no interest in my parcel. She was too busy going on about this order the king gave her to make me "clean" and "presentable."

I stripped out of my clothes at the edge of the tub. I was hesitant to step into the downpour, but I got in and found the water warm and pleasant. Babaga lived off the bare necessities, and none of the books we read mentioned anything about technocraft. This was all new to me, and I wanted to understand how it all worked.

As the water flattened my curly hair and the dark strands clung to my shoulders, back, and breasts in a hug, I dared to close my eyes. Two nights. If I got through this night and the next, the third would be a full moon. I would have power again when my moonlight reserves were restored—if they were allowed to be restored. Maybe I should have taken a chance on my terrible odds. Maybe I had sealed my fate by entering this kingdom. Paws Peak was as big of a prison as Babaga's woods.

No. It was much worse. Nothing like my woods at all. I had a small amount of moonlight left. But what good was it now? Patience was not my friend.

CHAPTER 5

AERRE

WE WEREN'T moving fast enough. The idea of infiltrating Paws Peak to take back the princess was a pain, but I knew we'd manage. What I didn't know was if we'd manage it before she was sealed by the Mate Claim. Would we need to hunt down the werewolf who claimed her too? It would be one of the princes, meaning more trouble. I wondered if we'd be able to do any of it without pinning Wolf Bridge as the culprit. I knew a worse war than I had ever seen in my lifetime was on the horizon because the Lost Princess existed. But I didn't want to bring those problems to Wolf Bridge. I wanted my sister and mother safe.

The world was about to fall apart, and it was all because of a damn werewolf princess. As if I didn't need another reason to despise those monsters.

I glared at Rodrick, who was leaning against the metal door on his side of the roader, head resting on the window as the vehicle bumped along narrow passages through the trees and growing mountains. We had to chart our own course since taking the paved road all the way to Paws Peak was only asking for trouble. We had to go incognito.

"We aren't moving fast enough," I announced.

"I'm moving as fast as I can without rolling us over," Todd said testily and shifted gears once again. His white hand was sweaty against the black leather steering wheel, veins popping out in a distinct blue. It was a bit warm in here, but he was probably mostly nervous since we were moving slower now because of the terrain and because we didn't want the roar of the engine to announce our presence.

"The princess is going to be sealed by the Mate Claim," I muttered. "Prince Charles will be the one to claim her, according to that conversation Todd recorded with his bugs a week ago. What are we going to do about Prince Charles? Kill him? We're at a stalemate with Paws Peak, with pretty much everyone, and now we're going to incite their wrath?"

"We're going in *quietly*, Aerre," Caspian chastised as he brushed the dark curls of his unruly hair away from his eyes. "But yeah. I'm not going to lie. This stalemate is coming to an end one way or another. It would be that way whether *we*, Phantom Fangs, did something or not."

I knew that, but it didn't make the painful twisting in my gut feel any better. I believed in Caspian. I thought he had the power to change this world, but I didn't want change to come at the cost of my family's safety. I wanted change to guarantee their safety. That was out of my hands, though.

I knew Caspian getting the princess first was the only decision we could make. If anyone else got her, that would mean certain doom. So I did my best to swallow my fears and uncertainties. Caspian hadn't led me astray yet. Werewolf or not, friend or not, I trusted the Phantom Prince with my life. I hated werewolves. I was sure that would never change after what happened to my sister, but I became tethered to Caspian and joined his team because he was my best option. He kept my family safe.

"Damn it," I muttered. "What if we can't handle the Lost Princess? The legend says she has great power."

"There's four of us and one of her," Caspian replied.

I rolled my eyes.

"And she's a werea," Rodrick commented with an irritating grin, flashing white teeth from within a short brown beard that was kept meticulously trimmed. "I've met few men and ain't ever met a woman yet who can best me physically."

"She surpasses physical strength if the rumors are true, you ox. She's supposedly like a container for moonlight, and you know how powerful moonlight can make a werewolf—even females."

Rodrick gave this lazy grin that made me wish I could punch him in his stupid face. I didn't fight Rodrick with fists. Although, I was often tempted to. He was literally an ox of a man, sturdy and stubborn. He was branded like one too, with all those inky, coiling tattoos he had. He was also an agitator spy. I was sure of it. I didn't have any proof, but I was determined to make him slip up and expose himself.

He gave me this knowing look and a slight nod of his head as if he knew what I was thinking. He probably did. I never let it rest. I couldn't. Rodrick could ruin everything for me. I thought he was the one who would bring bloodshed and kill my family, but the Lost Princess was beating him to it. I couldn't stand him. He was tethered too. He should have understood where I was coming from. He should have been an ally, but no.

Agitators wanted to see the world burn. They almost succeeded when their predecessors, the humans from Glory Valley, almost destroyed all of Prime with the Hellfire Strike. Every surviving kingdom, werewolf and vampire alike, had an unspoken truce as they teamed up to destroy Glory Valley after that, but some people inevitably survived and hid away, becoming agitators who reared their heads at random intervals, trying to build up their kingdom again, perhaps.

Rodrick was an agitator Wolf Bridge caught trying to steal tech. He should have been executed, but he somehow found out about Caspian forming Phantom Fangs two months ago. He asked to join. What did Caspian do? He fucking let him. I've been trying to convince him of his mistake ever since. Once an agitator, always an agitator. Maybe they didn't have much power anymore, but they could still cause plenty of trouble.

Agitators wanted to destroy the werewolves and vampires. While I wasn't against that, I was against what it would mean for all of the people living inside of Wolf Bridge, my family included. I was certain Rodrick was a part of this team so he could find the opportune moment to sabotage us. Caspian should have known that. If he did, he was doing a fantastic job of ignoring it. And that made me furious.

Soon, Rodrick would betray us. I had to stop him before he did.

Pressure built in my eyes, and I realized I was leaking moonlight. Wisps of blue played at the corners of my vision. I closed my eyes when Rodrick tensed and flexed his mounds of muscles. I wasn't going to start a fight in here. I turned forward and opened my eyes again when I had locked up my moonlight reserves. The blue was gone along with the pressure. I had to save my strength. I couldn't afford to act recklessly.

"Almost there. Then I just have to hack into the spires," Todd announced as he maneuvered through more trees.

Caspian nodded. "Get ready."

CHAPTER 6

SORISSA

*T*HIS YELLOW dress was like nothing I had ever worn before. It was made with materials that were quite obviously "expensive." The labor that went into crafting the intricate lace was something I only had a small understanding of. I knew how to sew and make my own clothes, but I wasn't into beautifying. I made my clothes with practicality in mind. This dress was not practical, and the lace was an unnecessary embellishment.

The dress wasn't the worst part, though. I was wearing layers of frills underneath and a devil-conceived contraption called a corset. It squeezed my waist and pumped up my breasts so they were almost bulging out of the strapless top of the dress. It made it difficult to breathe. I humored the human woman decorating me like a fine ornament. I let her put "makeup" all over my face. I let her tie up the long curls of my hair. But this corset was the last straw.

"I'm taking it off," I said.

The woman's face paled and her hands flew to her cheeks.

I was about to rip right through the dress when the door to my room flung open. The scarred alpha waltzed in with Den and Nash at his side.

"*This* is a princess," he said as he looked me up and down, eyes lingering on my abused breasts. "It's time to meet the king and his favorite prince."

"I can't breathe," I replied.

"Don't be dramatic. I'm sure your maid left you just enough breathing room. Doing a poor job means being demoted to meat. Isn't that right, woman?"

She trembled under his gaze and bowed. "Yes, Captain Leer."

"So your name is Leer?" I noted. "It suits you."

"Enough talk, Princess. We can't keep our king and prince waiting."

He grabbed me by the arm, and I stumbled in the ridiculous high-heeled shoes I was wearing. I was not a klutz, but I wasn't used to walking like this either. I tried to yank my arm from his grasp, but he held fast as if he were expecting me to try this.

"Get used to it," he said. "You should rest your hand gently on my arm. Then I won't have to force you. It's the proper way things are done."

I noticed a difference in Leer. He was portraying a calmness he didn't have before, even though I knew uneasiness rested below. He was trying to make a good impression on his king. He felt that the way I conducted myself reflected on him. Nash and Den were silent, falling into step just behind me and their "captain."

I took as deep of a breath as the corset would allow and relaxed my arm. *Patience. Play along.* Leer softened his hold and I rested my hand "gently" on his arm. He stayed true to his word, releasing me from his iron grip.

Soldiers watched us as we moved down long polished halls. My shoes clicked against the almost slippery surface and reverberated all around us. The slightest sneeze or cough wouldn't go unnoticed in a place like this. It didn't help that everyone else was so silent. The soldiers stood in their assigned places and looked more like statues than living beings.

At the end of the largest hall, there was a set of double doors that reached all the way up to the high ceiling. They looked extremely heavy. They must have been because I noticed a much smaller, inconspicuous door carved into one of them. That door was the one that opened to allow us entry. It was another one of those designs I thought superfluous, but that seemed to be just how things were in this kingdom. Many things were purely for the visual aspect of it while few others were there for function. It made me wonder why they insisted on so much gray.

This was the throne room—based on the metallic throne at the head of it, elevated on a platform standing at least six feet higher than the floor. A very old werewolf sat there. The back of the throne, like the double doors, reached the high ceiling, well past his head. His throne and crown looked like they were made of the same metal. They had spiraling patterns that reached up into points and gentle curves, part of the same "kingly" sculpture. However, the king himself was what made the sculpture pop. He stood out from the grays with his long white hair, plump form, and wrinkled brown skin. He wore grays similar to the uniformed werewolves, but he had much more yellow than a small paw-print badge on his right breast; he wore a long yellow cape that pooled at his feet like captured sunrays. There was a werewolf standing beside him as well, dressed much like himself. He looked like a much younger version of the king, his hair brown instead of white.

I noticed more windows with that pearly material making up their frame. More moons of the same material were embedded in the floor underneath them. Now, instead of red, they reflected the blue of moonlight. It almost made my hair stand on end, as if I could feel its energy. But that seemed unlikely, given I couldn't absorb moonlight until the moon was full.

"Bow down," Leer murmured when we reached the foot of the raised throne.

I followed Leer, Nash, and Den to the ground, bowing lower than I thought necessary. And it was quite a feat. I didn't know how I managed to do it without puncturing a lung or tearing the damn dress I was wearing.

"So this is our princess." Footsteps clicked on the polished floor. "Rise." A hand touched my shoulder and I righted myself. The king had descended his throne and stood in front of me. He was a little bit taller than I was, but not by much. I could look into his eyes easily enough. I held his gaze unwaveringly even as his fingers rubbed my shoulder in a manner that made my skin crawl. He wore the same hungry look as all the other werewolf males I had met. That was the best way I could describe their looks. I didn't like being viewed as a piece of meat. I wanted to tear out his steel-gray eyes. I was not a submissive.

Anger roiled inside of my stomach. My patience was running thin.

"You and your werewolves are excused, Captain."

The king jerked his head toward Leer, who gave a small bow and promptly left the way he had come with Nash and Den on his heels. A shiver ran up my spine with the resounding click of the door closing, leaving me alone with the king and the young werewolf who had to be his son. The king grinned, revealing a couple metal teeth among mostly white. "You are a beauty. Don't you think, Charles?"

"Quite the beauty," the younger werewolf replied as he came to stand near us. He was the first werewolf I had met who looked like he could be around my age.

I smiled back at the king and prince and then took a step back. Thankfully, the king didn't insist on holding my shoulder to keep me right next to him like Leer had. The instant I was freed from his touch, I felt a little better, but I still couldn't breathe. In fact, I was feeling light-headed. I needed to keep control of my breathing because any uneasiness would cut off my air and the corset would win if I didn't. I couldn't lose to a stupid article of clothing after all of this.

"We thought you died with Howling Sky," the king said. "Ah, but how rude of me. I'm King George ve Paz of Paws Peak." He held out his hand to the younger werewolf. "This is my son, Prince Charles ve Paz of Paws Peak. We are honored to finally meet you, Princess Sorissa va Lupin of Howling Sky."

"Long titles," I said.

"King George" laughed boisterously. There was a wicked gleam in his cold eyes. I said the wrong thing. Maybe it was best to resort to silence like I had with Leer and his underlings.

"It turns out your mother managed to save your life," George continued. "And she made a deal with a witch. The Witch of Witch Woods. All for you, her little Moonlight Child."

This time, I stayed silent. But I had questions. Many questions.

"Here you stand at the ripe age of eighteen like you were promised all those years ago, like nothing had happened, like Howling Sky hadn't fallen."

"I have no idea what you're talking about," I blurted.

"No matter. It's all in the past anyway. You needn't think on it. All you need to know is that I am the King of Paws Peak, soon to be High King of Prime, the entire world, and that Prince Charles is to be your mate. All you have to do is bear my son's cubs and make sure you look beautiful for all the werewolves in Paws Peak. You are a rarity. Wereas have always been uncommon, more so in recent times, but you are one of a kind. Anyone who catches a glimpse of you is lucky."

George paused to tear his cold gaze from me to look at his son. "It's a good thing I didn't select one of our four wereas of mating age to be your mate, Charles. Princess Sorissa was delivered to us just in time. Then again, even if I had, you would have just sealed her with the Mate Claim as well. It would have all worked out. Although, you would have had the beginnings of a harem." He chuckled. "Bitches often get jealous of such arrangements." He returned his gaze to me, and I swore the gray of his eyes darkened. "I'd claim you myself if I didn't already have a mate."

He reached out his hand and placed his fingers under my chin. I clenched my jaw as he propped my head up and turned it left and right before returning his hand to his side. "Radiant and soft to the touch," he murmured. "But alas, it's best to leave the kingdom to younger and more capable hands. I am getting old at two hundred and seventy-nine. I saw the Hellfire Strike with my own eyes, thought for sure it was the end of the world, but Prime still stands and so does Paws Peak. Tech returned from the ban and once again thrives. You still live. And the Prime War isn't over yet. I'll finally have my time as High King, and then Prince Charles will have his."

George had no interest in giving me a proper history lesson. He only wanted to boast. He was talking to me like I was another one of his prized accomplishments, a trophy. A conquest. I had been condescended to ever since I left my forest, ever since Babaga forced me out. I was not a token, some werea to be won. I was alive. I had free will.

"I don't want to stay," I said curtly. "I want to go back to my woods."

George's eyes widened and his jaw grew slack. Then he laughed again, louder than before. His voice rang throughout the throne room, and it kept ringing when he stopped. "This is your home now, Princess Sorissa va Lupin of Howling Sky. It's time you learn your place. I know you've been away from your own kind for your entire life, but you'll learn quickly." He turned to his son. "Claim her. It will make her more docile and less like a raging, hormonal bitch. Well, except for when it comes to how badly she'll crave you, how her body will need you."

What world were these werewolves living in? I didn't know much about claiming or mates, but I was pretty sure it wouldn't transform me into something else, something like what George described. I couldn't stop the reflexive action of baring my teeth at these males. Would another werea understand me better or would she be as upside down as everyone else I had met outside of the woods? I guessed she'd be the same. How else would a werea be able to stand being George's mate?

I growled but quickly silenced myself when I saw the dangerous look in George's eyes. *Patience. Patience. Patience.* I couldn't take on an entire kingdom. I couldn't even take on three werewolves—especially when they had moonlight to spare and I had but a drop. Why had Babaga done this to me?

"Out of my sight," George ordered.

Charles stepped out from behind his father's shadow. He grabbed my arm and spun me around, his other hand at my waist. My ribs ached from the corset and my panicked breaths made it worse. I wanted to struggle and fight, but I was certain it wouldn't do me any good. Maybe it would buy me some time, but I wasn't sure if I should risk it. I didn't know what to do. I didn't know what Charles was going to do to me. I didn't know what claiming entailed, only that it would make me his mate. Being his mate would lead to sex, and I didn't want that.

What could I do to stall? Did any of it matter? Would I survive long enough to recharge on the full moon? Would I be allowed to? Was the Mate Claim permanent? My werewolf education was sketchy at best.

I couldn't wait much longer. I needed to somehow slip away from the prince, grab the parcel I left in that room with the maid, and sneak out of this place. Running and hiding was my only option, my only chance. I had to fade away into the night.

CHAPTER 7

SORISSA

I LET Charles drag me back through the open halls. My eyes wandered, looking for any possible escape routes. It didn't look any better than the last time I came through. There were werewolf soldiers standing guard everywhere. I didn't know for sure if I could outrun them or not, but it seemed I would have to put my speed to the test. I didn't know the exact details of what Charles had in store for me, but I wasn't going to play along. Not anymore.

Living here with how these werewolves treated me was a worse fate than death. I wanted no part of it, and I refused to be their prisoner.

My arm felt like it was on fire. I jerked back, trying to escape Charles's grip, but all I did was wrench my arm worse. It was unfair that the base strength of males was so superior to mine. I could have used a trick of some sort to get free, like hitting a weak point, but I wasn't very experienced in that kind of combat. Underhanded combat. I relied on strength just like these males seemed to. I did know basics. Eyes, neck, soft parts of the body were good to aim for. This dress and these heels hindered my movements, but I'd likely have to try it. It didn't look like I was going to be lucky enough to find a break in the guards. When was the best time to act? Where and when would I have the best chance to escape? Yes, I would rather die than live here, but that didn't mean I wanted to die.

When we passed the room my parcel was in, I asked, "Where are we going?"

"To my bedchamber," he replied.

"To claim me?"

"Yes."

"What does that entail?"

"It entails you being bonded to me for the rest of my life," he said in a bored tone. "You'll bear my cubs and bring wealth to the entire kingdom. It's like my father said."

"Don't I get a say in this?" I asked, and I hated how my voice trembled with the question. I was angry, but I was also scared.

"No. Everyone's convinced the last male vampire is

dead. Werewolves are on top right now. Paws Peak will rise to the very top and become the High Kingdom. We'll rule what's left of the world. Then we'll make sure the vampires are extinct. Once the war ends, we'll start rebuilding the world, make the badlands livable again. You're a key component in all of this. You'll mother a new generation of powerful werewolves because you're the Moonlight Child. When I claim you, the entire world will know of your return and that you belong to us, Lost Princess, and Wolf Bridge will have to see reason."

"No!" I exclaimed. "I won't let you claim me."

"You don't have a choice." He pushed me forward, trapping me against a gray wall as he fumbled with a door to my left. "Guards, clear out so my new princess and I can have some privacy."

The guards in the area bowed and began to leave without a word. Just like that. This was it. My chance was coming.

He wrapped his arm around my waist and squeezed when he got the door open. He lifted me off my feet and knocked the air out of my lungs at the same time. My vision was darkening around the edges; between Charles and the corset, I was barely able to take in any oxygen.

I sucked in a breath of air when he deposited me stomach-first on his large bed. It was even bigger than the bed in the room my parcel was in, making it far less utilitarian. I felt tension at my back and heard ripping fabric as Charles laid into the yellow dress and the deadly corset. I could breathe normally again. I tried to take in big gulps of air to regain my strength quickly, but Charles pressed me into the bed, making it hard to move. I attempted to kick him, but my legs were locked in between him and the bed. I screamed, but he pressed my face down into the yellow duvet covering the mattress, muffling the sound. Then I felt a sharp pain explode between my neck and right shoulder.

This time my screams were involuntary. The pain got worse and worse as he sunk his teeth deep into my flesh. I had been bitten by a grizzly bear before, but this was somehow much worse. It was as if his teeth were iron heated in burning coals. Tears stung my eyes, and I dug my fingers into the bed, grabbing fistfuls of the soft fabric that promised luxury, but it was all a lie.

The prince moved the skirt of the dress and caressed my thigh as he pressed every hard edge of his body into me. He rolled his hips against my butt. I winced as the buckle of a belt or some other hard metal on his crisp outfit jabbed into my sensitive flesh. Then his weight lifted, slightly. There was a clink and swish of fabric. I knew this was my chance. I used all of my strength to push off the bed, and I kicked. I kicked him right in between the legs with a well-placed and pointed heel. He let out a high-pitched wail as he crumpled to the ground.

I wasted no time shaking off those hindering shoes, hopped off the bed, and ran. The yellow dress I wore was in tatters and falling around me. I ripped off what got in my way as I reached the door and fled the room. Charles growled at me and screamed, "Bitch, get back here! Guards!"

I slammed the door to stall for time. The hall was clear because of Charles's previous command. I picked the direction I was fairly certain would lead me back to the room where Babaga's parcel was hidden.

Hot blood dripped from my neck. The torn skirt of the yellow dress caught under my feet, and I almost tripped. I ripped more fabric away, revealing the puffy white underclothes covering my thighs. I felt sluggish, and my feet almost turned me back around. There was this tugging feeling that stemmed from that bite, like the farther I got away from Charles, the worse it hurt. Or like I was a runaway marionette tied to a string that wouldn't stop tugging. I ignored the pain and pressed forward.

The room my parcel was in wasn't far. I didn't run into any soldiers and was able to slip in unseen. No one was inside. The room was dark and empty. I navigated the dark with my hands outstretched, found the bed, and reclaimed my parcel. It was untouched, just how I left it.

With my parcel in hand, I snuck to the door and opened it a crack. I didn't see anyone, but I could hear the distant echoes of werewolves on the move throughout the large halls.

I exited the room and ran. My feet slapped against the polished floor, producing my own distinct echo. It rang in my ears louder and louder with each step I took. I was about to round a corner, but then I saw soldiers farther down. I looked behind me and caught a glimpse of Charles. His hazel eyes were gleaming, and he let loose an angry howl.

I was trapped.

CHAPTER 8

TODD

IT WAS chilly outside but stuffy inside the roader. Caspian set up a camouflage tarp that worked great with the trees we were hidden in. They were already greener than the last time we had been here a week ago, providing better coverage. Paws Peak couldn't see us, and we couldn't see them, but I was close enough to connect to the four spires, one actually. Now I just had to hack into their system.

Sweat beaded on my forehead. I wiped it away with the back of my hand and stared at the glowing screen of my pactputer. I returned my hand to the detachable keyboard and typed in a few more lines of code. I said I could get inside, and I could, but I knew it wouldn't be easy. I hadn't done it before. I practiced for it, using the information we gathered last time we were here, but practice was always different from the real thing. I was getting close, though. The last step was to plague the spires, and the entire Paws Peak system, with my virus.

That was why I was sweating. My virus was also untested. I didn't think there was any better time to test it, but the Lost Princess was a big deal to everyone else. I knew she should be a big deal to me too. She was, in a way, but I didn't really want to acknowledge her existence or what it meant for the rest of us. Namely, me and my tech.

Things were going fine before she popped up out of nowhere. I was working on my tech, improving it in peace, and now the whole world was probably going to get destroyed before I even realized half of my potential. I was well on my way to revolutionizing technology, and it was all for nothing. I didn't care if generations after me got to use it or not, but I did want to live for at least an average werewolf lifespan of three hundred years, creating and discovering. With the Lost Princess found, all I could see in my near future was the end of the world. For that, I decided I hated her.

I didn't care about "saving" the princess. I cared about my virus working and doing its job.

I entered a new line of code and watched the pieces

snap into place. I was in. I glanced over my shoulder at Caspian. Unlike Rodrick and Aerre, readying our weapons and checking our supplies in the back of the roader, he was intent on watching me. He was looking at the pactputer screen with a grin on his face, his teeth a stark white compared to his black skin. Could he read into my code? Did he know I was inside a spire and therefore connected to the entire system? Anytime my Phantom Fangs teammates made expressions and didn't use words, I questioned what they meant. Even when they did use words, I often questioned what they meant. Unlike machines and tech, they were hard to pin down because they could lie and feel emotion.

"You close?" Caspian asked. He didn't know. I read him wrong.

"I'm in," I informed. "I can loop their visual feed so you three can go in unnoticed."

"You're brilliant, you know that?"

In fact, I did, but I learned agreeing with things like that or saying things like that didn't make decent relationships. The only kind of relationships I wanted were those that amounted to me not being bothered any more than necessary. Emotions were an annoyance I tried to ignore.

"One problem," I said as I studied my screen. "The Paws Peak system is taxing my virus. I'm not going to have control for long. You'll have to be quick before it's overwhelmed and Paws Peak discovers our presence."

"Great. How long?" Caspian asked.

"An hour tops, but I'd halve that to be safe." I searched through and saved information from the enemy system while I was linked up to it. It was a good idea to harvest as much information as I could during the time limit. One day I might be able to control the Paws Peak system for good if I understood it better. And, right now, Phantom Fangs needed a map. Paws Peak wasn't small.

"Intelibands on and ready to go?" I asked.

"Ready," Caspian, Rodrick, and Aerre replied in unison.

"I'm downloading a generic map of the kingdom and a detailed map of the castle. Done and uploading. Should be accessible any second now."

"Got it," Caspian said.

I watched as my teammates each drew up the map as a 3D hologram from the handy piece of tech I developed to wear easily on the wrist. Intelibands weren't as powerful as my pactputer. They didn't have the power to do anything on their own. My pactputer was their central hub, but they were handy sources of information as long as I kept them updated and relevant to the task at hand.

"Commsbuds check," I said and waited as my teammates inserted the pebble-sized tech into one of their ears. I pressed my own commsbud into my ear, activating a temporary audio feed that would transmit to the commsbuds linked to mine—thanks to my pactputer again.

"Testing."

"Received."

We were good on my end, so I returned my attention to my pactputer screen as my teammates suited up in dark, bulletproof combat gear and equipped themselves with tactical belts, packs, and weapons.

It was ironic. The Paws Peak system wasn't half as sophisticated as the one I modified and practically rebuilt in Wolf Bridge. I figured attaching my virus to one spire would be enough, and it mostly was. Paws Peak didn't have a central hub. Everything I did revolved around a single, powerful source that reached out its digital brain-waves to digital limbs. In Wolf Bridge, that was the Heart. Paws Peak had a weaker system because the four spires had to communicate and take on tasks equally. I was off-setting the balance because my little virus wasn't prepared to stretch itself between all four spires. One spire dealt with surveillance, and that was the one I commandeered since it was the only one I *needed* for this mission.

Maybe I could make adjustments to my virus and assimilate the towers into one control center. I'd work on it, but I'd also operate under the assumption that the alarms were going to sound on us before too long because part of the problem was my pactputer. The tech field it emitted was as strong as it was going to get. If I could have packed up the Heart and brought it here, this would have been a different story.

"We're lucky the castle is built so close to the east side of the wall," Aerre commented. "Shouldn't have to do much navigating through the kingdom towns. Who knows how long that would take. Now, if only we'll be lucky enough to get to the princess before she's claimed."

"Stop bitching, Aerre," Rodrick said.

"Don't wait on me," I said quickly. "I'm good."

"Then we're heading out," Caspian concluded.

The three Phantom Fangs members opened and slammed doors shut again as they exited the roader. I rubbed my ears as they popped. It was like getting sealed away into an airless, noiseless bag. When the team was near, there was an imbalance of noise, peaks and drops. When it was me, the roader, and my tech, it was the ambiance of a consistent dull, mechanical thrum.

I stared out a portion of a window that wasn't covered by the camouflage tarp. Phantom Fangs was quickly disappearing into new foliage. Soon, they were out of sight. This strange sensation filled my chest as if my heart had dropped from its designated spot. I didn't like watching their backs, but I hated it most when they were completely out of sight. I didn't know what that meant. I didn't understand my own emotions because I tried to ignore them.

Turning my attention back to my pactputer screen, I focused on my agenda: keep Phantom Fangs safe from prying eyes and therefore rescue the Lost Princess of Howling Sky. That, I could do.

CHAPTER 9

SORISSA

*T*HERE HAD to be a way to escape. I didn't want to get captured again when I had been free for mere minutes. There were werewolf soldiers in front of me, and Charles was behind me. I spotted a shadowed nook I had almost overlooked. It wasn't a dead end like I would have thought at a glance. It was the beginning of a narrow staircase. I ran for it.

"Bitch, get back here!" Charles bellowed. "I will make you submit. I'll make you beg for me."

His voice bounced off the polished walls of the hall but quickly silenced as I descended the spiraling staircase. My fingers brushed across gritty stones that didn't match the rest of the castle. There was a distinct musty smell that assaulted my nose. When I reached the bottom, a labyrinth of catacombs was waiting for me. I picked a random direction and ran. I knew I was still being followed, but the sounds were muffled down here, less abrasive. The floor was a dampener of dirt and decaying stone. I took a right, ran into the rusty bars of old cells, and almost dropped Babaga's parcel. I startled when I came face to face with an emaciated female. Her hair was wild and ratted. Her eyes were bloodshot.

"You lost?" she hissed.

I scrambled backward just to hit another cell.

"I think she's lost," a voice from behind me said.

I yelped in surprise and looked behind me to see another female. They weren't werewolf. They weren't human. Their scent tickled my nose and made my hackles rise involuntarily. They laughed at me and licked their lips, showing sharp and pointed teeth like daggers: vampires.

Another female screeched from down the winding corridor. Their skins were varying shades of gray as if they had lost all pigment. They were nothing but bones and their eyes bulged. They were like living corpses, not the proud, beautiful creatures I read about in… I berated myself for always going back to fairytales. They had no place in this world.

"I-I need help," I admitted, not that I was sure these vampires could do anything to help me or that they'd want to.

The vampires in the cells across from each other cackled in unison.

"A werewolf asking for *our* help. That's a first. Are you the reason the guards are down here for the first time in a week? Your dress is in a sorry state."

"I'm not one of them," I said vehemently.

That area between my neck and right shoulder pulsed angrily like a throbbing vein about to explode. I pressed my hand to the sore spot and winced. Warm blood coated my fingers and my body flushed with heat. It was tugging at me again, urging me to go back in the direction I came—urging me to return to the prince. What had he done to me? I shook my head and ignored the absurd thought.

"I'll break you out," I offered. I could have really used some temporary allies.

The vampires screeched and giggled. I wished they'd keep it down. I was pretty sure I could hear footsteps coming this way.

"Perhaps you could free us with your moonlight form, werea, but then we'd kill you for everything your species has done to ours."

"I'm not one of them," I said, exasperated.

"All werewolves are the same."

Giving up, I said, "Never mind. I'll figure this out on

my own."

The vampires continued their cackling as I ran, determined to lose my pursuers.

"Run, little werea," the vampires sang. "Run."

I was lost.

My feet were cut and bleeding from all the running combined with the unforgiving rocks jutting out of the dungeon ground. I fell back against a grabby rock wall and sat down. The tattered dress I wore was barely covering me, doing little to protect me from the chill. It was filthy. No one would have ever known it was once a bright yellow.

I propped Babaga's parcel up against the wall and placed my hands on my arms as I tried to rub away the goosebumps. Then I inspected my feet, but there wasn't much I could do. I couldn't clean them and that meant I had to grin and bear the pain while hoping I didn't get a nasty infection.

At least I felt safe. Sort of. I was fairly confident the soldiers wouldn't find me if I took a short moment to catch my breath—unless they knew this place much better than I did. For all I knew, I could have been running in circles this entire time. I had no idea how long I had been down here, running like a chicken with its head cut off. I didn't know the way out. Maybe that meant I'd end up starving to death down here like those hungry vampires. I hadn't even seen any rats for us to feast on.

I closed my eyes for a minute, pressed my hand to Charles's bite, and felt that tugging sensation again. I had been ignoring it, but I supposed it would lead me back somewhere. I didn't know for sure that it would lead me back to Charles, but it was the feeling I had. It was like instinct. I tried to remember if biting was part of the Mate Claim.

I supposed I remembered illustrations of mated wereas with a scar similar to what this bite would inevitably leave on my skin. That was the extent of my memories on the matter, though. It wasn't like Babaga gave me books detailing the process of claiming or mating. It was all mentioned in passing in the werewolf fairytales I knew. The stories themselves were typically about a quest of some sort: finding food for the pack, a werewolf coming of age, using moonlight to slay a great beast.

There were so many stories in my head, but none of them were like the story I was living. Unless I thought of myself as one of those werewolves on a quest. I was forced to leave home, taken to a strange land. But what was my quest?

I rubbed the sore and still bleeding bite. It hurt but eased the tugging. I didn't know what Charles did to me, but I really hoped he didn't have the same tug toward me.

What if he did and that was all it took to find me? I wasn't moving now. It would be easy for him. Was this all it meant to be a werea? Was this why not a single werea went on an epic quest in werewolf fairytales? Why were males simply called werewolves while females were called by a different name?

I had never seen a werea treated badly in the books Babaga gave me, but I never saw them treated equally to a male. I had the ridiculous notion that I would change that when I got out of the woods, that I would be the alpha of my own pack one day. I wished I could return to such naivety.

I wiped sweat from my brow and raked my fingers through my curly hair to integrate the loose pieces back into the hairstyle that maid took a lengthy amount of time to do It wasn't very effective, but it was better than nothing. A single simple braid would have been nice.

Shivers pulsed through my body as I continued to sweat. It was like I had a fever. I was certain my bronze skin was burning, but I felt so cold. Maybe Charles's bite shot venom into my blood.

I glanced at Babaga's parcel and saw a tear in the brown paper. There was no better time to look at it. I was too tired to stand, so I grabbed it. I untied the twine and the brown paper fell away with a single pull. It was a book I didn't recognize.

Its spine was woven together in a crisscrossing pattern. The smooth leather making up the cover was dyed a dark purple. I traced the shiny gold lettering on the front of it. The script was beautiful with bends and loops that outdid mine. I never enjoyed Babaga's penmanship lessons. But I did like to read. I liked to read books by werewolves, humans, and vampires. I read so many fairytales that they often ran together—even from species to species. Though they had different journeys, different customs, the stories all had the same heart, the same questions, the same lessons. Based on their stories, the three species didn't seem that different to me.

I didn't know what Babaga was trying to do, feeding me fairytales and keeping me locked away all these years just to kick me out and sell me to a bunch of brutish werewolves. She didn't even give me all their fairytales. Surely this Moonlight Child blessed by Lureine, Lost Princess, Howling Sky, and whatever else these werewolves used to describe me, was fairytale material. Or maybe not. If fairytales were nothing but lies and the Moonlight Child was truth, one was fiction and the other was actual history.

What was the point in feeding me lies, then?

I ran my hand along the spine of the book and looked at its front cover. This time, instead of admiring the finish on the gold lettering, I read the words: To my pride and joy, the Moonlight Child blessed by Lureine, Princess Sorissa va Lupin of Howling Sky. There was more written below. With the greatest love, High Queen Alana va Lupin of Howling Sky.

My bottom lip trembled. Babaga knew all along. All of this. What these werewolves had been saying to me, she had a book all about it. I was a *princess*. I had so many questions and angry words to say to Babaga, but I bit my tongue and opened the book to the first page instead.

The 2nd Month of Winter, Day 59. 2525.

Little Sorissa, I wanted to write you a first journal entry the day I found out I was pregnant, but patience was in order. I had to be sure since we no longer use technology, including the technology to peer inside a mother's womb. A werea has never been wrong about knowing the gender and number of cubs growing inside of her anyway. I had a feeling you were the only cub inside of my belly. I know you are, and I know your worth. It's with certainty that I have told the wonderful news to your father and High King. A few days later, I leave you this: your name and your first journal entry about thirty days into my pregnancy. Almost ninety days remain, little one. I cannot wait to meet you and hold you in my arms for the first time.

I've thought about your name for the past thirty days and always come back to Sorissa. It's a beautiful name, regal, and befitting of your bloodline. Your breeding is the finest, made even more so because you are the only cub inside of my womb. Such an occasion is so rare I've never heard of another instance of it. Moonlight Child. Werewolves have womb-mates—usually a minimum of six cubs, all male. The imbalance of male and female is the opposite of vampires. They have many more females and few males. It's the way of it, I suppose. Something to do with our biology perhaps. But, for werewolves, all wombmates must share their mother's nutrients, and more importantly: moonlight.

As an unborn cub, you take and keep all moonlight I absorb on a full moon. After you are born, moonlight will be fleeting, something you will use and need to recharge, but as you are, the moonlight you intake will make you stronger than any before you. You will be able to store and use vast amounts of moonlight the likes of which none of us have ever seen. That is the future I see for you, Moonlight Child. You have been blessed by Lureine. You are not only a rare and valued werea, you are unprecedented.

I hope you will be the start of a new age. War is your history, but I don't want it to be your future.

Vampires target wereas while werewolves target male vampires, or vampyres as they are called among their own kind. The goal is to drive the other species to extinction. Humans almost took care of that, though. They almost drove us all to extinction when they initiated the Hellfire Strike. They have made the world small, but the fallout has rested for a hundred and fifty-six years. There is hope that the badlands can be revived, but the Prime War will have to end first.

The Prime War has existed for as long as Prime itself. Werewolves, vampires, and humans have fought for the ultimate power, the power as ruler of all of Prime. The humans, from the former kingdom known as Glory Valley, were responsible for the Hellfire Strike. They launched the attack when they must have seen how inevitable it was they would lose the war. The attack killed many of their own kind after all, including the humans kept as meat and blood inside of werewolf and vampire kingdoms. However, they failed to destroy everything and were quickly disposed of by their enemies.

Alas, I don't mean for your first journal entry to be so dreary. You are the Moonlight Child and of the High Kingdom: Howling Sky. Your fortune is good. Your future is bright. Three werewolf kingdoms remain: Howling Sky, Wolf Bridge, and Paws Peak. One vampire kingdom remains: Crimson Caves. No human kingdoms remain. Werewolves have all but won the war, and you will lead us into a new era.

I am happy to see the war ending. I have lived well over a hundred and fifty years now. I saw the Hellfire Strike firsthand. It destroyed the kingdom I was born and raised in along with countless others. It would have destroyed me too if I had not been promised to High King Kashe ve Lupin of Howling Sky two hundred years ago. Kashe was a prince then, but he has grown and claimed the highest station in all the world. I have given him many cubs during that time, but you are my only Moonlight Child.

With you, final negotiations are being made. Wolf Bridge remains neutral, waiting to see how everything plays out, but Paws Peak has resented Howling Sky attaining High Kingdom status. However, Paws Peak will stop resisting and werewolves will unite under Howling Sky if we promise you to one of twelve royal werewolf cubs just born to King George ve Paz of Paws Peak. We will mix royal blood and the three werewolf kingdoms will stand united. Details must be addressed for uniting our kingdoms, but, as I've said, your future is bright.

You, my beautiful Sorissa, are so very valuable. I'm sure your future mate will rule this world and that you will bear him many cubs, powerful male werewolves with expansive moonlight reserves thanks to your own. Your mate will expand this broken and tiny world into something glorious, a proper place for you to raise your cubs. You will likely be remembered as the most influential werea in our history, the mother of the new, more powerful generation.

My heart pounded so hard in my chest I could hear

it in my ears. The words I had just read swirled in my vision. They were a jumbled mess I couldn't sort through or process.

I clapped the journal shut when that throbbing bite acted up again. I strained my ears and picked up the sound of muffled footfalls. They were close. Way too close. I hadn't noticed because I was so engrossed in my "mother's" journal.

I jumped to my feet and pain flared anew in my soles. In fact, my entire body was riddled with pain. I was more convinced than ever that Charles had somehow poisoned me with his bite.

Limping, I checked the different corridors, trying to find the one farthest away from Charles and the guards. One direction beckoned me to it, and I didn't consider why. When I took a step toward it, the pain in my body subsided some. Then I saw Charles emerge at the end of the corridor. I couldn't trust my own instincts because even they were betraying me. How did everything turn out so wrong?

"Got you now, bitch."

CHAPTER 10

SORISSA

I RAN, journal in hand. Charles's screams tried to follow me, but I rounded corners quickly and found my way back to the vampires I had talked to in their cells. This time, I didn't stop to chat. I knew my way out of the dungeon now and decided to risk ascending. It wasn't like struggling down here was doing me any good anyway.

"Run, little werea," the vampires whispered in a chorus.

I ignored them and kept running. I found the spiraling staircase luckily unguarded. A bright light was above me. It was a relief from the dimness in the dungeon because now I could clearly see where I was going—not that I needed to dodge jutting out rocks up here, but still.

Once I emerged back onto polished gray floors, I was greeted by an abundance of those glowing orbs: light-bulbs. They supplemented the light of the sun, drowning out the almost ripe moonlight that drifted in quietly through high windows and reflected off that odd pearly material. I felt the pull of power. If only the moon had been full, I would have been able to recharge.

My eyes snapped to a corner where I saw shadows moving. I was certain it was a guard. I was also certain Charles was right on my heels. I swore I could hear his voice pricking at my ears from down the steps like demons chanting. Also, that bite was reacting again, promising relief if I went back down the stairs. I gritted my teeth and cursed these lowlife werewolves and their underhanded tricks.

I didn't know where to go, so I simply moved. I ran down the hall with no clear direction and hoped a soldier wouldn't pop out at the end of it. My feet stabbed with pain each time they hit the floor. The distraction of pain made me miss the shifting shadows in another deep and dark crevice to my right. Phantom hands caught me and dragged me into their shadows. I couldn't yelp because one of those hands sealed my mouth closed. I almost dropped my journal, but I managed to hold on to it.

My instincts told me to bite, to kick and run for it, but I waited. I let whoever grabbed me hold me still. I was back in the echoing halls and could clearly hear my pursuers. They were getting close. However, their jumbled mess of shouts suggested they had lost sight of me and didn't know where I was. I held my breath as they passed by the crevice in the hallway without even thinking to turn their heads. Apparently, my feet hadn't had enough grime and blood on their soles to leave an obvious trail to my location. Or they were oblivious. Regardless, I was grateful for that.

The soldiers passed by without issue, but then I saw Charles. He hesitated. I thought he'd turn his head to the shadows. My bite burned at the same moment like it was calling out to him. My heart sunk because I was certain he knew I was there. He only needed to take a few steps inside of the shadows. Maybe he only needed to turn his head.

I pursed my lips behind the stranger's hand and silently cursed Charles. I cursed whatever spell or poison his bite held. I would never be his mate. Mate Claim or not, I refused, and nothing would change that

Charles moved forward, catching up to the soldiers and leaving me alone with a phantom. At first, I was too relieved to do anything but sink back a little. The bite was burning and pulsing, but I refused to give in to it and reveal myself. Charles couldn't have me. He didn't own me. No one ever would.

The figure behind me stirred. I became aware of how solid he was at my back, not a phantom at all. I looked down at the hand covering my mouth. The skin was dark like the shadows. He felt big and solid like a male, and the subtle tingling in my nose told me he was a werewolf. I just knew. His warm breath drifted down to my ear, reminding me of how close Charles was to me, reminding me of the bite he gave me.

When I was certain the way was clear, I bit this werewolf's hand. Then I stomped on his foot. He hissed in pain and drew back for a moment—but it wasn't a long enough moment. He grabbed me again and twirled me around so I was facing him this time.

"Let me go," I warned in a low voice, "or I'll tear off your balls and make you cry like a wounded dog."

My fingers were likely boring holes into the journal I clung to desperately. Every muscle in my body was wound up so tightly I was almost shaking. I was on the verge of doing something underhanded myself: leaping forward and scratching his eyes out like a cat. But the expression on his face caused me to falter.

He was covered in dirt and grime like I was. He raised a full black eyebrow at me and wore a slight frown. His black hair was just long enough to show off charming curls that curtained his forehead and part of his ears. His face was hard and chiseled like all male werewolf faces seemed to be. He didn't have any facial hair. His skin would have looked endlessly smooth if not for the confused expression he was giving me. However, his eyes were the feature that ended up holding me captive. They were dark like the rest of him. The shadows we were in made it hard to discern everything about him, but I swore I could see flashes of blue in his eyes like sapphire dust.

"Please don't do that," he said. He kept the volume low, but the baritone resonance of his voice made me shiver all the same. If he wanted to, I was sure he could speak with great power. Then he added, "I'm trying to get you out of here, out of Paws Peak."

My mouth dropped open.

"You do want to leave, don't you? I mean, based on the way you were running like your tail was on fire." He gave a small smile, flashing white teeth.

Could I trust anything this werewolf said? My experience so far said no. But I was getting desperate. It wasn't like I had a plan. I didn't really think I could get out of here on my own without moonlight. If he was one of the soldiers—which I supposed he could have been since he was wearing a similar uniform with a small pack and a belt of weapons, though it was black without a trace of yellow—I was already caught so why play around with me?

The truth was, I had nothing to lose.

"Fine," I said. "Get me out of here."

The werewolf bowed. It was a small, elegant bow and nothing like what I had experienced from other werewolves so far. It somehow seemed genuine.

"You are Princess Sorissa va Lupin of Howling Sky, aren't you?" he asked when he stood up straight again. His eyes lingered on my tattered dress for a moment before moving to my bite and then meeting my eyes again.

"Apparently," I replied.

He grinned. "Fantastic. I'd get you out of here even if you weren't, but the Lost Princess, specifically, is who I came to rescue." He held out his hand. "I'm Caspian."

I couldn't pinpoint what made his words sound so sincere, but they did. I hesitantly held out my hand to his. He took my hand with his big one, eclipsing it. His touch was gentle, another difference between him and the other werewolves I had met so far.

"Nice to meet you," he established. "Now, let's get you out of here." After reclaiming his hand, he pressed his pointer finger to his ear. "Found her. Clear out and don't waste any time."

"Who are you talking to?" I asked as I looked up and all around us. I was the only one here.

"Stay close to me, Princess."

Instead of answering my question, Caspian took my arm and tried to force me out of the shadows, but I was done being forced to do anything. Plus, dragging me along was just a ridiculous handicap. I was perfectly capable of keeping up on my own, hurt feet or not. I ripped my arm from his grasp and bared my teeth.

"I'll stay close to you, and I won't get in the way," I told him.

"Right," he said uneasily. "I apologize."

He took off down the hall, and I kept right on his heels. He kept looking over his shoulder as we advanced like he was worried I would fall behind. He led the way through a couple different halls that were empty.

"It seems Prince Charles made the mistake of grouping all the castle guards together. He's making this too easy," Caspian commented as he looked over his shoulder at me again for the fiftieth time.

He tapped the glass face of a broad rubber and metal band on his wrist. A bluish light beamed out from it. I almost leaped back in surprise, but the light coalesced into an image, and I moved closer. It was a semi-transparent map. I swung my hand through the air to see if I could touch it. My hand passed right through.

"What is this?" I asked, mesmerized. I tried one more time to touch the map, but I couldn't. All I could do was disrupt the image.

"Do you mind?" Caspian remarked as he moved his arm and, consequently, the image away. "In answer to your question, it's the castle's layout."

"What are those little moving lights?" Everything else on the map stayed the same, but these two lights were moving slowly.

"My squad. We're going to meet up with them in a moment. This way, Princess."

I followed Caspian to a wall that didn't look like anything special. It wasn't polished though. This whole wall resembled the state of the dungeon below, rough and unrefined gray stone. Caspian was running his hands along it as if he was inspecting it for something. What that could be, I didn't know.

"Wasting time," I muttered.

"Ah, there it is."

Caspian's fingers hit a button I didn't see on the wall. A rectangular slab of rock screeched as it rubbed against the rocks next to it and sunk into the floor. This werewolf was a master of sneaky technocraft. Sort of sneaky.

I covered my ears in distress. "Why not announce our presence to everyone inside the castle?" I asked.

"We'll be gone before they get here," Caspian said. "And I don't think Paws Peak uses their secret shortcuts much anymore. I dare say they forgot about them. That's how I got in here." He gestured to the new doorway. "Wereas first."

I scowled at him but moved forward. I wanted to get

out of here more than I wanted to fight about all this ridiculous werea business. I had to crawl inside of the secret passage since it definitely wasn't large enough to stand in. It was cramped, damp, and full of spiderwebs. I barely ducked out of the way of a huge web as a spider the size of my fist came out to hunt. I heard the screech of rock again and the wall closed back up, leaving me in complete darkness.

I looked over my shoulder to see Caspian holding a metal torch with a ray of light shooting out from its head. The light shined on that big spider, now near Caspian's face. He ducked, repeating my maneuver, and bumped into me. His chest touched my butt and my lower back, and my mind flashed back to Charles pressing down on me in his bedchamber. I froze.

"Apologies in advance," Caspian said as he laid his palm flat against my butt and shoved me forward, "but I really don't want to get up close and personal with that hairy eight-legged behemoth back there. Could you please get moving?"

He was practically on top of me again because I was frozen in place. He reached forward and stole my journal, replacing it with the metal torch. "I'll hold on to this for you," he said.

I pinched the skin on my elbow to clear my head. Then I pushed the awful memory of Charles aside and crawled forward, guided by the light of technocraft. Once I was moving, Caspian allowed as much personal space as was possible inside of this narrow tunnel.

It was all more of the same for minutes that felt like hours. I thought I might die of claustrophobia when we reached a dead end. We were going to die trapped inside of a castle wall. I imagined my bones sitting here, joining the spiders and their webs, never to be seen again. Just when I thought I'd fall into hysterics, Caspian reached past me and pushed another hidden button. Stone moved. The night and houses outside of the castle opened before us. I took in a relieved breath of fresh air as I scrambled out into bushes that were partly concealing the entryway. I wanted to stretch my limbs but stayed low as guards passed by on the road a few feet ahead.

Caspian dropped down into the bushes beside me and closed the wall once it was quiet again. But it didn't stay quiet for long. The grating stones turned heads, and there were many more guards out here, in many more groups, than what we had seen inside of the castle.

Caspian touched his ear again after checking his map made of blue light. This time, I noticed there was something sitting in his ear. It looked like a pebble. He spoke. "Faster, Phantom Fangs. We're not going to get out unnoticed at this rate."

A siren blared into the night. It was joined by four

others. Then a voice spoke out across the entire kingdom. "Intruders. Intruders have infiltrated Paws Peak. Red alert."

"Damn it, Rodrick. Was that you?" Caspian said as he continued pressing a finger to his ear and grabbed my arm with his free hand. He succeeded in moving me a few steps before I ripped out of his grasp again. "Sorry, Princess," he said, clearly agitated. "I really need you to keep up though."

"I'll keep up," I assured. "Why lug around extra weight when there's absolutely no reason to?"

He sighed and conceded. "Follow me." He pressed his finger to his ear again. "Todd, get ready to roll out."

CHAPTER 11

SORISSA

I HAD many questions, like who were Rodrick and Todd, but I kept them to myself as I followed Caspian. He weaved his way past guards and through the houses clustered closely together. We didn't have to go through many before nearing the kingdom's large wall. At this end, it was almost right next to the castle. I wondered if Caspian would use technocraft to open up more secret entryways because I didn't see any gates and the wall looked pretty much impossible to scale—at least without my moonlight form.

Before Caspian and I cleared the last of the houses, I saw two figures running ahead, also headed for the wall. Not just the wall, a specific area. There was a long rope ladder dangling down the side. It looked flimsy, but it must have been strong enough for Caspian and his "squad" to get inside. The sight would have been a relief if I hadn't seen the soldiers marching across the top of the wall. They spotted the ladder too, and now it was a race to see who could get to it first.

"Get ready to climb," Caspian said.

The two figures, werewolves according to my instincts, I saw running ahead reached the ladder before the soldiers. I didn't have time to take in their features, but I did notice they wore the same black uniform as Caspian. They climbed fast as some of the soldiers on the wall aimed knives and others held up small metal sticks to their eyes. One of the sticks exploded. Something shot out of it and hit the ladder just as the two werewolves reached the top and took out metal sticks of their own. More like hand-cannons. Loud bangs filled the air, competing with the droning sirens.

Caspian tugged on the ladder once we reached it. It was barely hanging on by two ropes. The left side looked precarious. It was weakened by the blast that came from that destructive technocraft hand-cannon. It would snap if we climbed it.

"Wereas fir—"

"Yeah, wereas first," I said, cutting Caspian off.

My hands were clammy as I gripped the ladder and lifted myself upward. It jiggled with my weight. I would have to be very careful. If a gust of wind came in too strong, that would be it. It was ripping more and more by the second.

"Climb, Princess!" Caspian shouted from below me. "They won't let us fall."

As if to answer him, one of his teammates, braided blond hair and lake-blue eyes, did something to reinforce the ladder. The right side was no longer taking on extra weight for the left. It was stable.

"Get your asses up here!" a werewolf with long brown hair pulled back in a ponytail and rough facial hair that somehow screamed "warrior" bellowed. He also had black markings all over his skin.

I climbed like I never had. My muscles combusted with the effort, but it was worth it when I made it to the top. I watched in awe as the warrior werewolf held up his hand-cannon and pulled back a trigger with his finger. An object shot out from the nozzle. It moved so swiftly I lost sight of it. I stared lamely in the direction of soldiers where it must have landed. Then red bloomed out from the yellow paw-print insignia on a soldier's uniform. He gurgled, and blood dripped down his lips just before he hit the stone ground with a hard thud.

"Keep moving, Princess," Caspian said as he gave me a firm push on the back. "Climb down the other side." He whipped out his own hand-cannon and shot more deadly projectiles.

I did what I was told, finding another ladder like the one I used to climb up here. I began to descend. If I made it down this one alive, I'd be outside of Paws Peak. I'd be in free land.

A blue light I was intimately familiar with flared from above me. Someone, or multiple someones, was using moonlight. Howls pierced through the bangs and sirens. A werewolf in moonlight form latched his big, canine teeth onto the ladder and yanked his powerful wolf head back. I held on for my life as the ladder fluttered like a flag in the wind and came crashing back against the wall with my weight. I yelped upon impact. I got some new scrapes and bruises, but I was still hanging on. I was alive.

The warrior werewolf with the ponytail roared. He was emitting moonlight as well, but he stuck to his base form. He wrapped his arms around the wolf that tried to shake me off the ladder and threw him in the opposite direction. I realized he probably just catapulted him off the other side. I could have done all that and more if I had moonlight to spare. I had to admit it was amazing to see others like me, seeing what they could do with a power I felt was solely mine.

I kept moving.

When my feet touched solid ground and grass, my heart soared for the first time since leaving Babaga's woods. I took off running into nearby trees and was soon accompanied by Caspian and the other two werewolves who helped us. The blond one was quiet but visibly relieved. The warrior wore a toothy grin and a wicked gleam in his green eyes. Caspian was smiling tentatively and searching ahead.

"Almost there," he said.

Almost where? These werewolves did just help me escape Paws Peak, but I wasn't keen on going anywhere with anyone after what I had been through. Caspian did something with my journal, stored it in his pack probably, and I wanted it back.

A familiar growl rumbled in the trees and branches snapped. Then a roader burst out of the foliage. Its four eyes cast bright beams of light right at us, and its wheels were squealing. I was sure it was going to plow us down. I was ready to dive to my right, but Caspian picked me up, sweeping an arm under my legs and catching my back with the other. The roader came to a complete stop in the same instant.

"Let me go!" I screamed and kicked. I pummeled my hands against his broad chest, but I was too exhausted and hurt to put up much of a fight. My body was growing heavier by the second, and that bite was throbbing.

"Once we're inside the roader," he replied. "It's too dangerous to stay out here."

So, for the first time since I met Caspian, he forced me to do something. He forced me inside of the roader, onto the backseat. This was starting to get too familiar.

He didn't get in back with me. The blond and the warrior did, sandwiching me in the middle like Den and Nash had. There was another werewolf with extremely pale and freckled skin wearing a black cap at the wheel in the front of the roader. Caspian got into the seat next to him, and the roader roared to life. It looped around, taking us in the direction opposite of Paws Peak.

It was a bumpy ride since this roader was carving its own path, through bushes and small trees while turning away from large trees, instead of following one. The growl of other roaders joined in. They were a good distance behind, though.

"Don't stop," Caspian ordered.

"Wasn't planning on it." The werewolf wearing a cap jerked the wheel, and the roader flew out of thick foliage and off the side of a mountain. We were airborne. My body became weightless. I scrambled for something to ground me and strapped myself in with a seatbelt.

"Shit!" the blond werewolf to my right exclaimed as he grabbed a handle above the window to his right. "Todd, are you trying to kill us?!"

The warrior to my left howled and exclaimed, "Hell yeah!" as we touched down on rocky ground.

The roader almost somersaulted, but the back wheels managed to ground themselves as we continued on a steep descent.

"You wanted to lose them," Todd, the werewolf at the wheel, said calmly.

"Yes," Caspian murmured. He was holding a handle too, muscles tensed. "I'd also like to live to see another day."

The descent was steep for only a few minutes. Then we were on somewhat flat ground again with a clear shot to a dirt pathway. That leap was pretty crazy, but I doubted anyone from Paws Peak would be able to catch up to us now.

I was impressed.

"Well, Todd, you never cease to amaze," Caspian said, releasing his death grip on that handle.

"I didn't know you had a thrill-seeker side," the big warrior to my left commented. He was still grinning, practically exuding adrenaline.

"I just do what needs to get done."

"By the way, guys, this is Princess Sorissa va Lupin of Howling Sky," Caspian announced. "Princess, this is Todd, our fearless driver. The big guy with the tattoos to your left is Rodrick."

"And the killjoy to your right is Aerre," Rodrick chimed.

"Can't you two ever get along? If it's not one, it's the other."

I rubbed the bite in between my neck and right shoulder. I wasn't hurt badly or beyond repair anywhere—I didn't think. If I did have a serious injury, it was this bite. It sure was persistent about calling my attention to it. I was doing well more or less ignoring every other ache in my body.

I caught the blond, Aerre, staring at me in my peripheral vision. He didn't stop when I met his gaze. His lake-blue eyes were glued to my bite, and I suddenly felt self-conscious. I rested the palm of my hand flat against the bite to hide it.

"Right, and I still have something that belongs to you," Caspian remarked as he pulled my mother's journal from his pack. He reached it out to me, and the roader hit one last bump before landing on the much smoother trail. Caspian almost hit his head on the ceiling. "Thank the Gods for seatbelts."

"Thank the werewolves who first made roaders," Todd countered.

I took the journal from Caspian's outstretched hand. "Thank you." I looked around the full roader, at each individual. "All of you." They were an unlikely pack somehow. None of them really fit together. They looked nothing alike. Caspian's skin was the darkest I had seen yet, nearly black. Todd, on the other hand, was almost as pale as Den. Aerre wore a flawless golden tan, and Rodrick's skin was an even brown almost hidden by all the black tattoos. From the short time I had been with them, they also acted nothing alike. I doubted they were related.

However, there was one thing they had in common. I didn't feel threatened by their presence. I didn't exactly feel lesser either. Yes, Caspian had still made some comments about wereas I would have preferred he hadn't, and Aerre was giving me an odd stare, but it was different. I didn't think Caspian was trying to make me feel lesser, and Aerre wasn't giving me a hungry look. Their actions were different too. They gave me their names up front. But that wasn't enough. This was just like when Leer had taken me away from my woods.

Clearing my throat, I added, "But you can drop me off here." Whether they treated me "better" or not didn't matter. I wasn't going with them.

"We can't," Caspian said after a pause. "We have to take you to Wolf Bridge. You'll be safe there."

"It wasn't a request," I retorted.

"She's got the 'boss everyone around' part of being a princess down," Rodrick mused. "Doesn't look much like one though. Is what you're wearing supposed to be a dress, Princess?" His intense green eyes dipped to my breasts. My nipples were barely covered after the beating the dress went through. What was left could hardly be called clothing at all, but I didn't care. I was just glad Charles cut through the back of that corset so I could breathe.

"I'm not bossing anyone around," I argued. "I was stating my rights as a living being with free will to make my own decisions for myself. I'm not doing this again." I bared my teeth and growled. "I'm not going to another kingdom where I'll just get locked up. I'd much rather be out there in open land, out on my own in the wild. That's something I know, where I belong."

The roader was moving fast as ever, but we weren't careening down a steep mountainside, and my chances of landing without breaking a bone were good enough for me. I moved fast. I unbuckled my seatbelt, locked my mother's journal in my teeth, and leaped for the door on Aerre's side of the roader because he was smaller than Rodrick—not that he wasn't still a hard body of muscle. My options were limited.

And I chose right.

Aerre had been staring at me, but he didn't see this coming. He froze in surprise just long enough for me to open the door and tumble out of the speeding metal beast. I hit the ground, back-first, rolling around in the dust. That contact with solid ground reminded me how cold it still was, like winter was determined to linger.

More pain exploded across my body, but I ignored it. Before I stopped spinning, I dug into my nearly empty reserves of moonlight. It was a drop of cold water splattering against the back of my skull. I had one tiny burst I could use and now was the time. It might be enough to zip me to a thicket of trees, where I'd be able to hide from these werewolves.

My body hummed. Blue light of all shades steamed out of my pores. My body morphed. My bones were first; they grew, shrunk, and rearranged themselves to form my other skeleton. My organs followed suit, and my skin was pliable putty. The dress I was wearing officially gave up the ghost at this point. It blew away in the wind as pieces of dirty yellow and once-white undergarments. I kept my mother's journal carefully locked between my jaws, and my paws caught the ground. I was running. Black fur sprouted and coated my entire body. My shift into a wolf was complete.

Just as soon as I had accessed my moonlight form, I could feel it slipping away. My sharp eyes caught sight of thick foliage and trees where I could hide, and I ran. I had only seconds.

I glanced behind me, hoping the werewolves in the roader would leave me be. My heart dropped, and I pumped my legs harder. Three massive wolves were on my tail: two white, one gray-brown. The roader was in the process of turning around. They were all coming for me and fast.

It wasn't going to work. This was why I hadn't used this drop of moonlight sooner. My legs were slowing, re-belling. My moonlight form was fading away, and I was panting with the effort of holding on to it by sheer will-power alone.

Then something hit me. Hard. It was one of the white wolves. This one was speckled with gray. He tack-led me to the ground. The force knocked my mother's journal out of my mouth. It went skidding across dirt and grass, and I was grounded, back against the earth. Still, I hung on to my moonlight form as I growled, struggling to break free of the bigger wolf pinning me down as I nipped at him. I howled in gut-wrenching defeat as I fought to keep my moonlight form. I couldn't push him off when I was at war with myself.

The wolf above me shifted. When all the white fur was replaced with black smooth skin, I saw the Caspian I recognized.

He was good at catching me.

Blue was drifting from him, and his eyes were glow-ing with power. He was still using moonlight to keep me down even though he had shifted.

"Shift back," he commanded.

I growled and tried to bite him again, but he used a

strong hand to hold my muzzle shut. I hated this weakness. I hated being without moonlight.

The blue emanating from Caspian heated up, glowing white-hot. I thought he would try to command me again, but then it faded. The moonlight encompassing him receded, and he let my muzzle go.

"Please, shift back," he repeated, kindly this time, asking. "I can see you don't have any moonlight left. I don't know how you're still in your moonlight form."

I looked past him to the moon overhead. It was so close to full, but close wasn't enough. I couldn't stop panting. I'd have no choice but to give up this form no matter what I did, so I let it go.

My black fur withdrew. My flesh and skeleton reverted. I was back to my base form. The bare skin of my back was cold against the earth, but there was sweat on my brow from all the exertion. Heat radiated from Caspian's skin, and I was hyperaware of the places he was touching me. His inner thighs pressed against the outside of my own, and his hands were on my wrists. Then he moved. He got off me and stood up without me having to ask him to, to beg him to. He wasn't like Charles.

I splayed my legs, planting my feet wide, and sat up, using my arms for support, but I didn't go any farther than that. I had never seen a male of my own kind naked before, obviously, and I couldn't take my eyes off him.

His black skin reached every inch of his body like I knew it should, but seeing it was different. Seeing the muscles rippling underneath that same skin without layers of clothes to conceal the definition, each and every curve and indent like he had been meticulously sculpted, was mesmerizing. I was curious just like I had been curious when Leer, Den, and Nash had come to take me away, but this wasn't the same. Caspian and his werewolves were close to my age. Looking at Caspian like this, right now, made my core simmer.

Caspian wasn't looking at me, his head was turned over his shoulder as he spoke to the others, telling them to bring me clothes or something. I wasn't paying attention. My eyes were wandering down his chest, and my fingers were reaching out tentatively to touch him even though he wasn't within touching distance. His broad shoulders and chest tapered down to narrow hips and a patch of curly pubic hair. My eyes rested on his half-erect penis. It was growing more erect, swelling. Engorging.

"My eyes are up here, Princess."

Caspian's baritone voice startled me out of my stupor. I slowly looked up to meet his gaze. There was discomfort in his sapphire-speckled eyes. The skin was pulled too tight at the corners like he was trying to stop himself from grimacing. There was also something familiar. His gaze was heated, hungry like Den's had been, like

Charles's, like every werewolf I had met in Paws Peak.

He cleared his throat. "You are not shy."

I scowled. "What?"

He raised an eyebrow at me, the same expression he made when I told him I'd rip off his balls if he didn't let me go when we first met. His eyes shifted downward, between my legs, then they shot back up to my face. This time he did grimace.

The heat was still in his eyes.

The roader rolled up next to us as Aerre and Rodrick walked next to it. They were fully dressed. Aerre thrust a pile of clothes at Caspian and said, "Get a grip."

Caspian took the clothes and immediately started dressing after turning his back to me.

Todd hopped out of the roader, but he held back a few steps with Rodrick. Aerre came to me next. He was carrying more clothes. He shifted them to one arm and held out a hand to me. I took it, and he helped me to my feet. His hand was warm. So warm.

"These weren't made for a werea, so they'll likely be big, but it's better than nothing," he said, handing me some baggy undergarments, a large long-sleeved shirt made of wool, and loose pants with long legs that I would have to roll up.

I accepted the clothes. I was freezing and grateful for them and immediately began dressing. Aerre tuned his head over his shoulder, reluctant to look at me. I watched as the little lump in his throat dipped as he swallowed.

When I was dressed, Todd walked up to me. He was holding my mother's journal. "Dropped this," he said as he brushed off the dirt.

"Thank you." I was glad to have it back in my arms.

Todd bowed his head and scratched the back of his neck. Strands of fire-red hair peeked out from under his black cap. As if he just realized what he was doing, he abruptly stopped and pulled the cap down, hiding all traces of red—except for the tint of red showing through the freckles of his pale cheeks. I had the urge to touch his cheeks, to check if they were as warm as they looked. But I didn't.

I sighed and made a decision: if I was a captive again, I would make the most of it—and I could only hope this experience would somehow be better than the last. And I didn't have to give up my freedom forever. The full moon would come the night after the next. It wasn't too long to wait if these werewolves kept treating me as well as they had so far. I could handle it.

And, though I didn't want to admit it, I didn't actually want to be alone. Somewhere in the back of my mind, I still hoped there was a pack out here I could befriend. Werewolves, humans, vampires, none of it mattered to me as long as there was kindness and the possibility of understanding. Those things led to friendship. Those things led to family.

I missed my family. I wondered if I should have hated Babaga for what she did to me, but I couldn't bring myself to. I missed her. I missed the woods.

"I have a lot of questions," I said quietly.

"Can questions wait until we're back in the roader and moving?" Caspian replied.

"I don't have a choice, do I?"

"I suppose not." He frowned. "It really is for your own safety, Princess. And I'll answer any questions you have. How does that sound?"

It was my turn to raise an eyebrow at him. Did he genuinely care about my willingness to go with them? It seemed like it.

"Okay," I said.

"Great." He smiled. "Let's hit the road."

I looked from him, the first potentially nice werewolf I had met and the first I had seen naked, to redcheeked Todd, no-nonsense Aerre, and carefree Rodrick. They were nothing alike, but they shared Caspian's potential for kindness.

Maybe I could befriend these werewolves.

CHAPTER 12

CASPIAN

*M*Y BODY was aching with a need I had never felt before. The Lost Princess of Howling Sky was a temptress—or I was so deprived of sex I had lost all self-control. I tended to do my best when leading with my head, or my heart as Aerre might have claimed, rather than with an alpha's instinct and power or whatever. But I couldn't deny that the princess did something to me. I blamed it on indecent exposure and that neglected sex drive I mentioned. It never seemed to mind being neglected before.

This was going to be a long drive.

The princess was looking at me expectantly from the backseat of the roader. I was glad I was sitting up front with Todd—and I also despised it. I was jealous of

Rodrick and Aerre, sitting next to her, nearly touching her. The Lost Princess was the most beautiful creature I had ever laid eyes on, the first werea close to my age I had the privilege of being near; she just turned eighteen and I was twenty-three. Her comfort and trust were my top priorities, but "instinct" was fogging up my head. She was covered in dirt and grime, but that didn't matter. I could see through it—or my imagination had run wild too.

I studied her dark brown hair. It was slipping out of a pile that was carefully placed on top of her head, revealing natural curls. The patches of her skin that glowed through the grayish smudges of grime was a warm bronze. Her eyes were dark, a warm brown with a reddish tint like a sunset. She was wearing some generic clothes we brought along, and they were baggy as hell on her, but I knew what she looked like underneath. I tried to swallow the lump in my throat that was making it hard to speak. Her body was lean with muscle she must have gained while living her entire life in the Witch Woods. I held back a shudder when I remembered the perfect curve of her breasts, her nipples taut from the cold. Wide hips, smooth thighs. Gods, and then the way she had her legs perfectly splayed to show me everything.

I had to push those thoughts aside before my hard-on, pressing insistently against my combat pants, got painfully uncomfortable.

It was unfortunate she didn't feel the same way. Well, not that it changed anything, but I wasn't getting the same wave of heat from her that I had projected. I wanted to take her right then and there when she was naked underneath me. Admitting that made me feel a little queasy. That kind of impulsiveness wasn't like me. And it was obvious this werea was clueless. Almost completely. I was certain she had never been with a male, though that bite between her neck and right shoulder would usually mean otherwise. This was another alpha, or just a typical werewolf, instinct-based observation, but I was convinced Prince Charles hadn't sealed the deal.

She wasn't bound to him, and that was a great relief. But it also didn't change anything for me. My desires could and would never be acted on. I wouldn't pursue her to any degree because I couldn't have her. It was *truly* unfortunate because there was much more than a physical attraction pulling me toward her. She made me smile easily, with no effort, without even realizing I was doing it. I wanted to know her.

"Caspian," Sorissa said, exasperated, "you said you'd answer my questions, but we've been sitting here in absolute silence."

"You haven't asked any questions yet," I defended. "Wereas fir—"

"Stop saying that."

"Why?"

"I don't want any special treatment from you. Any of you." She made a point to look at all of us, requiring eye contact. She even stared at the rearview mirror until Todd glanced up at it to meet her eyes indirectly. "You're werewolves. I'm a werewolf too."

"But you're a female," I replied.

"So? Females are supposed to be shy? I'm not shy. Obviously. I'm assertive."

A grin was on my face before I even knew what happened. Then I was laughing. Todd wore the hint of a smile. Rodrick laughed that low laugh of his that meant he was very amused. Aerre had his face screwed up like he was trying not to smile. What was this werea doing to us?

"Obviously," I restated. I liked her more each time she opened her mouth. "Do you know a single thing about modesty or did your witch let you run bare-ass naked in the woods all the time?"

She looked offended, the way her mouth slipped open and her eyebrows furrowed into a cute scowl. "Of course not! The woods were way too cold for that unless I was in my moonlight form." She didn't answer my question about modesty. "And *my* witch has a name. It's Babaga."

I admitted I had no idea what kind of relationship

the Witch of Witch Woods and the Lost Princess could have, but I hadn't expected this.

"You act like you don't care that a witch kept you locked up in some isolated woods for all these years," I said.

She frowned. "She loved me."

"Did you love her?"

"I still love her."

"Really? Because you didn't seem all that happy when I found you in Paws Peak. She sent you there, didn't she?"

Her frown deepened.

"Caspian," Aerre warned, "enough."

Right. What am I doing? The dejected look on the Lost Princess's face made my stomach twist up, and I felt guilty.

Since Phantom Fangs was formed, I spent a lot of my time keeping Aerre and Rodrick from killing each other, but there were also times like this when Aerre put me in my place. I wasn't sure he realized it, but he was my oldest and closest friend. I relied on him more than anyone. He was much more of a brother to me than my blood-related brothers.

"Sorry," I said. "So what do you want to know, Princess? I'm supposed to be answering your questions, right?"

"I want to know why," she said softly. "Why were you looking for me? Why did you take me from Paws Peak, and why are you taking me to Wolf Bridge now?"

"Because you're the Lost Princess, Princess Sorissa va Lupin of Howling Sky. We wouldn't have known about you if we hadn't been spying on Paws Peak a week ago, though. They wanted to use you. Thanks to Todd's bugs, you're safe. Keeping you safe is the reason we're taking you back to Wolf Bridge, like I said before."

"Bugs?" Her small nose wrinkled with the face she was making. "What could bugs tell you? Todd can communicate with insects?"

Todd's eyes widened as he gripped the steering wheel tighter and made a jerky turn to follow the road.

Rodrick let out another rumbling laugh. "I like this girl."

Todd reached for his utility belt and produced one of his bugs. It was the size of a lady-bug, so it was close enough to an insect. "This is one of my bugs," he said, reaching back.

The princess took the black dot from him and held it between her fingers as she squinted at it.

"It's tech," Todd continued. "It can stick onto almost anything when you peel off that thin film, and it transmits audio to my pactputer."

"Pactputer?"

"More tech."

"But you can hear whatever these bugs hear."

"…Basically."

"Fascinating," the princess remarked as she inspected the bug with newfound interest. I was shocked by the sincere tone of her voice.

"The only bad part is that the range is limited," Todd continued. "My pactputer is a hotspot. It produces a tech field. So, unless those bugs are within the tech field, I don't get any audio."

I wondered when I should step in. Todd was about to go off on a tangent. I could tell. The werewolf hardly ever spoke a word without coaxing it out of him, but if you got him started on tech, it could be difficult to make him stop.

"We would have gotten to you before Paws Peak had if our roader hadn't broken down," Rodrick commented. "Todd's a certifiable tech wizard and whatever but even he can't be prepared for everything."

"Todd has great skill in technocraft," the princess said with a nod.

"T-technocraft?" Todd sputtered.

"Right, the magic you used to bring all this metal to life and mold it to your will."

"It's not magic. It's science, engineering, programming. I build and invent things, but none of it is alive."

"Not like you or me, but it seems alive in a way. It's amazing."

Todd's cheeks went bright red. It was easy for that color to permeate his pale skin, but he wasn't one for emotion, so I hardly ever saw it. In the short time the Lost Princess had been with us, I'd seen it more than ever before. She caught his attention, an accomplishment no other living being had ever achieved.

I glanced at the bite marring the princess's skin. She had cuts and bruises in several places, but that wound was the worst. We could mend the others, but a claiming bite would be tricky—even though I was almost certain the Mate Claim wasn't fulfilled. Prince Charles would have seen the princess back in the shadows if it had been. He would have sensed her, turned his head.

Maybe I should have hunted Prince Charles down, but that would have been a declaration of war—not that stealing the princess was any less of a declaration since we were seen. Paws Peak still might have blamed us, but they would have had no proof until the King of Wolf Bridge had decided to announce her presence. It would have worked out better in terms of war and politics. As for Prince Charles, hunting him down and eliminating him right then would have been a problem. He was surrounded by guards. I would have put the princess at greater risk. I made the right choice. I hoped.

It was time for me to ask a question I had been avoiding because I didn't want to somehow be wrong about the Mate Claim.

"Princess, that bite. Prince Charles gave you it, right?"

"Yes."

"Did he seal it?"

"I don't know."

I ran a hand down my face. "Did he have sex with you?"

"No. I kicked him in the balls."

Rodrick laughed again. This time his laughter was a roiling rumble that filled the roader. "Gods!" he exclaimed, slapping his knee. "I wish I could have seen his face. Did he cry?"

"Like a cub whining for its mother."

"Little fighter takes shit from no one."

The princess grinned at Rodrick. A full-on grin. She wasn't the least bit intimidated by him.

"Good," I murmured. "You aren't bound by the Mate Claim."

"What is the Mate Claim exactly?" she asked.

"A werewolf bites a werea and has sex with her to seal her to him. That werea is bound to the werewolf that claimed her like a tethered would be. She has to obey, and even if she was stolen away by another werewolf, she wouldn't be able to bear cubs for any werewolf but the one who sealed her with the Mate Claim."

"Tethered?"

"Do you know nothing at all?" Aerre asked testily. "A tethered is a human turned werewolf."

The princess cocked her head, and Aerre turned his gaze to the window.

"Prince Charles put an unfulfilled claim on you," I continued. "You aren't bound to him, but he still has first rights. That mark will stay until he fulfills his claim. I think it can be broken if another werewolf claims you and seals you first, though."

"That's not happening," she announced. "I don't belong to anyone." She shot me a severe look. "Is that the real reason you are taking me to Wolf Bridge, so I can be a breeder for you instead of Paws Peak?"

"No! Well, sort of?"

Her eyes got darker.

"I mean, we're not going to force you to do anything."

"You forced me to come with you."

Now Aerre was looking at me with accusing blue eyes. He was daring me to act and do what I wanted to do instead of what I was assigned to do.

"You're right, Princess. But I meant what I said. So, if you want out of this roader, give the word. We're far enough from Paws Peak now that you'll probably be fine. We'll stop and let you go," I said. And I meant it. It would be the first time I went against a direct order, but I meant it. I'd be damned if it didn't worry me, though. The implications of returning to Wolf Bridge without her would be dire. Then again, I didn't have any intention of leaving her out here on her own.

No wonder *my father* didn't trust me. I saw the Lost Princess as much more than a key piece in a lingering world war that just wouldn't die.

The princess took another long look around the roader, carefully observing each of us.

"I don't want to be alone," she whispered. Her bottom lip quivered, and her eyes glossed over with tears. My chest tightened at the sight. "If I go to Wolf Bridge, will I just be a breeder forced to mate with some werewolf the king chooses?"

"No," I said firmly. "You will not." I meant that too, even though it wasn't my place to make such promises.

She nodded like my words were enough. "Maybe I won't mind Wolf Bridge if everyone there is like you four. You're different from the werewolves in Paws Peak."

"That's because we aren't maneaters."

"Maneaters. That explains a lot," the princess murmured. "What are you then?"

"Shields. We protect the humans in our kingdom, and we definitely don't eat them."

Rodrick folded his arms, and Aerre looked out his window in resignation. They were both tethered to me. They were both human and still were in a sense. It wasn't perfect. Wolf Bridge wasn't perfect, but it was better. It had potential to continue to be better. Most importantly, the world had the potential to change. I wanted that. That was why my squad was made of a bunch of misfits. A former agitator, a human born and raised in Wolf Bridge, the smartest werewolf I had ever known from a line of maneaters, and a prince whose title was hollow.

Things were simpler when I was a cub who snuck out of the castle so I could make a friend. A real friend. Someone who wasn't my brothers, because I didn't fit in. Someone who was different and would see me differently. I picked Aerre, a human. He wasn't half as naive as I was, though, and he rejected me time and time again. But I was stubborn and patient. Patience was what had seen me through to this point, and it was what would continue to see me through to a new world, a kinder world more like the one I saw as a kid. I hoped so anyway.

I glanced back at the princess to see her dozing. I didn't blame her for being exhausted. She held on tightly to that book she was attached to. I never did read the title and wondered why it was so important to her.

"Take a nap," I said. "We'll wake you up when we get to Wolf Bridge."

She shook her head, but she could barely keep her eyes open. "I'll stay awake."

I smirked. "We'll see about that, stubborn princess."

CHAPTER 13

AERRE

I COULDN'T stop my foot from tapping the ground. I wasn't jumpy or hyperactive by nature, but when I got agitated, it just happened. It was like my body had to find a way to deal with the discordance in my head, and that resulted in whatever this foot-tapping shit was. If there had been more room in the back of the roader, I might have been cleaning or polishing our weapons instead.

The princess fell asleep. Her full eyelashes pressed lightly together like butterfly wings, illuminated by the moon. How she managed to look so delicate and beautiful while covered in filth, I didn't know, but it made me uncomfortable.

She was clutching some book or journal to her chest.

I couldn't read the title since it was covered. If I really wanted to know what it was, I probably could have asked Todd. He might have read it when he picked it up after Caspian tackled the princess to the ground. I didn't care that much.

What I did care about, at the moment, was how the princess was sleeping so peacefully with her head resting against Rodrick's densely muscled and tattooed arm. For some reason, the sight made me more agitated. Maybe it was the fact that the princess was so unsuspecting. Rodrick was the worst choice for her to show this kind of vulnerability. He was her predator and was probably contemplating how to discreetly slit her throat right now. As an agitator, the punishment he would receive for that would be worth it.

I couldn't take my eyes off him.

"What are we going to do about the Mate Claim?" I asked, directing my question at Caspian. "Prince Charles will be able to track her, won't he? Just because she wasn't sealed, doesn't mean he won't sense her, right?"

"I don't know about that. I hid the princess in plain sight and Prince Charles had no idea," Caspian replied. "But he did hesitate for a moment."

"Maybe his sniffer is broken," Rodrick mused.

I shot him a glare, and he grinned through his stupid beard.

"He'll know, or King George will," I insisted. "Paws Peak will attack Wolf Bridge."

"Maybe."

"They will! We were seen. There aren't any other werewolves around."

Caspian shrugged like none of this mattered. "Okay, but there's a chance they'll negotiate. Not everything has to end in violence."

"Is that why you didn't tell us to hunt down Prince Charles as soon as you saw the bite on her skin? Or did you somehow know Prince Charles hadn't fulfilled the Mate Claim? If he had, you would have had to kill him or she would be bound to him until he died. She would be useless to your asshole father. Did you think about that? You don't really know if she can escape Charles's claim if another werewolf tries to claim and seal her, do you? What about your promise to her? You never think things through."

"And you think your way into endless circles, never finding a right or a wrong," Rodrick jabbed, "confrontational asshole."

"That's not true." I hated that he was somehow right.

"We know Paws Peak wants to be the next High Kingdom, but that title died with Howling Sky eighteen years ago. We also know that if someone took the title, it'd be Wolf Bridge," Caspian said. "We don't have lunalite, but that won't help Paws Peak when we have superior tech. There's no way Paws Peak will get inside our walls. Right, Todd?"

"Probably," Todd answered.

"That wasn't the comforting answer I was hoping for."

I growled. "We failed the mission! The princess might never be free of Prince Charles unless he's dead, and you fed her a bunch of *bullshit*."

"I didn't lie," Caspian defended.

"You did."

"No one's ever heard of the Mate Claim being stopped halfway, but Prince Charles passed by the princess when she was practically right in front of him. I wasn't completely talking out of my ass."

"You better hope so because otherwise we're going to have to kill Prince Charles, and it'll be a lot tougher than if we had just done it in the fucking first place. You should have killed him when he was right in front of the princess, then."

"With a shitload of guards? The princess's safety was my top priority."

The princess stirred, likely disturbed by our raised voices.

"Just shut up, Aerre, before I lose my temper," Rodrick said menacingly. He hardly ever lost his temper. He was the go-with-the-flow member of this squad—even when he was bashing heads—but not right now. He moved slightly, making the sleeping princess's crunched position propped up against his arm a little less crunched.

Rodrick continued, "You're whining for no reason just like you always are. We got the princess. We'll figure out the Mate Claim. We'll be back in Wolf Bridge soon enough, and then your homesick bellyaching will be cured until we leave again."

That last bit was oozing sarcasm. I growled. Rodrick growled back. The princess stirred again, letting out a little sound of displeasure.

"Stop," Todd ordered.

Rodrick and I stopped out of pure shock. Todd never got into this stuff. He withdrew. He never said a word unless he was directly asked a question, or if the conversation was about tech.

"You'll wake her," he said.

The fight left my system, so did the urge to tap my foot. Silence engulfed us, aside from the hum of the roader engine. I looked at the princess as she drifted back into a deep sleep. It was dark out, but the headlights and dim light inside of the roader provided adequate visibility. I could see the slight rise and fall of the princess's chest even through the large sweater she was wearing. I almost swore I could hear her heart beating. It was like I was hypersensitive to her presence, but I couldn't explain why that would be.

This werea had been through a lot in one day, and yet she was taking all of this extremely well in my opinion. She was born with the kind of confidence that was almost intimidating. I would have also called her naive, but that wasn't true. She wasn't naive. She was new to this world. She was practically a newborn in it. However, I had a feeling she'd grow up fast. Her fate was to be treated as a piece of property. Werewolves couldn't even be bothered to treat their own females right.

This world would tear her down like it did my sister, and I had to play along with it. I hated werewolves. That included the princess, but that didn't mean I wanted her to suffer. I didn't think any female, human or werewolf, should have to go through what my sister did. I couldn't believe any male, werewolf or human, would take advantage like that. It was wrong. So wrong. It was her first day out of the Witch Woods and Prince Charles already succeeded in violating her partway. Perhaps vampire females were lucky in that sense since they greatly outnumbered their males; the same couldn't be said for their males.

I tasted bile in my mouth. I was complicit in whatever happened to her next. I wasn't stupid. It would be more of the same, but it was my only option. I didn't rebel. I was a good submissive, a good tethered, a good dog. Rebelling got people hurt and killed. That wasn't worth the outcome to me.

Fuck werewolves.

Fuck agitators.

Fuck vampires.

I hated them all.

CHAPTER 14

SORISSA

*T*HE VAGUE awareness of a loud clang roused me. I must have been exhausted because I wasn't a heavy sleeper. I wasn't a light sleeper either, but a sound that loud should have woken me instantaneously. Instead, I stirred slowly. I moved my head, rubbing my forehead back and forth against something firm and warm. I wasn't touching skin, but the warmth reminded me of skin. It was nice, soothing and comforting. I didn't want to open my eyes.

I snuggled closer, tilted my head upward, and then I opened my eyes. I was met with forest-green eyes staring back at me. I blinked, surprised. I glimpsed a couple white scars marring the brown skin on his face and even some

hidden in his facial hair before he moved like he was trying to shake me off of him. I sat up rigidly straight at the
same time.

I was still buckled inside of the roader, and we were
still moving. I squinted at early morning light streaming
in through Rodrick's window. Truthfully, I was a bit
mortified. I had been sleeping against his shoulder. Yes,
these werewolves were much kinder than the ones I met
from Paws Peak. I even hoped I could find a place in their
kingdom, but I couldn't become complacent. There was
a big possibility I'd still end up having to escape alone,
having to run from here. Being alone was better than being forced to mate with a werewolf I didn't even know.

Did I really think these werewolves could be different, or was I simply delusional? I hoped for the former
but feared the latter.

"Good morning, Princess," Caspian said as he
looked back at me from the front of the roader. He was
wearing a soft smile that seemed easy for him to give.
"You woke up at the perfect time. We're inside Wolf
Bridge."

I looked back and forth between Rodrick and Aerre,
trying to decide which window I'd get a better view out
of. That turned out to be an easy decision. Rodrick was
huge and blocked a lot of his window, so I picked Aerre.

But then I caught Aerre staring at me. There was something sharp in his look, something I wasn't sure I liked. He seemed angry. I wasn't sure if that anger was directed at me, but I felt it regardless.

I turned back toward Rodrick. I had been sleeping against his arm, so maybe he wouldn't mind me being close again. I just wanted to peek outside of the window. The view from the front window was too bright.

Leaning over, I experimented with getting close to Rodrick without touching him. He tensed and folded his arms, but he directed his gaze outside of the window. I placed my hands on his right leg to get a better angle. That made him really tense, but he sat back in his seat, giving me as good of a view as he could.

This kingdom was bright. Paws Peak was a lot of gray metals accentuated with yellow. Wolf Bridge was a lot of tan clay-based structures accentuated with dark blues and warm orange-reds. Based on looks alone, I liked Wolf Bridge better. The streets were wider, and the houses had a little more room. They were close and cozy, but they weren't practically built inside of each other to save room. These buildings also looked much more similar to Babaga's cottage. I didn't see tech or things I didn't recognize.

I saw humans, a lot of them, walking the same orange-red streets the roader was traveling. These humans actually smiled. I didn't see many werewolves, but there were a few scattered here and there. They wore dark blue soldier uniforms with silver accents and a orange-red insignia of two wolves whose noses were joined together like a bridge. They didn't seem to bother the humans. Some of them were even talking to humans and smiling. Was this the difference between "maneaters" and "shields"? If so, I liked shields many times better.

I thought I heard the sound of rushing water, but I wrote it off as part of the growl the roader made constantly when it was awake. But eventually we made it to a humongous bridge, and I couldn't deny the sound any longer. It wasn't the roader at all. I dug my fingers into Rodrick's leg, expressing my anxiety-mixed excitement. Wolf Bridge was split by a far-reaching chasm. It had walls clearly outlining its territory like Paws Peak had, but they stopped where the chasm began. However, those areas had extra fortifications, tall watchtowers likely equipped with weapons.

"Careful with the goods, Princess," Rodrick murmured. His voice was so low I was sure only I could hear him. I softened my dagger-like fingers so I wasn't digging into his leg and offered an apologetic smile, but he wouldn't look at me. Was he angry too? What happened while I was sleeping?

"This is the bridge our kingdom was named for,"

Caspian informed. "It has a lot of history. It used to kind of be a toll bridge. It was the most popular way for kingdoms on either side, east or west, to cross the Quicksilver River. It was a power play really, and our kingdom naturally grew out from either side of the bridge until it became what it is today.

"At one point, this bridge was the only way across the river, so it kept Wolf Bridge an influential and neutral kingdom. Things got hairy with war and demanded alliances of course, and Glory Valley ended up making a bridge of their own to cross the Quicksilver River. War is pretty complicated and messy. Stories like this just go on and on, war and more war. But I like the idea of a bridge uniting species, inviting peace."

Peace. I was right. Caspian, Rodrick, Todd, and Aerre were different. I was sure of it. And I wanted a reason for why I liked them because I did. I liked them.

I moved away from Rodrick and squeezed my mother's journal as the roader began its journey across the bridge. It was so wide it didn't feel like we were on a bridge at all. The base was made of the same orange-red rocks as the streets. The railing was intricate, swirling and sweeping. The metal looked like white gold. It was dazzling in the sun. I saw a hint of white, frothing water to either side, past the walls to the north and south. The Quicksilver River was wild and sent up a misty spray from time to time. The water particles twinkled in the morning light like stardust. It was one of the most beautiful things I had ever seen.

Would I be able to call this place home? My mother's journal made that question hard to answer. Nothing would let me forget that I was valuable, that I was a "werea." I didn't want to be treated like a sack of coins in fairytales. I didn't want to be traded or hoarded. I was alive, and I wanted to be treated as such.

When we crossed over the bridge, landing on the east side of Wolf Bridge, the kingdom seemed to transform. Some of the buildings here looked like the ones I first saw, but they were quickly getting bigger, and I was starting to see things I didn't recognize. Tech. It had to be tech. Tall poles had neat rows of wires connecting them and other poles. Other poles had huge lightbulbs inside of them. The roader's eyes were likely lightbulbs too, I realized.

The roader turned down another street, taking us north alongside the river. That was when I saw the castle. It was the largest building in the kingdom. It was made of mostly tan stones and had a large tower that looked like it had several floors and large verandas to walk outside on from every level. At the very top stood a tree-like object, minus the leaves; it was too high up to know what it actually was, but that was what it looked like.

Just like I was first brought to a castle in Paws Peak, the same thing was happening here. I tried not to replay the events in my head. Maybe this would be different, a good introduction.

I tried to stay positive, but we went to a roader stable, got out of the roader, made our way to the castle, passed by guards, and entered the castle much the same way I had with Leer and his submissives. At least I wasn't being dragged along. My werewolf entourage gave me a wide berth, and their presence didn't feel heavy. I held my journal closer, seeking comfort, but it wasn't comfort from my mother that I wanted. I wanted Babaga. The werea on those pages, the werea who was my "mother," was a stranger to me. Reading these pages would help me understand things better, but that was all. Judging from that first entry, I didn't think I even liked her.

We passed soldiers and moved through a long hall lined with ornate silver fixtures that held glowing light-bulbs The floor was carpeted in dark blue, saving this castle from the fate of being a complete echo chamber. It felt softer. More inviting.

At one point, the hall opened up into a large foyer. When I looked to my right, I saw a silver archway leading into a large circular room. There was something trapped inside a big bubbly glass cylinder, glowing brightly in the center of it. It almost hurt my eyes. I didn't think that was a lightbulb. I blinked and squinted, and then the light dimmed. Some werewolves wearing white coats stepped out of the open room, bypassing a couple of soldiers standing guard at the archway.

"Maintenance is done. You can open the tower again. The Heart looks good," one of the werewolves wearing a white coat announced. His eyes widened when he spotted us. "Todd! Welcome back. It's always an honor to be in your presence."

"Maintenance for what?" Todd asked. His face stayed neutral. I hardly recognized him as the Todd with red cheeks, the one who seemed shy when he was talking to me. This Todd was somehow cold and detached, like talking to these werewolves was a chore he'd rather not do.

"Just making sure the energy chamber can hold all of that electricity. We thought we saw a fracture in the glass, but everything is fine."

"I'll have a look at it later."

"S-sure. Is… is that the Lost Princess?"

Now all eyes were on me. It was like being appraised for my worth based on my weight in gold. It didn't matter that I was filthy, cut, and bruised.

"Yes," Caspian replied. "So, if you'll excuse us, we have to report to the king."

"Ah, yes, of course. Have you warned him you're

coming?"

"No. He'll like the surprise. Don't tell anyone she's here. The king will want to announce her arrival."

Everyone was stiff. Rodrick and Aerre were as quiet as mice. Caspian was all formalities. Todd was distant. Did they hate it inside of the castle?

The werewolves wearing white coats nodded and made a hasty escape. The soldiers straightened up and moved out to the far edges of the silver archway, apparently allowing entry into the circular room once again: the tower. The Heart.

"What's the Heart?" I asked as we began moving forward again.

"The center, the power source of the entire kingdom," Todd replied. "The big lightning rod at the very top of the castle attracts lightning during a storm and sends the electricity down to a fist-sized lightning stone, which takes any electrical energy and multiplies it tenfold. It's extremely rare, and it's hard to contain." He glanced over his shoulder at me, and his cheeks reddened. That was more like it. This was the Todd that I liked. "Sorry, I tend to go on about this stuff. You probably hate it."

"I like it," I said.

His face turned a brighter red.

I couldn't help myself. I sped up to him and reached out my hands to touch his cheeks. He flinched, but he let me do it. His cheeks were as hot as a furnace! I grabbed his black cap and pulled it off of his head, revealing a mess of short red hair.

"You're burning up!" I exclaimed.

"May I have my beanie back?" His voice was quiet, head bowed, and he held out his hand to me, pleading.

"It'll only make you hotter."

"Please."

Something was wrong. Did I hurt him somehow? Confused, I returned his "beanie." He hastily pulled it over his fire-red hair, hiding every last strand.

"I'm sorry," I said. "I didn't mean to upset you."

"Todd is a genius," Caspian said as he wedged his way in between Todd and me. He was giving me his easy smile, acting as if I hadn't just done something wrong. "No one knew how to handle that lightning stone before he came along. Thanks to him, Wolf Bridge is the safest place in the world. Right?"

"Probably," Todd muttered.

Caspian laughed. "He's just being modest."

I liked how Caspian praised him. Unlike Leer, Caspian cared about his team. A lot.

"I'd like to see the Heart and learn more about it," I said hopefully.

Todd glanced at me and then at the dark blue floor. "Okay."

"Another time, though," Caspian added. "We have other things to take care of first."

"Great, we have another tech-head," Rodrick teased. Aerre rolled his eyes.

"What do you like to do for fun, Rodrick?" I asked.

"Fight."

"Me too. Maybe we could exchange methods."

Rodrick smirked, and Aerre let out an exasperated sigh.

We went through another hall, shorter this time, and reached large wooden double doors. They weren't the same ridiculous size as the ones in Paws Peak. But I wasn't surprised to find a spacious throne room behind these ones as well. A throne. A king wearing a jewel-encrusted silver crown. He was speaking to other werewolves until he saw us.

"We'll finish this later," he said. Then he stood and opened his arms wide and smiled. "Welcome home, Phantom Fangs."

I lagged as my escort took the lead, all four of them bowing down on one knee in front of the king. I stayed where I was. I had no intention of bowing. I didn't know this king. Did he deserve my respect or was he like the king in Paws Peak?

"Your Highness, I present to you Princess Sorissa va Lupin of Howling Sky," Caspian said.

The king's smile broadened. Something about that smile was a bit familiar. As I looked at him, I thought of Caspian. They both had the darkest skin I had ever seen, sunny smiles, curly hair, and dark eyes speckled with light. But the king had a beard, and they were dressed quite differently. The king was wearing a luxurious outfit of mostly dark blue and accentuated silver while Caspian wore black tactical gear. If they were related, they had a very different relationship than the last king and prince I had met.

Warily, I watched the king descend the stairs to his throne. He bypassed Phantom Fangs, kneeling on the carpeted floor, and came to me. I had the urge to step back, but I stood my ground.

He held out his hand and said, "My name is Philip."

I didn't take his hand. He drew back easily like I hadn't just offended him, and his eyes began probing me. He was likely taking in my state. I was hardly fit to be in his presence right now if the cleaning and dressing routine at Paws Peak was anything to go by. His eyes glazed over my mother's journal and lingered on my bite. The twinkle in his eyes dimmed.

"It seems you've been through a lot to get here," he said. "Rise, Phantom Fangs."

My escort stood up in unison as if they were one thinking-and-feeling body.

"You're all dismissed except for Caspian. You did good work. Caspian, I want you to take her to her room, where she can clean up and rest."

Todd was the first to leave. His feet moved quickly, just shy of a run. Aerre and Rodrick left at a more moderate pace, but they made sure to time their leave a minute apart. I didn't like watching their backs. I didn't like the feeling of them leaving me. I turned to Caspian, reminding myself I hadn't been completely abandoned.

"We will speak again, Sorissa," Philip said. "Please, make yourself comfortable until then. This is your new home, and I want you to enjoy it."

I nodded. So far so good, I supposed. This was definitely a step up from Paws Peak.

Caspian stood patiently until the king walked away from us and ordered a guard to bring back the werewolves he was talking to so they could finish their business. Even then, Caspian waited. His jaw was clenched. He was looking in the direction of the king, but not at the king. I hadn't seen him look directly at the king the whole time since we entered, I realized. There was an angry vein pulsing in his throat.

"Caspian?"

He held out his arm to me, exactly how Leer had at Paws Peak when he escorted me to George all properly cleaned and dressed. I hated that the action alone dredged up the sour memory, and I hesitated.

"Take my arm?" he asked.

I bit my lip and shook my head. "No."

"Okay then." He dropped his arm and walked past me. "Let's get going. I'm sure you're dying to get washed up. I can put an herbal remedy in your bath. It'll sooth and clean your cuts."

If he was offended by my refusal, he didn't show it.

"Thank you," I said.

I followed him out of the throne room, keeping one step behind him. We eventually made our way up a couple flights of stairs and down a hall lined with doors precise distances apart. I figured one of these doors would lead to "my room."

"Caspian, is this bite Charles gave me really no issue? And don't treat me like I'm stupid or fragile. I can handle the truth."

"I didn't lie to you before, Princess. I don't think it's a big deal. I'll explain to King Philip that the Mate Claim wasn't fulfilled." He looked straight ahead as he talked to me. "In the worst-case scenario, I'm wrong and you are bonded to Prince Charles, but that's not a problem either. We'll just have to hunt him down and kill him."

I stopped dead in my tracks. "Why are you talking like this? Your voice was so warm before we entered the throne room. You haven't smiled since we entered or since we left."

Caspian sighed and finally turned to face me. "I'm tired. You probably are too. Yeah, you slept in the roader, but that thing is not comfortable."

"You're avoiding my question."

"This is what I can tell you: I promise to get you out of the Mate Claim that was forced on you one way or another. I'll see to it personally. We can't very well have you 'mated' to a werewolf you don't love, right?" He gave me his easy, warm smile.

"That sounds more like you," I noted. "Thank you for helping me. I mean it."

Caspian's grin broadened. He held out his hand and made a big show of bringing it to his chest, palm flat against his heart. Then he bowed. "It's my pleasure, Princess."

When he straightened, I shifted my mother's journal to one hand and grabbed his arm with my other hand like he asked me to earlier. "Let's go," I said. "I trust you."

CHAPTER 15

CASPIAN

*T*HERE WAS a room all prepared for the Lost Princess. The king made sure that was taken care of as soon as Phantom Fangs verified she was real, from that intercepted conversation in Paws Peak, and that we'd be bringing her back to Wolf Bridge in a week's time. We couldn't very well let the Moonlight Child fall into the hands of King George ve Paz of Paws Peak. King Philip never even made that sound like an option. He all but assured Wolf Bridge that the witch had reached out to *us*. He was that confident Phantom Fangs would deliver her, and it did.

We did.

I wasn't stupid. I knew Princess Sorissa wasn't here for strictly her own benefit, but that didn't mean I couldn't work in the shadows to try and make it so.

She said she trusted me.

I was glad the castle was carpeted since the princess was forced to walk barefoot at my side. She hadn't complained about the lack of shoes, but I felt bad. Her feet probably hurt from all the running she did back in Paws Peak. I saw cuts. Luckily, they didn't look too bad.

I would have volunteered to carry her if I hadn't thought she would refuse me without even considering it. The fact that she was holding my arm at this moment was a huge accomplishment. I wished my arm hadn't been covered by the long, tight sleeve of my Phantom Fangs uniform so I could feel her skin. It was probably for the best that I couldn't, though. My mind kept wandering back to her naked underneath me.

Think about something else, I silently chastised myself. Gods knew I didn't want to deal with another hard-on and these pants.

"Here it is," I announced when we reached the wooden door leading to her room. I opened it and presented the large room to the princess. The color scheme was the same as the rest of the castle. There was a large circular bed in the center with delicate white lace draping down from the ceiling. It was meant to be soft. Feminine.

"What do you think?" I asked.

"It's really big," she said.

She let go of my arm and walked over to the bubble-glass doors sealing off the balcony. She slid them open and stepped out, allowing sunlight to trickle unfiltered into the room. I joined her as she leaned against the silver railing.

"I like this view," she said. "You can see the mountains in the distance." She was still holding that book. She pulled back her hair with her free hand when a gust of wind blew, tucking the dark curly strands behind her ear. I could have stared at her for hours, filthy or not. She was literally as beautiful as a painting. This moment had all the dynamics and colors needed for a masterpiece.

I followed her when she went back inside. She touched the edge of the circular bed and sighed. "The bed is too soft. So is this floor. I don't feel like I fit in here."

"Once you're cleaned and dressed up like the place, I'm sure you'll fit in just fine," I said. I walked over to her closet, which was basically another room, and presented all the different dresses the king filled it with. At the very least, I was sure one of them would fit her for now. Her measurements could be taken to replenish the closet with only dresses that fit her now that she was here.

The princess joined me in the closet and crinkled her cute nose. I had to laugh. What was that reaction? Any other werea I knew of, albeit elders or young cubs, would have died at the sight of these dresses. They were the best of the best, befitting only a princess.

"I definitely don't fit here," the princess concluded. "If I have to wear another corset, I swear to the Gods I will tear every last one of these dresses to ribbons."

"Is a corset that bad?" I asked.

"The worst. I couldn't breathe and all because they wanted to make my waist smaller and force my breasts to reach my chin."

"Gods." That earned her another laugh. Her frankness was refreshing. "No corsets then. You certainly don't need a skinnier waist and your breasts reaching your chin would be a sight to behold."

"I'm glad we agree."

"I'll send a maid in to assist you shortly, but I'm going to get your bath running so that the herbal blend is perfect for you."

"You're not going to have the maid do it?"

"I'd like to get you into that bath sooner rather than later. Don't your feet hurt?"

"A bit."

"Then please allow me to do this for you, Princess."

"Sorissa. You can call me Sorissa, Caspian. That's who I am, not some princess."

"I'm afraid we'll have to agree to disagree on that one."

She grabbed my hand before I could escape the

closet. "We're friends, aren't we?"

I hesitated before saying, "I sure hope so."

"Call me Sorissa."

I sighed and slipped out of her grasp to make my way to the bathroom on the other end of her quarters.

"Caspian!" she exclaimed, chasing after me. "Why is it so hard?"

I ignored her for a moment to consider her question. I looked at the variety of bath salts and herbs stored in jars on silver shelves lining a wall. The large bath in the center of the room was more like a pool. It was a downgrade into the floor and took up most of the room. If the princess really wanted to, she could swim in it.

I turned on the faucet, sending water out from the miniature waterfall connected at the head of the pool. I checked the temperature and made sure it was perfect before moving on. The princess was determined to be my shadow, standing right behind me with her arms folded and a defiant expression on her face.

"It's not so hard. It's just improper," I explained.

"Why? What is your title?" she asked.

"I don't have one."

"Don't lie. You're at least a captain or something similar."

I took a jar of mild lavender-colored salts, a collection of herbs, and sweet-smelling flowers. I placed them on the edge of the bath and started sprinkling in the proper amounts.

"I'm like a captain, sure, but I don't have the title. Phantom Fangs is treated as one entity," I explained. "It's the only title I have."

"You resemble Philip."

I finished prepping the bath and started screwing lids back on jars. "I won't deny it."

When I turned around to put the jars back in their proper places, the princess had dropped all her clothes onto the tiled floor. Once again, she was bare-ass naked in front of me without a fucking care, perky breasts, full hips, and perfect legs spread in an elegant and strong stance. I nearly dropped all the jars onto the floor. Thankfully, I avoided that disaster, gathering my wits about me in time to shove them back onto the shelves. I stayed facing the wall, allowing myself a moment to breathe. I couldn't turn back around. I couldn't see her like this again. My body was already burning at the thought.

"We really need to have a talk," I said.

"About what?"

I closed my eyes as water splashed. I could imagine her sinking into the bath. I could see every curve of her as if I was looking. So much for avoiding this hard-on. I opened my eyes again to stare at the shelves.

"Modesty," I gritted out.

"Okay, what about it?"

"You should have waited to undress until after I left."

"Why? Babaga and I bathed together in the woods."

I pressed my fist to my forehead and turned around. I kept my eyes grounded, but I really needed to turn off the water before it overflowed.

"That's different," I told her. "You and Babaga are both females." I reached the faucet and turned off the water all without looking at the princess. It was one of the hardest things I had ever done. I turned back away from her so I wouldn't be tempted to look and ended up staring at the pile of clothes on the floor. That book she was so attached to was sitting on top of them.

"So?" the princess asked.

"The only werewolf you should ever be naked in front of is the one who becomes your mate."

"I should only ever be naked in front of a male if my hypothetical mate is putting a baby inside of me," she said bluntly.

"Something like that." This conversation was unbelievably awkward. I wanted to say this was all common sense. It was for every werewolf raised by werewolves and not some backwater witch. That was the worst part. The princess wasn't trying to play games. She just didn't know these things. She didn't get hot and bothered at all when I was naked in front of her, as far as I could tell, but I was losing control. I was losing control again in this stupid bathroom. I adjusted my pants to relieve some of the discomfort, but it didn't help the ache. Gods, I ached in a way I didn't even understand.

"What about my moonlight form then?" she asked. "I'm never supposed to shift?"

I wasn't sure how to answer that. Wereas were never encouraged to fight or do anything that would require them to shift from what I knew. They were kept safe. "I guess not," I finally replied. "Let's stop talking about this. I'm not explaining well."

"The bath is really nice. Thank you, Caspian. Your herbs are magical, just like the herbs Babaga used back in the woods." She let out a contented sigh.

"Glad to hear it."

I stared at that book sitting on top of her clothes. It had gold writing on the cover. "What's this?" I asked as I read: To my pride and joy, the Moonlight Child blessed by Lureine, Princess Sorissa va Lupin of Howling Sky. There was more written below that: With the greatest love, High Queen Alana va Lupin of Howling Sky.

"A gift from Babaga. I'm going to read it later. I was going to read it in the bath, but I don't want to ruin it by getting it wet."

"May I take a look?"

"Since you asked so nicely."

I picked up the journal and flipped through a couple pages. High Queen Alana va Lupin of Howling Sky was a memory, but she left a never-before-seen record in these pages. It wasn't burned with the rest of Howling Sky. She truly did manage to escape and presented her daughter to the Witch of Witch Woods. I knew the cost of asking that witch for a favor. It was obvious to me that the High Queen paid with her life.

What last words did she leave her daughter?

"I guess those are the words of my mother," the princess said. "It's weird to think of some queen as my mother. Babaga never told me anything about her or this journal until she decided to give me away yesterday. She didn't bother telling me anything useful about the world outside of the woods either. I feel so stupid out here."

"You are smart and brave." I placed the journal back down on the pile of clothes. It didn't feel right to pry. The High Queen's words weren't for my eyes. "I should get going."

"Will I see you again?"

"Most definitely, along with the rest of Phantom Fangs. In the meantime, I'll send you a maid."

"Promise."

"I promise." I looked over my shoulder to see the princess resting her elbows on the edge of the bath. Her wet hair cascaded down her front and back, effectively hiding her breasts—but not effectively enough. I couldn't see past her torso, but that didn't matter. Her breasts were enough to get me hot. Her nipples were hard, bronze skin taking on a reddish tinge from the warm water.

Fuck, I was weak.

"Later, Sorissa," I said. "I'll keep my promise."

I was rewarded with seeing her face light up in a smile before I made a hasty exit.

What was I doing? Pretending I could be anything other than the princess's bodyguard was a dangerous game to play. If she was going to mate with any werewolf here, it would be one of my brothers, not me. King Philip would make sure of that, but he'd do it so subtly the princess would think it was her idea. He was good at that: manipulating. One way or another, she would willingly end up on King Philip's side. I doubted there was anything Phantom Fangs could do about that. I had a growing idea of a world I wanted to see, but Phantom Fangs was under King Philip too. If I never broke away, maybe I'd never see it.

CHAPTER 16

SORISSA

I WAS still staring at the door leading out of the bathroom long after Caspian left. I would have preferred him to stay, but a moment alone wasn't terrible. I wasn't exactly looking forward to my new "maid." I hoped she wouldn't be like the last one.

Closing my eyes and letting the warm water engulf me all the way up to my chin, I replayed in my head what Caspian told me about modesty. Honestly, whatever he was trying to get at was a bit confusing to me. I didn't feel like I had done anything wrong, but it was like I had offended him somehow. I remembered him naked after he chased me down when I fled the roader. I wondered if it was okay for males to be naked in front of me as long as I wasn't naked in front of them.

My mind wandered around in the memory of Caspian naked. His black skin was beautiful in the moonlight. It brought out a blue undertone I hadn't noticed before. His body was so perfectly sculpted, smooth and hard edges combined to make him so very beautiful. A lump formed in my throat. I tried to swallow it when I thought about his penis, how it was swelling, growing erect. My brain went blank for a moment when that happened, like a snuffed-out candle. Was that his body's reaction to seeing me naked?

I flushed, heat originating from the base of my stomach. It was a recreation of the blooming feeling I had when I first saw this scene with Caspian. This feeling. Just thinking back on that moment, naked with Caspian, made me feel like this again. But this was stronger. There was no shock or fear to pull me out of it. I didn't understand. I had never experienced this feeling. My sex tingled, and the bite Charles gave me burned at the same time. It startled me at first, but the burning quickly subsided. The heat, the pleasurable almost humming heat in my core, did not.

My mind drifted to Todd, and I smiled. The memory of my hands on his reddened cheeks was fresh. The cute way he talked so passionately about what he loved was endearing. I thought of Rodrick and his size, the largest of Phantom Fangs. Maybe it would have been prudent to find him intimidating, but he only riled me up. He only made me feel safe. Aerre came to mind next. I thought about how closed off he was, but I remembered his calm and collected attitude when he provided me with decent clothes to stave off the cold. I saw through to his kindness. Each one of them had that: kindness. And each one of them was beautiful. I wanted to get to know them better. Phantom Fangs was what I had hoped to find when I left my woods.

A little gasp escaped my lips when that tingling feeling in between my legs got stronger. It built into a surge of pure energy that was too much. It was just sitting there inside of me with nowhere to go, making it painful, making me ache. I had no idea what was happening to me.

I closed my eyes and pictured Phantom Fangs naked. I placed my hands on my tender breasts and tried to massage away the discomfort I felt there first. The ache ran deep into my chest. I ran one hand down my stomach to my sex, the area containing the densest energy. My lips parted softly as I gently explored the sensitive flesh in between my legs, imagining Phantom Fangs doing it instead. The warm water ensured my touch was slick and light. Instinctively, I rocked my hips forward. It ramped up the building sensation in my body, a sensation I was sure couldn't build any more. Frustrated, I whimpered, but my hips rocked forward against my hand again as if they had a mind of their own and knew how to find some sort of release.

The pressure continued to build as I hit a rhythm that almost felt good, sliding two fingers across my slit and dipping shallowly inside. I had no idea what I was doing, but I was doing it. I moved faster and gripped the edge of the bath with my other hand for stability. I rocked and rocked until the pressure reached its peak, and my body shattered. I breathed heavily as I hunched over the edge of the bath and noticed the pulsing in between my legs. With each tiny pulse, the energy dissipated until I felt mostly normal again, aside from this strange sense of satisfaction.

Finally, my eyes fluttered open, and I wondered what just happened.

I wrapped my arms around myself. I concentrated on my breathing until it returned to a normal flow. The desperation was gone, but I couldn't stop thinking about Phantom Fangs. I couldn't stop myself from wondering what each of them looked like naked. I couldn't stop thinking about the warmth of waking up next to Rodrick, from the feeling of Aerre's hand clasping mine to Todd's cheeks, and Caspian's arm when I allowed him to lead me. I wanted to feel that again.

A knock startled me out of my thoughts. "Princess?

I'm Trace, your maid. May I come inside?" The voice belonged to a female, and that meant, according to Caspian, that it was okay for her to see me naked.

"Yes," I replied.

A lovely blonde emerged. She was human, tall and slender with full breasts. She had sun-kissed skin, and her eyes were the color of a cloudless sky during a summer day. She stood straight with her hands clasped in the front of her floral-patterned skirt. I could sense she was much more confident than my previous maid.

"I'm supposed to assist you in getting ready to see the king. He requests your presence at your earliest convenience," she informed.

"What about Phantom Fangs?" I asked.

"I'm afraid they won't be accompanying you for this. The king wants only you."

I didn't want to see Philip. I wanted to see Phantom Fangs, but I didn't say that. Caspian said I would see them again. He promised, and I wanted to believe him.

"You told me your name," I said. "The maid I had in Paws Peak wouldn't."

"Should I not have?"

I shook my head and smiled. "No, I'm glad you did, Trace. I hope we can become friends."

Her eyes shifted like she was uncertain about that, but then she returned my smile. "I would like that."

"You can tell me when I'm doing something wrong."

"I-I couldn't."

"Why not?"

"There is nothing you could ever do wrong, Princess."

"Caspian seemed to think so when I took off my clothes to get into this bath before he left the room."

I thought Trace might laugh. Her eyes were twinkling, and she was definitely holding back a much wider smile. "Shall we get you ready, Princess?"

"Why not?"

It wasn't like I had a choice. Wolf Bridge was a werewolf kingdom like Paws Peak. They weren't copies, but there were still plenty of similarities. I had to be ready for whatever Philip would throw at me because I wasn't naive enough—not anymore—to assume it'd end well.

The bath really did soothe my cuts. I hardly hurt at all anymore, and I didn't look like I had just gone through a rather stressful ordeal. Caspian knew what he was doing. His herbal blend worked almost as well as Babaga's.

By the time Trace was done with me, I was once again wearing a dress. However, Trace didn't bring up corsets once. I wondered if that was because of what I told Caspian. Then again, this dress was quite different from the one I wore in Paws Peak. This one was simpler, similar to Trace's. She said it was a spring dress. It had a flower pattern and the skirt cut off just above my knees. Since it was still chilly, I wore solid-colored tights and a solid-colored jacket, both a dark blue. I didn't feel trapped in this dress. I actually felt quite free and found myself liking it. She even left my hair down after drying it with a handy hairdryer.

"Your hair is beautiful," she told me. "It curls perfectly on its own when it dries."

The last thing she did was paint my face with makeup. This time it felt less like painting and more like powdering. I didn't mind it.

I found talking to Trace easy, too. At least she *would* talk. I doubted she would ever tell me anything even slightly negative, but she talked. Everything she said seemed sincere enough, so I wasn't really complaining. We didn't talk about anything "serious," but that was fine. I figured I'd save those questions for Phantom Fangs. Trace wasn't shy like my other maid, but she was still human, still my "maid," and I didn't want to cause her trouble even with Caspian's explanation about Wolf Bridge werewolves being shields. The memory of Paws Peak was too fresh. I was still an outsider, so what did I really know?

"Is the princess ready?" A male's voice and another knock outside of my room sounded.

"Yes," Trace called. "I'll send her out."

Suddenly, my stomach dropped. "Is there a way out of this?" I asked.

"You'll do fine," she assured. She took my hand and squeezed it as she walked me to the door. "Everything is going to be okay."

She released me and opened the door to a soldier, a werewolf I didn't recognize.

"Thank you, Trace," the werewolf said. He wore a grin that lit up his entire face.

Humans and werewolves had much better communication in Wolf Bridge, it seemed. No, it was more than that. This werewolf was beaming at Trace specifically. Trace's cheeks heated, but they only turned a fraction of the red Todd's did.

"Take good care of her," Trace said as she shut the door to my room purposefully slow, locking herself away inside.

The werewolf soldier looked at the door and sighed. He hadn't looked at me at all yet—which was a nice change. For once, I wasn't the focal point of a werewolf's attention. He was a handsome werewolf with straight black hair and wide dark brown eyes. At this moment, his entire countenance was sunny.

"Nice to meet you, Princess," he said with a bow. "I'm Koren, and I'll be your escort to the throne room."

He held out his arm to me. He was so friendly it didn't feel weird to take him up on the offer—not after Caspian had broken through to me.

"Nice to meet you, Koren," I replied.

I noticed touching his arm was not the same as touching Caspian, Todd, Rodrick, or Aerre. Koren was warm because he was alive, but that was all. There was something magical in the Phantom Fangs' touch. Even just being near them was magical. They had something no one else had.

Koren was lost in his head the entire time he was escorting me. I was almost positive he was thinking of Trace, so I didn't bother trying to speak to him. And I found it fascinating. He would keep smiling randomly for no reason. This was the kind of love portrayed in fairytales. Apparently, it was real, because Trace and Koren's actions fit line for line. This was the first thing I had seen outside of my woods that was exactly like the fairytales.

Koren brought me back to the throne room. This time, Philip was sitting on his throne, watching as Koren led me down the dark blue carpet. Five other werewolves stood at either side of him. There was a unity about them, in their faces, their builds, and dark skins. They were also dressed similarly, in dark blue suits decorated with patterns of silver that matched the crowns on their heads, though they were less extravagant. They looked a lot like Caspian, the same age too. Visions of George and his son Charles flashed through my mind with the feeling of deja vu.

When we arrived at the foot of the throne, Koren announced, "Princess Sorissa has arrived." He tugged away from my hand and bowed down on one knee.

"Thank you, Koren. You are dismissed," Philip said.

Koren stood up again, pressing his right hand to his heart with another tiny bow of his head. Then he turned on his heel, leaving me alone with Philip and the werewolves who had to be his sons.

Philip rose from his seat while his sons bowed to me, low on one knee. The king descended the few steps separating us and took my hand, kissing the back of it. His long black beard tickled my skin.

"It is good to see you again, Princess. I hope you were able to get some rest. You cleaned up nicely."

As Philip righted himself, releasing my hand, the princes rose from the ground. I gave them all a quick look. All I could think of was Caspian. I was positive he was somehow related to Philip and these other werewolves, but he wasn't here. I wondered why that was.

"These are my sons," Philip explained and pointed

out each of them. "Prince Alexander ve Casst of Wolf Bridge, Prince Julius ve Casst of Wolf Bridge, Prince Dominic ve Casst of Wolf Bridge, Prince Edward ve Casst of Wolf Bridge, and Prince Henry ve Casst of Wolf Bridge."

I wondered if it was really necessary to repeat their titles each time. I also wondered if I would remember their names, because I found myself not caring.

"I want to reassure you that we will do everything we can to free you from the unfinished claim Prince Charles put on you. It will be removed, and he will have no power over you anymore."

I thought about that bite on my neck. It wasn't bothering me much anymore, not compared to how it felt back in Paws Peak. I didn't like that the Mate Claim apparently had the power to turn a werea into a submissive. I didn't like the pull the unfinished Mate Claim had toward Charles. I wanted to dig at the bite. I wanted to tell everyone that I would never let the Mate Claim control me, sealed or not. I didn't belong to anyone. But I bit my tongue. My outburst in front of George hadn't gone over so well, and I didn't believe in repeating mistakes.

"How will you do that?" I asked. "Free me of the Mate Claim."

"We'll kill Prince Charles ve Paz of Paws Peak," he said simply. The way he said it made me think of Caspian and how he had said that same thing before, like killing wasn't a big decision. They said it with detachment. "You needn't worry about it. The situation is under control, so you should proceed as if you weren't claimed. Live your life here. If you find a werewolf you wish to take as your mate, pursue him. I've asked you here to introduce you to my sons. Any one of them would be happy to show you around Wolf Bridge or answer any questions you might have. Come forward, my sons."

Philip used different words than George, but the end goal was the same. He wanted me mated to one of his sons. He didn't say that specifically, but why else would he shove them in my face like this? I pretended to be interested, to inspect each son from head to toe, but it was all a show. I had no interest in going through this again. I had no interest in looking for a mate. I wondered how long Philip's patience would last. If he was anything like me, it wouldn't last for long. That thought made my skin crawl. All I knew for sure was that I needed to recharge on the full moon tomorrow night so that I had another option if Wolf Bridge didn't work out.

I thought of Phantom Fangs. I thought about how I wanted to see those four werewolves again. When I looked into one of the prince's eyes, I could only think about how his eyes didn't have those same luminous blue specks as Caspian's. I thought about asking Philip about

Caspian, but maybe that was something that would get me in trouble. I felt as if I were walking on a brittle rope. Speaking my mind, something I never had any trouble with, would send me plummeting into a deep, dark chasm. I decided to save my words for Phantom Fangs. They listened to me. I did not see the same thing happening with Philip or his chosen sons.

I did decide to risk one question though.

"Where is Phantom Fangs?"

"Indisposed," Philip dismissed easily. He went on to tell me all the "wonderful" things about his sons, but I only pretended to listen.

Caspian said Phantom Fangs would see to breaking the Mate Claim personally. Had they already left? Were they really going back to Paws Peak for me? Was it for me at all? What if they died? Thoughts of Phantom Fangs consumed me, and I hoped for their safety. There were many things I wanted to know about them, like why thinking about them made me so warm, why my flesh tingled at the memory of their touch. I wanted to understand, and I wanted to believe they were genuine.

CHAPTER 17

RODRICK

"WE SHOULD just head back to Paws Peak right now and kill Charles because the full moon is tomorrow night. It'll make everything more of a hassle," I argued. "Chances are they're low on moonlight right now. When they recharge, the fight we're taking on will get bigger."

"Sure, Rodrick, but we don't have much moonlight left either," Caspian replied. His arms were folded, and he was leaning back against one of the obnoxious tan pillars that lined the inside of the Phantom Fangs Lair. Those pillars had no purpose aside from the "aesthetic."

"We shouldn't be hasty," Aerre agreed. "They'll have their defenses up higher. Maybe they've changed their system now or found a way to lock Todd out."

"Doubtful," Todd said. "That would require an entire system overhaul. I should be able to get in any time I want. With my modifications, we shouldn't have a time limit either. The problem is my reach and power."

"I'm just saying we need to consider everything."

I stopped wasting my breath, and I stopped listening. Aerre would have us all spinning in circles for Gods knew how long. All of this deliberation was pointless. It would be so easy if they would just look at the obvious white and black, the right and wrong decisions. It frustrated me, but the squad didn't see the world as clearly as I did. And how could they? They were werewolves and a confused tethered.

I sat back and looked at the wall Todd filled with mounted monitors. I didn't know why he bothered when he hardly spent any time here. They oversaw Wolf Bridge from the vantage points of various cameras. We weren't the guard. We didn't take care of domestic issues. Maybe it was for Aerre's benefit, because plenty of the cameras were watching over the Tech Off Zone, the human-only zone; the lair was located on a border between that zone and the Tech On Zone near the castle, walking distances. I didn't know Aerre's whole issue because I didn't care to, but he liked to keep his eyes on his mother and older sister. That was the source of his constant homesickness. If he thought werewolves were so untrustworthy, I couldn't fathom why he was so against me and my "agitator bud-dies."

I saw things clearly, but not clear to the point that I knew the details behind everything. I knew Aerre was my enemy, an enemy of the rebels, and therefore wrong. It was really that simple.

We were all supposed to live in the lair, but more than half of the time that didn't seem to be the case. Aside from Aerre, Todd was always off in the Heart, Caspian was always sulking outside or inside of the castle, and I was always sneaking out. We were a single unit, but it was a rare occasion for us to actually be together outside of our missions. That suited me just fine.

"We just need time to prepare," Todd said when I started listening again. "I'm working on a larger tech field, one cast out by the Heart. Give me a couple days to see what I can do. If I can hack Paws Peak from here and reconnect with those bugs we planted, we'll have better intel for planning an attack. We'll know when to strike."

"You really think you can do that?" Caspian asked. "Paws Peak is miles away."

"That sounds like a huge leap from where you are," Aerre said. "Are a couple days really enough? We're kind of on a time limit."

Todd averted his gaze. It was a childish action, something he did when he didn't have a good answer.

Aerre continued, "Paws Peak could attack us well before you figure that out. They know we have the Lost Princess, but they still have a half-claim on her—or an actual claim. We don't even know."

He shot Caspian a glare, and Caspian replied with a growl that showed off his white teeth. "Enough, Aerre. I told you it's not a big deal. We're going to fix it. Stop fighting me."

It wasn't like our alpha to react aggressively to anything we did. He wasn't the type to play the power card because he liked to play at being the peacemaker—or he just liked the role of a mother. He hardly ever showed off his strength or "superiority." He never used moonlight to make us submit unless he deemed it absolutely necessary, and he certainly never brought up breeding. He never brought up the fact that Aerre and I were tethered. He also never brought up Todd's ancestors being maneaters. As far as raw power, involving moonlight, Caspian outranked Todd spectacularly too. That was because of breeding. But Todd's whole thing with tech made him irreplaceable, strangely important in a culture that valued brute strength. It was because Philip understood the importance of strength in brains too.

We were quite a crew of misfits. But that was what made Phantom Fangs interesting. We somehow worked together.

"We're going to give Todd a couple days," Caspian concluded. "If he can do it, Wolf Bridge has as good as won the Prime War. He'll also prepare a contingency plan because we can't wait too long to solve the princess's problem."

"And everyone will start fresh with new moonlight," I said, offering my last reminder of that crucial fucking detail. Werewolves relied way too much on their damn moonlight.

"It doesn't matter. We're going to wait and guard So-rissa until then."

That slip-up, the fact that he didn't use her title, got him stares from the rest of us. Caspian never missed titles—even with his own bastard father. Using the princess's name casually like they were old friends or maybe even *lovers*… it made my gut burn. I ignored it, but I didn't like it. I didn't like the subtle shift in our already precarious balance caused by the Lost Princess. Caspian wasn't thinking with a clear head. Maybe none of us were.

"Caspian," Aerre warned, "she's got an entire kingdom to guard her. We don't need to be her designated bodyguards. We need to break that claim."

"I can get this tech field to work. The Heart will make it work," Todd insisted.

"How come you never brought it up before now? It

must be a huge undertaking."

Suddenly, the clarity I had of the situation was gone. It all seemed so muddy aside from the princess herself, but decisions about the princess for the princess weren't how this was supposed to work. I had tried to ignore it, to forget her and focus on our task, but she had done something to me. All of us. She wasn't the Moonlight Child blessed by Lureine for nothing. I shouldn't have allowed her to get so close to me. I shouldn't have let her sleep against my arm in the roader, but I couldn't bring myself to move away and wake her.

I knew what I had to do. I had to hand her over to the rebels. That had nothing to do with breaking this claim on her. In fact, if Phantom Fangs postponed the whole hunting-Prince-Charles-down thing, that would work better for me. I should have been supporting it.

I had just been fighting for the wrong choice. For the wrong side.

Because the princess wasn't like other werewolves. She wasn't like anyone. She was pure, an outsider in a war that had tainted everyone involved with the shadow of death. She hadn't been corrupted, not by war and not by the witch or her witchcraft back in the Witch Woods.

I had to hand the Lost Princess over to the rebels. That was the right thing to do. It had to be.

But what would they do to her?

I was a human. I never knew my blood family because of werewolves and vampires. My only family was the rebels. The only *right* in this world was the rebels' goal to put an end to those monsters, who couldn't see reason, and this filthy war before everything was destroyed beyond repair. Even knowing all of that, even knowing the right choice, I didn't want to hand the princess over to them.

They wouldn't treat her well, to say the least, even though she hadn't committed any crimes. Even though she was innocent. The princess changed everything because I had never met a werewolf who was innocent, but this werea was. And she was malleable.

"Rodrick, are you listening?" Caspian asked.

I snapped to attention. "Nope."

"We're calling it a night. Todd's going to see what he can do with the Heart while preparing that contingency plan."

"We're not taking a vote?"

"No, we're not."

Upset balance for sure. Caspian was pulling on those power strings, making the decision he wanted, not considering the opinions of his squad, because he had already made up his mind. I had the sneaking suspicion that he chose this route so he could stay closer to the princess for a little longer. It was possible he really was thinking of the end game, but I seriously doubted it.

All because of "Sorissa."

The Full Moon Banquet was tomorrow night. Caspian's decision worked out better for the rebels than mine would have.

No one stayed at the lair after the meeting, another thing that worked out well for me. I slipped out onto the streets at night, left my inteliband, commsbud, and any other tech behind, and no one gave a damn.

The moon was bright, only one night away from being full. Tomorrow night, all werewolves would bask in its light and recharge. Even as a tethered, a lesser werewolf, I would do the same. My body was already humming with the energy, but I couldn't fully absorb any succulent moonlight until the alignment was perfect. I had to admit the stuff was addicting. I had to fight off a shiver at the thought of consuming that power.

I kept to the shadows, avoiding the electrical lights and their lit pathways. More importantly, I avoided important surveillance cameras. I knew all of Todd's dead spots. The guy was a genius, but he wasn't infallible—it also helped that Todd was Todd. He didn't care so much about what the denizens of Wolf Bridge were up to in every nook and cranny. He cared about tech and what he could make it do. It was convenient for me and perhaps a careless oversight on Philip's part—that or the king respected his citizens' privacy, though I highly doubted it.

As I took small back roads and stuck to shadows, I thought about how I'd deliver the princess to the rebels. It would be risky, but tomorrow night was what I had to shoot for. It was dangerous because all these werewolves would be replenishing their moonlight reserves, but that was also what made it perfect. Everyone got distracted on a full moon.

The Full Moon Banquet would be held, so there was also a party to distract them. Then there was the act of absorbing moonlight itself. It required stillness and concentration when the alignment was perfect. That was often joined by silence, closed eyes and ears, that sort of thing. It would have to work. It would be short notice for the rebels, but they'd get ready in time since I was on my way to meet with Jobe right now. All they'd really need to prepare for was transportation anyway. I'd tell him the plan. It was better to get everything done quickly and take everyone by surprise.

I came up on the south wall after passing through the Tech Off Zone on the west side of the Quicksilver River. It was quieter than the Tech On Zone at night since werewolves tended to be night owls and humans were encouraged to clock in and out with the sun. There was also less tech to deal with, even though they still had electrical lights to light the streets—not their houses—and cameras set up here and there. The Tech Off Zone felt like a medieval castle town aside from those two things. The Tech On Zone felt like a modern civilization prevalent with tech of all kinds. There was unity in the structures all throughout Wolf Bridge, but the architecture was the only unity. Wolf Bridge werewolves claimed to be shields. They treated humans just well enough to win them over. They kept them safe from maneaters and bloodsuckers and gave them decent lives so fighting for their freedom seemed detrimental. It was better to "fight *for* Wolf Bridge." Aerre fell into that trap.

Philip was a conniving king.

The south towers were sitting on either side of the Quicksilver River. They were ready to shoot down any intruders with the brilliant idea of scaling the steep fifty-foot drop off into the river to get inside the kingdom. They had rotating lights in their heads, basically making them armored lighthouses. I had the brilliant idea of scaling the slick river wall to get outside of the kingdom. I had done it before, so I knew it was possible. It just had to be timed perfectly. Thanks to my peak physical condition, that was possible. I was accused of being a carefree and impulsive brawler, and while that wasn't inaccurate, it didn't make me a meathead. Fighting wasn't just a way to blow off steam. It kept me sharp.

I waited for a moment to analyze how the lights rotated. The next time they shined my way, I reached into my moonlight reserves and sent the stuff to my eyes. When highly concentrated like this, I could keep the consequential blue flames of active moonlight to a minimum. With the night as clear as day, I tailed after the rotating lights to the edge of the drop-off and slid down, scaling the mostly vertical natural-rock wall with my hands extended and my feet planted firmly. If I fell into the Quicksilver River, it'd be over. The water rushed by at a lethal speed. It kept the rocks wet and slippery as it angrily spat over fifty feet up in the air.

I stopped sliding when I hit what would have been an undetectable narrow ledge had I not been enhancing my eyesight. I pressed back into the river wall and inched my way forward. The searchlights couldn't reach me here. I was hidden in shadows. All I had to worry about here was keeping my footing and being patient. Once I made it past the kingdom wall, I timed my ascension with the searchlights. Then I ran for the trees nearby. I blinked and shut off my moonlight consumption as if flicking a light switch. And just like that, I snuck out of Wolf Bridge.

I navigated through the trees until I reached a large

stone marking the spot where Jobe and I met regularly. He was Merik Rexx's main runner. He got the job done, so I didn't mind him, but I did miss reporting directly to Merik, leader of the rebels and the man who took me in when no one else would have. Orphans were often more of a nuisance than anything, but the rebels didn't feel that way. The rebels were made from families broken by werewolves and vampires.

"Rodrick." Jobe stepped out from behind the stone. The bridge of his corkscrewed nose and a pink scar on his right cheek peeked out from under his large hood. He wore all black and had become a shadow during his work as a runner. If I hadn't known for a fact that his skin was a medium brown, I would have said it was gray because of the tricks shadows played on the eyes. It didn't help that he looked like some harbinger of death.

He asked, "Is it true? Is the Lost Princess real?"

"Yes," I replied. "She's inside Wolf Bridge right now. I can break her out tomorrow night, or at least bring her to the south wall where I always sneak out. I might need your help from there, but I can probably get her out myself if I knock her out. I'll need to return to Freedom with you because my cover will definitely be blown after a stunt like that."

Jobe nodded, and his cloak rippled around him. "You really think doing this on a full moon is the best idea?"

"It's the only option. Do I need to explain it to you?"

"No. I'll take your word for it. You've never been wrong before. Just tell me what you need me and the rebels to do."

"Just make sure you have enough guys to sneak us out of there if there's trouble with the watchtowers and the river—which there shouldn't be. I can handle it."

"Always so much resting on Rodrick's shoulders," Jobe remarked. "Merik told me to relay a message. He says you've been doing good work. Those pieces of tech you've managed to steal and hand off to me have been a great asset in helping Freedom build into something more than a temporary camp. Eventually, we'll be able to bring Wolf Bridge down. We're working on developing new tech based on what you've brought us and what we know of the Heart, but it's been a bit difficult with our meager resources. This Todd Bizimunt is quite a genius. His tech outdoes the tech we've been able to analyze from Paws Peak."

"You could say that. The guy definitely has a brain that works differently than anyone else's," I agreed.

"The vampires and their tech are a wildcard, though. They may have retreated as far as they can from the war since Phantom Fangs made its debut a couple months ago, but we think it's for something big. No one knows what they've been up to underground. Whatever it is, it can't be good. Everyone believes Phantom Fangs killed their last male. It explains their sudden withdrawal, but they could also be planning for something big like when they took down Howling Sky."

"The vampires have nothing on Todd. One thing at a time," I said. "We'll cripple the werewolves first. Besides, we *did* kill their last male. You weren't there. I was. Todd used his underground radar shit to scope out the area all around Crimson Caves on our first mission. That was how we found him. They kept him isolated outside of their caves in a metal prison underneath earth they dug up themselves. I always knew the bloodsuckers were crazy and that they kept their males separate, but hell. Not like that. Not even inside of their own caves." I shook my head because I didn't want to remember the rest. "Doesn't matter. Made things easier for us since infiltrating Crimson Caves is going to be way more difficult, but we'll have to do it eventually to eradicate any pregnant females. The vampires will be done after that whether we slaughter them all quickly or let them die out slowly."

"Indeed. The war is coming to an end. If we have the Lost Princess, we'll be able to make that happen sooner. The werewolves will try to bargain with us. She's too valuable not to. And since no one knows where Freedom is, since we've been so spectacularly ignored, it'll be even better. We'll rise up from the ashes and show them humans aren't to be trifled with."

"Yeah," I agreed. "Let's bring back real freedom and human dignity, starting tomorrow night."

"Tomorrow night then."

I followed Jobe to his motorbike. It was much smaller and much quieter than a roader, perfect for a runner. When he took off, I lost sight of him pretty quickly in the dark. The hum of the engine lingered in my ears a little longer.

A frown crept onto my face. It felt like there was a heavy rock glued to my chest. I was second-guessing myself, unsure of if I did the right thing or not. I never second-guessed myself. I knew I was doing the right thing. I was tethered, but I was a human first. My allegiance was to humans, rebels. They were white, everything else was black. I knew that. I never doubted that.

But Caspian could have killed me when I was captured outside of Wolf Bridge on a mission to steal tech, a rebel, an enemy of Wolf Bridge. They all knew what I was. I was an "agitator" to them, and I was marching on my way to death for that. I was fine with that, but I knew I'd be better use alive than dead. When I overheard Caspian was putting together a squad, I volunteered. It was a joke. I never thought he would actually take me up on it.

I didn't know why he did or why he never bothered to keep a sharp eye on me. I understood Aerre's frustration there.

Did Caspian think me being tethered to him meant I couldn't be a problem? Or did he really believe in change? I knew Caspian wanted more, but I also knew he was playing safe. He would never make a real change. It would be too big. He was wrong. I told myself over and over that he chose black, so why was I thinking about this now? I already knew the answer. Caspian, Aerre, and Todd were my enemies, but they also had my back when we were on missions. Like a real squad. I was meant to be a warrior, not a spy.

Perhaps the princess really did have witchy powers. My resolve came unhinged with her arrival, and that was unprecedented. Beautiful monster. Spitfire. Little fighter. She was only eighteen and so commanding. I was a punk at eighteen and probably not much better now at thirty.

I shut my thoughts down and returned to Wolf Bridge the same way I had escaped. I just emerged from climbing back up the water-slick ravine when I noticed movement in the shadows. *Shit.* I scrambled my way toward some shadows as well, hoping I hadn't been seen, but I had. And it was fucking Aerre who had seen me.

"What the hell are you doing out here?" Aerre asked, glowering at me. "Sneaking in and out of Wolf Bridge and simultaneously trying to get yourself killed by the river. You are an adrenaline junkie, or you have a death wish."

"I get antsy when I'm cooped up," I said with a shrug. "Needed some fresh air."

"Don't lie, agitator scum. I know exactly what you were doing."

Fucking Aerre. He wanted to protect his family, but he was going about it the wrong way. He chose black. That little tear-up I was having earlier got cured quickly. It was obviously complete bullshit, and I did do the right thing with Jobe.

"Where's your proof?" I asked. "As far as you know, I was just out for a midnight run, which is, in fact, what I was doing."

"Rodrick," Aerre pleaded—yes, pleaded—"why can't you understand? You're going to get my family killed."

"And your family is all that matters."

Aerre fell silent. He put his commsbud in his ear, pulled up his wrist, and tapped the touchscreen on his inteliband. I rolled my eyes when he brought up Caspian's name and pressed call.

"I caught Rodrick sneaking out," Aerre said. "The south towers and the fucking Quicksilver River. Guy's a maniac, Caspian."

I dug into my core, accessing that cold pool of

moonlight that rested there until I activated it, transforming it into fire. I concentrated the moonlight in my ears and kept the blue glow to a minimum. Aerre didn't need to know I was listening in.

"Fine." I heard Caspian's slightly distorted sigh. "Bring Rodrick back to the lair. We'll talk."

Hah. That was just like Caspian. Maybe he didn't believe Aerre since he had been trying to get me to fall ever since Caspian put me on this team.

Aerre growled. "You aren't taking this seriously. What possible reason would Rodrick have to sneak out like that other than to contact agitators? He's going to ruin everything."

"I'm not going to let anything happen to your mother and sister, Aerre," Caspian said.

"I'll bring Rodrick to the lair." Aerre ripped out his commsbud and closed down the call from his inteliband as he screamed, "Fuck!"

"You're going to wake people up," I said, releasing my activated moonlight and allowing what I had left to drip back into my core.

"Are you coming or do I have to force you?"

"I'd like to see you try that." I laughed. "But I'm coming without a fight."

"Perfect," Aerre muttered.

I didn't like Aerre, and I didn't hate him. I knew what

was right and wrong.

But Phantom Fangs was a loose thread dangling from my resolve. The Lost Princess kept tugging at it, threatening to unravel it all.

CHAPTER 18

SORISSA

*P*HILIP DIDN'T make me stay in the throne room for long. Maybe he could sense I was distracted, or maybe he saw that I had no interest in the sons he was showing off. I spoke to each of them, but I couldn't remember the conversations. I didn't ask any of them to show me around. My mind had been preoccupied with Phantom Fangs. It still was. I wanted them to show me around.

My freedom in Wolf Bridge far outdid Paws Peak. I was allowed to wander the castle, and I did before getting lost. I was trying to find my way back to the Heart to see if I could find Todd there, but I got tired and hungry. I ended up asking a guard to take me back to my room. He also provided me with a prime cut of smoked venison for dinner, which I was allowed to eat by myself in my room. In hindsight, I could have just asked the guard to take me to the Heart. He probably would have. So far, Wolf Bridge wasn't terrible. I kind of liked it, but I wanted to see Phantom Fangs again. Nobody would tell me where they were. That was something I asked the guard. I just kept getting told they were indisposed.

After getting dressed in a lightweight gown that was actually comfortable, and seemed to be designed for sleeping, I stared at my mother's journal, resting on the headboard of my rounded bed. I sat on the fluffy mattress, and it tried to swallow me up. All I could think about was falling through a puffy cloud in the sky. I didn't know if I'd be able to sleep on it. Then there was the sheer fabric cascading from the ceiling. I didn't know what the point was when it was too sheer to even hide me from view.

I took my mother's journal and leafed through the pages. I was curious, but I wasn't sure I wanted to read any more of it. The werea on these pages was a stranger to me. She was my mother, but I felt no connection to her. This was all Babaga left me. She was telling me I didn't belong with her, that I belonged to this stranger—or at least to her legacy.

I navigated to the page where my mother's second journal entry started.

The 2nd Month of Winter, Day 60. 2525

It's every mother's dream to give her cubs the world. I'm glad I'll get to give you the world, Sorissa. I think about you so small inside of my belly and how you grow bigger every day. Your father rests his head on my stomach at night because he wants to feel as close to you as I am. He loves you, and he'll get to hold you soon enough, but no one can take a mother's place or the connection I have to you inside of me. Right now, you are all mine.

King George ve Paz of Paws Peak has chosen your mate, his son Prince Charles. You are betrothed as of today. He is a fine young cub, one I'm sure will grow into a strong werewolf deserving of you.

One day, when you are sealed to your mate, you will know what I mean when I say this time with you inside of me is precious. This private time with your cubs is the most beautiful thing. I will raise you to be the best of nurturers, the most elegant and poised of all wereas. Such a presence will need to be upheld as the Moonlight Child blessed by Lureine and mother-to-be of an all-new generation. All who see you will revere you.

I know I've put a lot of emphasis on your future, your legacy, but I can't help it. Thinking about all you will do makes me giddy, Sorissa.

For now, know that I can't wait to show you the world. This private time with you and me is glorious and quiet. No words need to be spoken. But I look forward to the day you open your eyes, and I too can hold you in my arms. When I can speak to you and have you speak in return.

You are loved, Sorissa. So loved.

I closed the journal. My mother's words tied my stomach into knots. She was referring to me as a breeder again, and then she proceeded to tell me how loved I am? I didn't understand. Worse, she said Charles was meant to be my mate. Babaga read this journal, then? That was why she gave me to Paws Peak? But what happened to my mother? What happened to Howling Sky? Both were dead according to what George said to me in Paws Peak, but how? Why? The Prime War?

War. And more war. That was all this world was. It was in my mother's journal. It was all around me.

Kingdoms and their citizens died, and only their memory remained. If even that.

Whenever I would ask Babaga about the world out-side of the woods, she would deflect my questions. She would tell me to read the books she brought me. Were-wolves, vampires, humans. Babaga never said much about the three species. She seemed to think their fair-ytales were all the education I needed. She told me once that their hearts were inside these old fairytales and that hearts told a different story than cold, hard facts. Maybe she was right. If I had grown up on these war stories in-stead, the actual history of this world, I would have had a different outlook on all three. But the history was the truth. The fairytales were a dream. I wished Babaga had told me the truth.

What did it matter what was inside a heart if it was never allowed to manifest anyway? That seemed to be something left to individuals, not entire kingdoms. Indi-viduals were hearts. Kingdoms were a collective of cold, hard facts. That also made things more complicated. Was it okay to like Phantom Fangs when I didn't necessarily like Wolf Bridge?

I placed my mother's journal back on the headboard. It was late, and I had been up all day, so it seemed like a good time to try and get some sleep. I was exhausted. I crawled under the covers of the fluffy, puffy bed and closed my eyes. Sleep refused to find me.

I tossed and turned because I was tired, and I really

did want to sleep, but my mind wouldn't rest—and the bed was too soft.

Phantom Fangs.

I wondered if Trace would have told me their location if I had asked. By the time I got back to my room after Philip showed off his sons, she was gone. I hoped that meant she got some time to herself. Maybe some time with Koren.

But I didn't want to be alone anymore. It was suffocating. The world was bigger than ever, with more people than ever, but I felt alone in this room. Isolated.

What if I searched for Phantom Fangs myself?

Before I could think it through, I hopped out of bed and went to that humongous closet in search of some shoes. I found a pair that felt kind of like slippers, but they had good, sturdy soles. They looked funny with the nightdress I was wearing, but I didn't care about that. I only needed them to be functional.

I crept to my door, though I didn't know why. No one here had told me I couldn't do anything yet. The memory of Paws Peak wasn't even a day old, though. Caution was in order.

I opened the door a crack and peeked outside. The coast was clear aside from a guard disappearing down a hall after making one of his rounds. This was my chance to sneak out. I took my first step forward and felt my heart pound against my rib cage with each following step.

CHAPTER 19

AERRE

"*T*HAT'S IT?" I demanded. "You're just grounding him to his bedroom?"

"You don't have any proof, Aerre. Not about him being in contact with agitators," Caspian replied.

"So you won't do anything until I get you proof. The implications of him *sneaking* out aren't enough for you."

"Aerre, I just think you've been obsessing over this too much."

"How? He was going to be put to death for being an agitator, for trying to steal our tech. Then you decided to put him on this squad and your father backed you up. We have *the* fucking tech guy in our squad, too!"

"He's tethered to me just like you are. That's why the king allowed it."

"So keep him on a tighter leash." I couldn't stop my teeth from grinding together or halt the growling rumble in my throat. "You're too trusting, Caspian. Or maybe you're just way too forgiving. Maybe that's why you allowed Zecke to walk after what he did to my sister. Maybe you're just afraid of real conflict because you bend over backward just to keep things 'peaceful.'"

"Am I excused?" Rodrick interrupted.

"No," Caspian said firmly, which surprised me. "Don't leave Wolf Bridge again. Whatever you both think, I'm not an idiot. I've included you, Rodrick, and treated you like the other members of this team. I know you didn't volunteer for Phantom Fangs and follow through because you were scared to die. You have your own reasons, and I won't throw around accusations—but Aerre likely isn't far off. I let you join this team because I've been hoping you'd see things from our point of view." He paused. "*My* point of view. There's a reason I have two tethered in this squad instead of limiting it to pure werewolves. There's a reason I chose a former agitator."

He sighed and pressed his hand to his forehead. "I want something more than *this*, this world, and I thought you did too. Don't sabotage us. Don't break us. I'm begging you as a friend and a teammate. What have these past couple months together meant to you? I had your back. I still do. Do you have mine?"

Caspian hadn't changed at all from when he was a kid. This was proof. He was trying to win Rodrick over the same way he had won me over when we were kids. I would have laughed if I hadn't thought it was so fucking pathetic. And confusing. Because it worked on me, hadn't it? Even though he was a werewolf, I was supporting Caspian right now because I trusted him with my damn life, my sister's and mother's too. He was far from perfect, but I knew his heart. Apparently, that was enough.

Rodrick was standing with his arms folded. He was looking Caspian straight in the eye, defiant as always, a lost cause.

"I won't leave again," Rodrick announced. His voice was solid, and I couldn't detect the lie, but I knew it was there. I knew he was lying.

Caspian shook his head. "I'm going to the castle. The king wants to see me. Behave yourselves."

"I'm always behaved," I replied.

Rodrick snorted.

"This really is your last chance, Rodrick," Caspian reminded. "So make your choice. I'll be back within an hour."

"Is it really a good idea to leave him here by himself?" I asked.

"Your choice, Aerre. You can go to your old home in the Tech Off Zone to watch over your mother and sister like you usually do, or you can babysit Rodrick. Either way, if he's not here when I get back… Well, I hope it doesn't come to that."

"What about Todd?"

"He's busy."

"Fine," I said reluctantly.

Caspian left the lair without another word. I got the feeling he couldn't get away from us soon enough. That left me alone with my favorite tethered.

"What'll it be, Aerre?" Rodrick asked.

I didn't want to babysit this oaf all night, and what if Zecke decided to slink back to the Tech Off Zone for my sister? He wasn't allowed there anymore. That didn't mean he wouldn't do it. Caspian was only going to be gone an hour. I was torn because none of this mattered to me if my sister and mother were killed. I couldn't stand another moment away from them. I hadn't gotten to check up on them since we came back from collecting the Lost Princess. The Lost Princess, Rodrick, everything was beginning to spiral. If we were met with more hell-fire, would I be able to get my mother and sister out before we burned up too? What about Caspian? Did any of this even matter? Was I just delaying the inevitable?

"Congratulations," I said. "You've got a free pass. Don't fuck up while we're gone."

I exited the lair and slammed the door behind me.

The nearly full moon made my skin buzz. My body was changed on a fundamental level when I became tethered to Caspian. I had instincts that were werewolf. This reaction to the moon was that werewolf in me, craving the power of moonlight. It got more intense as the full moon drew closer.

The south side of the Tech Off Zone was quiet this late at night. None of the lights were on inside of the houses. Aside from the moon, there was only the light cast by lamp posts. It almost looked peaceful—or deserted. It could have gone either way, but tonight it felt deserted. My heart was constricting in my chest. It was hard to breathe.

I walked silently down lit roads until I found the small house I grew up in. It didn't stand out from the rest of Wolf Bridge, certainly not from the Tech Off Zone. It was quaint, but it had everything we needed. It was warm, never let in a draft, and it was large enough for the three of us. The tan walls and dark blue detailing were a little scuffed, but no one would look at this home, or the Tech Off Zone in general, and think "poverty."

And that was because it was true. Life in Wolf Bridge wasn't terrible.

Most of the time.

It wasn't terrible enough to justify agitators.

I hung back in the shadows when a light turned on inside of the house. It wasn't the light created by an electrical bulb. It was the flickering of a gas lamp. That was something growing up in the Tech Off Zone had taught me: tech wasn't a necessity. It was a luxury. Wolf Bridge treated humans well enough that we wouldn't rebel. King Philip really had that logic down to a fine art. He knew exactly what to tug on and what to adjust. Those micro-adjustments meant everything. Take away too much and you had an uprising. Give too much and you had an uprising. Society was nothing but a scale always being adjusted to find a perfect balance that couldn't be achieved until something went too far and everything fell off into fire and brimstone.

It was amazing any of us existed when existence itself was so chaotic.

I found some crates that made it easy to climb onto the roof of the house across the street. From this vantage point, I could watch over my mother and sister effectively and quietly. I wondered what my mother and sister were doing up so late. They were in the kitchen, dressed in nightgowns, and their long blond hair draped over their shoulders. Mom often got the compliment that she looked more like Trace's twin sister than her mother.

If I activated the moonlight resting inside of me, I'd

be able to hear their conversation. It looked like it was getting a bit heated, a mother's scalding lecture.

I didn't have much moonlight left, but I decided it was worth using it to hear this conversation. I closed my eyes and concentrated on the dormant, dark energy resting at the base of my stomach. As soon as my consciousness brushed against it, it lit up into multiple shades of blue. It vibrated inside of me and phased outside of my flesh into harmless flames. I concentrated the moonlight in my ears, hiding the blue flames except for where they gently kissed my ears.

"I'm just worried, Trace. You need to be careful," Mother said as she took a seat beside my sister at the kitchen table. "You know what werewolves are… are capable of."

"Not just werewolves," Trace shot back. "Plenty of the men around here have made unwelcome advances toward me."

My hackles rose at my sister's words. She deserved the highest respect, and she didn't even get it from our own species. The worst part was I knew that. I couldn't stand by my sister's side and protect her since I was tethered now. It would have only made things worse for her. I had to watch over her in the shadows, at night, and just wait until things went too far. Because if they ever did, I would step in, rules or no rules, there would be no choice.

No man had attempted anything unforgivable, but Zecke had. He raped my sister. If that werewolf bastard ever came back, I would kill him and face the consequences. The only thing that stopped me from hunting him down was the fact that my sister and mother would share those same consequences.

I became tethered to help my family, but it also meant I could never see them again. It was an unspoken rule. Werewolves tolerated humans. Humans tolerated werewolves. Smiles and laughter were allowed, but they were all a facade. I was an outcast, a freak. Humans considered me a werewolf. They wouldn't speak out against me. They'd feign welcoming smiles. Werewolves still considered me a human. They tolerated me as such. Becoming a tethered and protecting Wolf Bridge was the best way to keep my family safe, but it left no place for me to fit in.

Giving everything I am to Caspian was the best way to keep Trace and Mom safe. They tried to talk me out of it. They even cried, but I chose to become tethered to Caspian anyway. I knew it wasn't perfect, but it was the best I could do. It was worth the sacrifice of belonging anywhere.

I gave everything to Caspian and gave up my life as a human when I turned seventeen. I'd never marry, never have a wife or kids. I was sterile and couldn't pass on my bloodline. I was nothing but a shield erected to protect a tenuous peace. I gave innocent princesses to corrupt kings so that they could be defiled to spare my sister that repeated fate.

Thinking about the Lost Princess made me cringe. She was an enigma. I was determined to hate her because she was just another werewolf in the end, but she stirred things in me, in Phantom Fangs. I tried to ignore it and to leave her out of my thoughts, but she kept coming in at random times. I had to keep actively burying her. Now that she was in King Philip's hands, there was no telling what would happen to her. Hate or not, the thought of what her own kind would do to her made me sick.

"I love him, Mom. I really love him," Trace said. "I didn't tell you until now because I knew you would react like this."

So my sister was seeing someone. I had my suspicions. I watched her get home late more than once. It had me worried before, but it made me more worried after hearing what she said. Werewolves... why were they talking about werewolves?

"Who is this werewolf, then?" Mom said the words and a shiver broke out across my skin. I didn't want to believe it.

"His name is Koren. Mom, he's so wonderful and sweet. He even gives me updates on Aerre, letting me know he's safe and when he's out on missions. He'd probably get a message to Aerre if I asked him too, but I know Aerre wouldn't approve, so I haven't. Oh, but I want to. I hope that little brother of mine is doing well. I wish I could tell him about Koren."

Mom somehow managed to frown and smile at the same time. "Me too, honey. Me too."

I wanted to scream. Mom needed to talk Trace out of whatever crazy idea she had in her head. A human in love with a werewolf? Talk about taboos, the ultimate of taboos. How could Trace even consider this after what Zecke had done to her? How long had this been going on and I had been fucking clueless?

"Trace, I know… you think you love this werewolf, but it simply isn't done."

Thank you, Mom.

"I know I do, and no one will change my mind. You'll like him when you meet him. Aerre would, too."

"*When* I meet him?"

"Things can change!"

"At what expense, though?"

"At no expense, Mother! We'll be careful. We'll take it slow. We can figure it out. Don't you feel like things are changing? I do. I think there's a beautiful future ahead of us."

Werewolves treated wereas as nothing but breeders.

They locked them away. Men and women were more or less equal in my experience. At the very least, women weren't locked away and told their only purpose was to breed. I had seen unwelcome advances from men toward women as well as women toward men among humans, but it was completely one-sided with werewolves. Vampires were the opposite of werewolves. Vampires ruled, and vampyres, males, were locked away. Very locked away. I shuddered at the memory. None of the three mixed. Interbreeding was impossible. Racking my brain to try and understand how my sister could say she was in love with a werewolf wasn't helping me find an answer. It just didn't make sense.

Then I thought of Caspian. I thought about how he'd be thrilled to hear this because this was the kind of world he wanted, wasn't it? It was certainly a whole new world if werewolves and humans suddenly married or became mates or whatever the term would be coined. If Trace loved this werewolf and he could treat her like a living thing, since she couldn't be used as a breeder... I couldn't fathom it. *Could* he treat her like a living thing or would he just use her for sex? Was he using her for sex now? He couldn't love her. Love across two different species that have hated each other for how many years? Impossible.

Is this the start of the future you see, Caspian? Is it going to be at my sister's expense, or are there other werewolves out there with a heart like yours?

Caspian would never take a mate, lock her away, and force her to be a breeder. I knew that when I looked past what he was because I knew him. I didn't know Koren.

I needed to do some investigating.

"Why don't you go to them?"

"Shit!" I hissed in surprise and nearly jumped off the roof. The drop of moonlight I had left settled back into my core as I looked behind me to see none other than the Lost Princess herself. Did she ever sneak up on me. She almost gave me a fucking heart attack.

She giggled softly, pressing her hand to her mouth like she was trying to hide it. The smile was clear in her dark brown eyes, though. I couldn't look away. Those eyes were dancing lights, reflections of the moon. Her eyelashes fluttered like butterfly wings, and her smile was the most beautiful thing I had ever seen. Her lips looked like they had been painted by a rose, but it was just their natural color and texture. Her bronze skin was luminous with a natural glow that somehow resembled moonlight. And she was wearing a sheer nightdress that made it impossible not to see her hard nipples, a reaction to the chilly night air. The fabric fell around her body so perfectly. It hardly hid anything.

My body flooded with heat, and I tried to ignore the ache in my dick. No one made me feel this way, certainly not since I became tethered, and I didn't like it. It reminded me of things I couldn't have.

Sorissa ran her hand through the long curls of her hair. "I'm sorry if I scared you."

"You're not supposed to be out here," I said.

"No one said I couldn't, but I also didn't ask."

"How long were you watching?" I managed to tear my eyes away from her to see Trace and Mom finally calling it a night. The gas lamp flickered off, and the house became as dark as all of those surrounding it.

"Long enough. You look alike. I'm glad your sister is my 'maid.'"

I had to close my eyes and take a deep breath before I exploded. My sister was even working inside of the castle? I thought she'd be working in the farms. Watching over my family at night obviously wasn't enough. Zecke had been stationed as a guard in the Tech Off Zone when he raped my sister. Caspian took the issue straight to the king. Zecke was reassigned to guard the east gate. Because of that, I would have preferred Trace not to be anywhere near the Tech On Zone, but I supposed the castle was as safe a place as any.

"Caspian must have picked her for that reason," Sorissa continued. "He knew we'd get along, though she was a little shy at first."

Did Caspian handpick Trace for this position? I

doubted it. She must have applied for a position in the castle herself. How my sister could stand to be surrounded by werewolves like that after what happened with Zecke, I had no idea.

"Koren seems nice. I like him."

"You've met him?" I asked.

"He escorted me to the throne room again after Trace got me all dressed up." She rolled her eyes. "At least she dressed me in something comfortable." She gave me a thoughtful look, eyes wide and questioning. "Can werewolves and humans actually breed then? You're a werewolf."

"No. I'm a tethered."

"A human turned werewolf. You said something about that before."

"Well, it has nothing to do with breeding," I growled.

"You don't want to talk about it."

"What gave you that impression?"

"Why are you angry, Aerre?"

I was angry for a lot of reasons. At least one of them involved her.

"I'm sorry," I said. I couldn't be this hostile around the Lost Princess. There was no telling how that could end for me. If she wanted my head, the king would give it to her. For some reason, my tongue was loose around her. I only revealed my true thoughts around Phantom

Fangs.

She reached out a slender hand and bent down to touch my forearm. I was still wearing my Phantom Fangs uniform, that meant long, tight sleeves, and I couldn't feel her skin against mine, but her warmth made me shiver anyway. It was disarming, a balm for the rage constantly boiling inside of me.

I didn't look at her, but I spoke. "A werewolf can change a human and bind them into servitude by biting them, a lot like that bite Prince Charles gave you. It's different of course. I have no idea what your bite feels like, but it all involves moonlight and the intent behind the bite. If I was still human and you bit me in your moonlight form or with moonlight concentrated in your teeth, you could either seriously injure me, depending on your intent, or you could tether me. Submission seals the deal. Charles bit you with the intent to claim you, but the Mate Claim also has to be sealed with a form of submission, sex, after the bite—apparently."

"I have a hard time envisioning Caspian making anyone submit," the princess commented.

"You'd be surprised, but he didn't make me submit. I chose to. Rodrick, too."

I shuddered at the memory of Caspian laying his teeth into me. I was seventeen and Caspian was only fifteen. Maybe it wasn't fair to ask him to do it, but I did. I chose it because it was the best I could do, the most power I could have, the way I could be with Caspian and get information without being frowned upon because he was a werewolf and I was a human. The bite and change following were probably the most painful things I had ever experienced. The loss of freedom. And worst of all, Caspian cried.

If the Mate Claim was even remotely a similar experience, I pitied Sorissa.

"So Caspian is your alpha. Rodrick's, too."

"Basically. He can use us however he wants to, and we can't say no." *Curse my loose tongue.*

"Where's your bite?"

"The back of my neck. It's faded some. Rodrick's would be a lot easier to see if he didn't have so many damn tattoos."

The princess stood up and touched the back of my neck, moving down the collar of my uniform. I tried to ignore the buzz she sent through my skin as her fingers brushed across my mark. Then she sat down next to me.

"I don't think Caspian sees you as expendable submissives. I don't think he sees you as submissives at all."

"You like Caspian," I noted. I was glad she did. If there was even the slightest chance Caspian could become her mate, I would support it. I knew he would treat her well. But I couldn't stop this pang of jealousy in my chest.

"You do, too," she said.

"Funny, Princess, but he's not my type."

She squeezed my arm. "I like you, too. I like Phantom Fangs. You're different from everyone else."

I laughed. "Because we're fuckups."

"You're kinder. It seems like what I say actually matters to you. You answer my questions even when you don't want to. You're the first friends I've made outside of my woods."

I wanted to say something to combat that, maybe tell her that she needed to get to know more people, but I couldn't bring myself to joke about that. The king would lock her away soon enough—unless she really did like Caspian and he could convince the king to let him take her as his mate. It was a long shot, but it was her best shot.

"You said I'm not supposed to be out here, but you haven't marched me back to the castle yet." Sorissa leaned against me. My skin felt like it was about to combust. It was then I realized she had been shivering, and her lips had taken on a bluish tint. Hesitantly, I wrapped my arm around her waist. It seemed to be the right thing to do since she melted into me, readily accepting the gesture.

"It's cold out here!" she exclaimed. "I should have found something else to wear, but the only things in that closet are dresses and more dresses. Where are all the pants and sweaters? It's spring, but the nights are still cold."

"Criminal," I murmured. I could barely manage that one word. This wasn't good. What was she doing to me? I wanted to be closer. I *needed* to be closer. My body ached, but my soul was aching at the same time. It was insanity. Was this unbearable attraction because of her power as the Moonlight Child?

"You should see your sister and mother."

"I can't."

"Because you're tethered?"

"Yes."

"Caspian won't let you?"

"It's not… it's not that simple."

"They love you a lot."

"I wonder about that sometimes."

"They do."

"Even though becoming a tethered betrayed them? Do you still love your witch even though she betrayed you?"

"I still love Babaga. She loved me, too. I don't know why she kept things from me or why she gave me away to Paws Peak after it all, but I know she did love me. I think she still does because love isn't something that breaks so easily, Aerre."

"It seems pretty fragile to me."

Sorissa shifted onto her knees and pressed her nose to my neck. Her hot breath tickled my skin, and I had to squeeze my eyes shut tightly to resist the groan on my lips. I needed to adjust my fucking pants, but I couldn't move because I didn't trust myself at the moment. I didn't want this. I so didn't want this.

But I did.

Each word she spoke, how easy she was to talk to, how she made my anger fade, each move she made, I craved it all.

She rested her hand dangerously high up my thigh and took in a deep breath through her nose. "You smell so good, like the breeze that came in from the east and into the woods sometimes. Babaga told me that breeze came all the way from the ocean."

Gods, the princess didn't know a damn thing about personal space. First, she fell asleep against Rodrick's arm, *Rodrick*, and now she was cuddling with me. She made me remember things I almost had, the girlfriend I was serious about before becoming tethered to Caspian. Genna was my first and last when it came to sex and thoughts of a future family. I was fine with that. But with Sorissa, right here, right now, I wasn't. I had moved on. Genna moved on and was married. Sorissa made me want things I couldn't have.

Suddenly, the princess pulled away from me. "Am I

making you uncomfortable? You keep shaking. Or are you just cold too?"

I stood up before I could give in to temptation. "I need to take you back to the castle, Princess."

"I'm sorry, Aerre." She stood and stared down at her slipper-covered feet.

"I'm not mad," I said. For the first time in a long time, I really wasn't. I was nearly jumping out of my skin, but I wasn't mad. "There's just this thing called personal space."

"Is it a similar lecture to modesty?"

"What?"

"Caspian told me I can only be naked in front of the werewolf who becomes my mate."

I shook my head but couldn't hide the smile tugging at my lips. "I don't know about that, but we're strangers and it's not typical for strangers to be so close."

"But it's cold."

I couldn't take my persistent hard-on anymore and tried to discreetly adjust my pants. The princess stared at me the whole time, so that was a failure.

She narrowed her eyes at me.

"What?" I asked, feeling like I was in trouble.

"Our bodies are magnetic."

"Okay?" I was fucking lost.

"Being near you, all of Phantom Fangs, makes my

body feel strange."

"Cor, give me strength," I said under my breath. I was not equipped to deal with this. I didn't know what to say. In hindsight, I should have called out to Lureine since he was the werewolves' god. It wasn't like the God of Humans could help me with a werea.

The princess closed her eyes and brushed her fingers down the front of her stomach, lower and lower, and I couldn't take another moment. I took her hands. She opened her eyes, startled.

"I *really* need to take you back to the castle," I repeated.

"I *really* don't want to go back to the castle. It's lonely. The bed is too soft, and I can't sleep."

"Too *soft*? People usually complain about the opposite. I complain about the opposite."

She shrugged. "Maybe you'd like to trade beds for a night."

I laughed. I laughed much louder than I should have.

"I won't be in the way," she insisted.

"You think you're going to come with me?"

"Sounds perfect."

I didn't have the strength to fight with her, not after she left me so thoroughly wrecked. At least I wouldn't be alone back at the lair. Caspian could take care of this. "Okay," I said, "but if the king comes calling, I won't be able to do anything about it. You'll have to go back."

"Deal." The princess smiled and squeezed my hands. "And call me Sorissa. Friends call each other by their names."

Friends, huh?

"I can't. It's improper."

"Aerre," she chastised, but I raised a finger to her lips to silence her.

"However," I continued, "I'll whisper it from time to time so only you can hear." I sighed in defeat and pressed my lips to her ear. I shuddered at the feeling of her skin and murmured, "Sorissa."

CHAPTER 20

SORISSA

*A*ERRE LED me out of the "Tech Off Zone." Not far, though. He led me to a large house near an odd border where tech suddenly grew prominent again after being so absent. There wasn't any sort of wall or anything separating zones. It all came down to tech, and if the tech wasn't immediately apparent, it came down to the size of the buildings.

"This is the Phantom Fangs Lair," Aerre said.

"Lair?" I laughed.

"Ridiculous name, isn't it? But it made sense to call it that. Phantom Fangs is a beast after all."

"I like it." I craned my neck to see the windows on the second floor. "It looks dark. Is everyone asleep? Will we wake them up?"

"Rodrick should be in. Caspian should be back soon if he isn't. If we wake them up, too bad."

I got the feeling Aerre wanted someone to be awake. He was a little jumpy after that conversation we had and since whispering my name into my ear. I still had residual shivers running up my spine from him doing that. I wanted to ask about this buzzing attraction. I wanted to understand it better and why it only seemed to apply to Phantom Fangs, but it was obvious Aerre didn't want to discuss it. I knew he and Caspian felt some kind of attraction to me too. Was it just because I was a *rare* werea to them? It was true I hadn't seen any other wereas, so that was possible.

Aerre opened the door to the "lair," and I followed him inside. It was riddled with tech. There were these rectangular contraptions projecting light and images from their mounted position on the wall. They showed scenes outside of the house in strange grays and almost greens. I wondered if it was because of the dark. I recognized some of the areas. I even saw a light post flicker on one of them. They were like Babaga's seeing mirror, a mirror she could use to see any part of the world. I had only glimpsed it a time or two since she didn't like me to mess with it, but it looked like tech and magic had a lot in common. It was almost comforting because it was almost familiar.

"Monitors," Aerre said as he turned on a light that flooded the room. "They let us keep track of everything happening outside."

"So many eyes," I murmured.

"Pretty much. Stay here, Princess. I'll be right back."

Aerre disappeared into a room, and I got closer to the monitors. It was mesmerizing, crazy to see what was going on in these different areas at the same time—though it was late, dark, and nothing was going on at the moment.

"Caspian isn't back yet," Aerre said when he returned. "Rodrick's sleeping."

"We should let him sleep, then. Where's this hard bed of yours?" I asked.

Aerre shook his head, but I saw a smile on his face. I liked it when he smiled. I hadn't seen that look on him before tonight. His lake-blue eyes were brighter than usual, and I really could see the resemblance to his sister and mother. I wanted to unbraid his hair and tangle my fingers in the long golden strands, but I stopped myself with the thought of "personal space."

"My room is this way."

Aerre led the way to a flight of stairs and opened a door to a room on the second floor. It was much smaller than my room in the castle, but it felt better, cozier. Even though the walls were primarily tan here too, they didn't seem as brazen. I caught sight of a rectangular bed also much smaller than mine. I walked over to it and plopped down on its edge. This reminded me of home. The frame was even made of a dark wood like my old bed was. I fell onto my back and spread my arms, savoring the firm mattress supporting me. Already, my eyes were growing heavy.

"I love it," I murmured.

"I'll sleep on the couch downstairs if you need anything, Princess," Aerre said.

I sat up when he was about to leave. "I don't want to steal your bed."

"I prefer the couch, and you're exhausted. Sleep."

"Are you sure?"

"I'm sure."

I couldn't resist the temptation after that. I pulled down the covers and got comfortable in Aerre's bed. I hadn't realized how tired I was until it became hard to open my eyes again after blinking. It didn't help that this bed smelled like him, like the ocean breeze. It was soothing and somehow reminiscent of home.

"Thank you, Aerre," I whispered.

Instead of leaving the room like I thought he would, Aerre walked over to me and bent down to whisper in my ear, "Goodnight, Sorissa. Sleep well."

The way he said my name made me shiver. His voice

was as powerful as his touch. I smiled and trapped this warmth inside, savoring each moment. I wanted to touch him, to combine his voice and his touch, but exhaustion was clouding my brain like a fog. When I blinked again, my eyes stayed closed and sleep took me.

AERRE

I lingered outside my bedroom with my back pressed against the closed door. I was being much too friendly with the princess, but I couldn't stop myself. She kept inviting me in. She called me a friend and told me to use her name instead of replacing it with "Princess." Maybe I had given in too easily, but what was the point in resisting when we were alone? She made me feel good like I hadn't felt in eight whole years. The last time I felt good was before Zecke hurt my sister. I changed after that, physically too since I became tethered to Caspian.

Right now, at this moment, I felt like myself again. And that was a big deal to me.

But this wasn't good. Sorissa was too good. She didn't hide things. She was honest and open unlike anyone I had met likely because she grew up sheltered in the Witch Woods, far away from everything else. She was a werea, but I just didn't care. I liked her much more than I should. And I prayed to the Gods this world wouldn't break her.

I made my way down the stairs and sat on the couch. I was exhausted too, ready to close my eyes and sleep at any moment, but I needed to check in with Caspian first. I plucked my commsbud from my combat belt, stuck it in my ear, and searched the inteliband on my wrist for Caspian's name. I was too tired to find one of the portacomms we had lying around somewhere. Typically, it was more convenient for making calls. The commsbud and inteliband combo was optimized for missions and a commsbud was too hard to keep track of when not in uniform.

"What's up, Aerre?" Caspian answered almost immediately.

"The princess is sleeping in the lair. She passed out on my bed."

There was an uncomfortable gap of silence before Caspian responded with, "Why?" At the same moment, the front door opened, and he was standing right there.

We both took a moment to shut off the call so we could talk in person instead. I explained how I was watching over my family and the princess happened to sneak up on me. I also explained that I tried to take her back to the castle, but she practically begged me not to. I left out the finer details.

"I couldn't say no," I defended. "She's very persuasive."

Caspian chuckled. "She is something. It's fine. Let her sleep."

"She said you gave her a lecture on modesty."

His chuckle turned into a cough. "Why'd she bring that up?"

"No reason," I replied a little too quickly.

"Lie, but I'll let it go. Where are you going to sleep?"

"On this couch."

"No. You're going to sleep on the floor of your room."

"But—"

"Sorissa isn't inside the castle so you're her personal guard now since you decided to bring her back here. Also, we won't bother telling the king the real story. We'll say she got lost. We'll return her to the castle in the morning unless I hear otherwise before then. I'm sure she was caught on camera."

He called her Sorissa *again*. "That's pretty bold, Caspian. I thought you'd want to return her immediately."

Sighing, he pulled off his combat belt and set it on the table near the monitors. "I like her. She's spunky, fun to talk to. She makes me laugh and smile like I haven't in so long, maybe ever. Things don't seem so bleak when she's around. It's like she isn't from this world at all. And have you looked at her, Aerre? Really looked at her. She's beautiful."

"Dangerous words, Phantom Prince. But I'm glad you feel that way. I'd feel a lot better if she became your mate instead of the mate to one of your bozo brothers."

"You know that won't happen."

"I know that you say you want change, but nothing ever changes." I sighed. This wasn't going to go anywhere, and I had questions. I shifted the conversation. "Why is Trace Sorissa's maid?"

Caspian paused. Maybe he was analyzing how I was on a first-name basis with the princess, too. "She requested to be," he replied.

"She did? Really?"

"Yes. It pays well."

"But all the werewolves surrounding her all the time…"

"She's safe, Aerre. She's just trying to move on. You should let her."

I bit my lip to stop myself from screaming. All of that anger Sorissa managed to subdue was coming back in full force. I wondered if Caspian knew about Koren too. I wondered if I even wanted to know.

"Do you know Koren?" I muttered.

"Yeah, he's a guard in the castle. Nice guy, friendly."

"Fucking perfect."

"Why do you ask? Do you know Koren?"

"No. I'm going to bed."

I didn't let Caspian get in another word. I went back up the stairs to my room. I moved without a sound when I saw the steady rise and fall of Sorissa's chest underneath the blanket keeping her warm. I ached at the thought of keeping her warm myself. The bed was small. If we both slept on it, she would have to stay pressed into me or risk falling off the side.

I grabbed some spare blankets and tossed them on the floor. Since she was fast asleep, I risked changing into more comfortable clothes. Like hell was I sleeping in this combat gear. I had just barely put on some pants when she stirred.

"Aerre?"

"Yeah?" I quickly tugged a shirt over my head.

"Is everything okay?"

"Yeah, it's fine. Turns out I'm going to sleep on the floor. That okay?"

"Yeah." She mumbled something else I didn't catch, still half asleep.

"Goodnight," I said.

"Night," she whispered and rolled over.

I stayed where I was, concentrating on her breathing. I wanted to use the last drops of my moonlight reserves to hear the depth of her breathing, calm like the leaves on a tree rustling in a soft breeze. I had the urge to adjust her blanket, to tuck her in more tightly, but I grounded myself to the floor and turned my back to her while closing my eyes.

My last waking thoughts were of Sorissa. I wondered what her power entailed or if it was of a physical nature at all. But she was low or out of moonlight too, or she would have given us more of a challenge when she leaped from the roader like a maniac. She was the Moonlight Child, but it was obvious to me that moonlight wasn't the extent of her abilities. I wondered how many would fall for her natural charm. And I wondered why I was so happy that she said *we* were magnetic. All of Phantom Fangs and her, the Lost Princess. It could never work, but I liked that it included me. I liked that I could make her hot.

The memory of her hands gliding down her stomach, pressing against the sheer fabric of her nightdress, searching for her sex, coaxed my dick to stand at attention. The thought of her touching herself because of me was just too fucking much.

I told myself to sleep, but it turned out that was going to be harder than I thought when the *werea* in the bed nearby had thoroughly ensnared me. It took her no effort either. I was lost. And I was hopeless.

CHAPTER 21

SORISSA

I WOKE up to morning sunlight streaming through a half-curtained window. The sun's warmth kissed my exposed skin. A discarded blanket currently resided on the floor. The light nightdress I wore was rolled up well past my thighs. I sat up and stretched, feeling rejuvenated. Aerre's bed was much better than the one in the castle.

I looked around the room. Aside from the mess of blankets on the floor, it was spotless. Aerre must have gotten up already, or did I dream that he was in the room with me? I wasn't sure. But I felt safe. Knowing this place belonged to Phantom Fangs was almost as reassuring as being with Phantom Fangs.

Phantom Fangs. Phantom Fangs. Phantom Fangs.

The name was a chant that echoed in my head. I wanted to stay with Phantom Fangs. I didn't want to stay cooped up in the castle. I didn't want Philip to show off his sons, sons he wanted me to pick from to choose a mate. I didn't want to think about mates. I wanted to get used to life here. I wanted to know more about Phantom Fangs.

I scratched at that bite between my neck and right shoulder. It hadn't been bothering me much since Phantom Fangs broke me out of Paws Peak. I had almost forgotten it was there many times. I was glad it didn't seem to bind me to Charles like Aerre was talking about. The bite was bad enough, but the Mate Claim, fully realized, sounded awful. So did being tethered. But I wondered how powerful these claims and resulting connections really were. Could Caspian really make Aerre and Rodrick do anything he wanted?

I hopped out of bed and smoothed out my nightdress. Then I crept outside of Aerre's room and heard voices from downstairs. Two voices, to be exact. A deep baritone and a bit higher tenor. They had distinct tones and inflections. I recognized them as Caspian and Aerre. The thought of seeing them both encouraged my feet to move faster. When I reached the bottom of the stairs, I was grinning.

"Good morning," I said when Aerre and Caspian

looked my way.

"Good morning, Princess," Caspian replied with a serious face. "I need to take you back to the castle. The king is worried."

"Sorissa," I corrected.

Aerre was silent, sitting at a table with his hands clasped. I noticed he and Caspian were wearing casual clothes today. They weren't equipped with heavy-duty belts, and the sleeves of their shirts were short. I could see the smooth skin of their arms up to their bulging biceps. The prominent veins in their arms had me feeling a bit lightheaded.

"*Princess*, we're going back to the castle," Caspian re-stated.

"No," I growled. "I'm not going back to the castle. You said I wouldn't be a breeder here, but that's exactly what your king wants from me."

"The king won't make you mate with anyone."

"But he'll shove all his sons, all suitors, in my face to try and convince me otherwise?"

Aerre covered his mouth. Judging by the twinkle in his eyes, he was trying to hide a smile or maybe a laugh.

I looked between the two werewolves and asked, "Are you going to force me?" The thought of that made my heart sink. It made me feel defensive and like maybe Phantom Fangs had somehow tricked me into believing they genuinely cared about me, or at least what happened to me. I also wished I had moonlight so they'd know there was no damn way they could ever force me to do anything. Tonight. Tonight, I would get to recharge as long as I wasn't locked up in some dungeon or something.

"We don't want to force you to do anything you don't want to do," Aerre spoke up. "But it would be wise not to challenge the king. We want to keep you safe."

"The king is just worried," Caspian said. He sighed, and his broad shoulders slumped forward. He looked tired.

They seemed sincere. Maybe Phantom Fangs felt like they had no choice. Maybe they didn't. Kings ruled kingdoms. Did that mean they ruled everyone inside? Were kings the only ones with free will in this world? If so, I was determined to find a way to change that.

I tucked away my aggression. "What if you show me more of Wolf Bridge first?" I said. "Then I'll go back to the castle."

Caspian picked up a small rectangular box with an antenna sticking out of it. He pushed a button and said, "The princess says she'll happily return to the castle after breakfast and a quick jaunt around the area."

When he released the button, a dismembered, crackly voice replied, "Very well. Make sure she has a good time and that you bring her back early enough to prepare for the Full Moon Banquet."

Caspian set the tech on the table and leaned back against it, folding his arms. Once again, the bulging muscles in his arms caught my attention. I loved the way his dark skin seemed to reflect blue and how Aerre's tan skin reflected gold. I was confident in my strength combined with moonlight, but without it, these werewolves made me feel small, even breakable—but not in a bad way. When I was sitting close to Aerre on the roof, I felt safe. When I fell asleep leaning against Rodrick, I also felt safe. They were somehow hard and soft at the same time.

"Satisfied, Princess?" Caspian asked.

"If you call me Sorissa, I will be," I replied.

Finally, Caspian grinned. I adored that look on him. When he wasn't smiling, something was wrong. It was natural for him to smile. "Sorissa. I brought you a change of clothes, pants and a shirt instead of a dress, because I had a feeling this would happen."

"Finally. Thank you, Caspian. And what's the Full Moon Banquet?"

"It's exactly what it sounds like," Aerre said. "Important werewolves come to the castle garden to dine, dance, and recharge in the light of the full moon."

"Will Phantom Fangs be there?"

"Yes," Caspian said. "The king requests our presence."

I liked the sound of that. It meant I could look forward to this Full Moon Banquet instead of dreading it.

"Where are Rodrick and Todd?" I asked.

Aerre stood up and pulled out a chair from the table. He looked at me and gestured to it, so I took the seat and thanked him. Then he placed a pan on what had to be a stove and pulled out some meat from a box that let out cold air.

"Todd is in the castle, in the Heart specifically, and Rodrick is out fighting," Caspian informed.

"Fighting where?" I asked and took in a big whiff of the meat now simmering inside of the pan. It smelled like beef, and the seasonings Aerre was sprinkling on it made the aroma even better.

"They hold fights in the square, in the Tech Off Zone, so humans can blow off some steam. It's friendly competition. The winner takes on new challengers until he's defeated."

"Werewolves won't fight Rodrick in the coliseum inside the Tech On Zone because he's tethered," Aerre commented. "Humans probably only humor him by fighting in the square because he scares them shitless, and they don't want to get on his bad side."

"Werewolves won't fight Rodrick because they're afraid he'll take them down," Caspian interjected.

"Then there's Todd. He hardly ever comes here. He

likes to sleep in the Heart. It's like his tech mistress or something, his one true love," Aerre mocked with a smirk on his lips.

"No. Todd's prepping for our next mission to break the Mate Claim you didn't ask for, Sorissa. He works harder than anyone," Caspian defended, but he wore a playful smile.

The mood in the house was easy, friendly. Aerre and Caspian were obviously good friends, and I loved that. It made my chest squeeze. It made me wish I could be as close to them as they were to each other. Aerre resented being tethered, but it didn't look like he resented Caspian. I felt like I could understand that.

Caspian was kind and sweet. Being tethered to him meant a loss of freedom, but if Caspian never pulled his alpha rank, were Aerre and Rodrick really tethered? The lingering idea that Caspian could make either of them do anything he wanted was what brought out any resentment. I didn't think it was right, but Aerre said he chose this. What did it all mean exactly? What was Phantom Fangs? What was the Mate Claim? Was a loss of freedom just how the world worked? Even I never had real freedom because I was never allowed to leave the woods, but freedom was something I highly valued. No one wanted to be forced to do something against their will.

"Hope you're hungry," Aerre said as he placed a plate

of steaming hot meat in front of me.

"Very," I said. I hadn't realized until right then that my stomach was growling. My mouth watered with the delicious aroma. It was cut into strips, very easy to handle with my fingers. I took one strip at a time and savored the taste as it washed over my tongue. A contented hum buzzed on my lips.

"This is delicious," I announced.

Caspian was still standing while Aerre sat at the table. Caspian was grinning at me instead of digging into his own meat. Aerre, on the other hand, was staring at his plate intently as he ate. I thought I saw a red tint in his cheeks, and he let out a little cough.

"Did you eat cooked meat in your forest?" Caspian asked. "Or did your witch serve it raw?"

My mouth dropped open after I swallowed. "We're not barbarians!" I exclaimed. "*Babaga* taught me to cook meat very well, thank you."

That earned me a laugh from Caspian and a smile from Aerre—though Aerre tried to hide that by shoveling more food into his mouth.

Finally, Caspian decided to sit down at the table and eat breakfast with us. Things quieted down, but it didn't feel awkward. Silence with them was natural and somehow full.

My eyes lingered on Caspian as I took in his dark,

handsome features. Everything but his eyes was so like the princes Philip introduced me to. And his eyes were like the king's. Even though the resemblance was so strong, none of them could hold a candle to Caspian. None of them made me burn like he did. I wanted to ask him about it, but I also didn't. I was relieved he wasn't among the princes. It meant we could have easy times like this without me feeling like he was trying to encroach on my already limited freedoms. But I wondered why he wasn't with the other princes. Did he not want me as his mate or was it something else?

I selfishly wanted to believe that Phantom Fangs was on my side—even if it meant going against their king. I wanted to keep this easiness I felt toward them, but I also wanted to dive in and really *know* them, each one of them. I wanted to be able to hold them close. Maybe that meant I wanted to make them my own "tethered." But I didn't want to *make* them do anything. I wanted them to stand by me because they wanted to. I wanted more than friends. I wanted a family.

CHAPTER 22

RODRICK

AERRE WASN'T even close to the only person who didn't like me in Wolf Bridge. That list was long. To the werewolves and humans here, I was an "agitator" still. People respected me to a degree because I was part of Phantom Fangs, but the square was the perfect place for them to let out their frustrations. They didn't have to hold anything back.

My current opponent was a big guy close to my size. He had a couple scars, but they were nothing compared to mine. His hair was shaved, meaning there'd be nothing to grab on to for dirty fighting. It was a smart decision, but one I had always ignored. Anyone who fought me could use the handicap of my long hair—not that the handicap ever worked out for anyone. I was undefeated.

We circled around each other in the dirt square bordered by the orange-red stones that made up the streets. It was located near some houses, which was unavoidable because the Tech Off Zone tended to be compact, but it faced the backs of these houses where no windows were placed. It was kind of like being locked inside a cell made of blank tan walls.

The guy snarled at me, but it didn't hold the same weight that same action would have coming from a werewolf. I smirked and kept moving until we circled the entire square. It was the way these fights started. It was a chance to size up your opponent or to try and fake them out if you decided to. I never did anything more than smirk. It was a subtle fake-out, but it relayed my confidence to the guy opposite of me. I could always see them stutter at least a little, suddenly second-guessing themselves.

My current opponent stuttered in his first step right when the fight began. We leaped for each other after completing the circle, but his one bad step sealed his fate. I slid my bare feet on the dusty floor of the square and slipped out of his way just to bring my elbow down at a sharp angle. It connected with the back of his neck. I held back just enough not to shatter it. He hit the dirt facefirst. He sucked in pained gasps, gagging on the dust. I kicked him over onto his back so he could breathe. He wasn't getting back up.

"Surrender or I'll have to throw you out of the square," I said easily.

I glanced at his buddy, waiting on the sidelines. His mouth was agape. I had heard them bad-talking, acting tough, boasting about how they were going to bring me down and put me in my place. Things didn't go according to plan.

"I give," the guy wheezed.

His buddy ran into the square to help him off the ground. Then he dragged his sorry ass away. Several pairs of eyes watched them leave with their shame. My fights tended to bring a crowd. Mostly human. Once in a while, I'd be honored with the presence of a couple observing werewolves. But I always got the attention of the guards stationed here. Their job was to supervise things and ensure nothing got out of hand. It was almost like the king gave a fuck sometimes. This was one of those times. I had an audience of humans and a couple of werewolf guards today.

"Who's next?" I asked. I pressed my fists together, ready to go again. I relished this sport. Fighting kept my mind sharp. It allowed me to think with an almost perfect clarity. There was nothing better. This was also why I was a better mercenary than anything. Fighting was all about acting and reacting in a quick succession. It was all about black and white decisions. It was deadly precision or death in a real fight. There was no middle ground. There were no mottled grays.

"Lucky bastard," a man on the sidelines muttered. Another guy spat at my feet. The guards didn't care about that sort of stuff. They were only there to stop physical violence from leaving the square. Everyone outside talked amongst themselves, trying to decide who to send into the square next to finally bash my head in for being "agitator scum."

I found it all more amusing than anything. I didn't need to be a hero even though, as a human rebel, I was fighting for all humans. Even the lost ones. In time, they would see the truth. They'd either die alongside their precious werewolves or they'd join the rebels. I had faith the majority would pick the right choice.

But I found myself questioning that when the memory of Sorissa seeped into the edges of my mind, pushing for the spotlight. I could see her there, in my mind's eye. I could see her naivety, her innocence in a world she was just born into. She was a werea, but she didn't fit werewolves. She didn't fit humans. She didn't fit vampires. She just was. And I wondered, *what* was the right choice?

Because I wasn't sure I had made it.

I needed to fight today more than I ever had. I

needed clarity, but the clearer my mind became, the more Sorissa shined. Could *she* be the right choice? Every option I had to consider paled in comparison to her. That kind of gut instinct was what I lived by, and it said this: handing the princess over to the rebels was the wrong choice. But it was the one I picked. Was that the result of loyalty? My loyalty and the choice between black and white never butted heads before. Now it did, and the more clarity I gained, the more certain I was that I had chosen *wrong*.

The air in my lungs rushed out like I had been punched in the gut. I remembered Sorissa sleeping peacefully at my side in the roader, touching me like it was no big deal, like it was natural. And she was beautiful. I had never seen so much beauty contained inside of one living thing. I hadn't wanted to admit it, and I still didn't, but she made me ache in ways that I never would have thought a werea would have been capable of. But that was how she was an anomaly. She wasn't a werea to me. She was just... Sorissa.

I had had women, beautiful women back in Freedom, but it was never anything more than a moment to enjoy. Sex was casual and nothing I ever gave much thought to aside from that it felt good. I didn't agonize over it. I didn't *need* it. But Sorissa created this ache. I couldn't stop thinking of her supple bronze skin. I wanted to feel that skin on my lips. I wanted to explore every inch of it.

"Rodrick!"

I knew I had lost it when the sound of her voice in my head became as clear as if she were right across from me. Prepared for disappointment, I searched the crowd, but I wasn't disappointed. She was right there. Not in my head. The people gathered outside of the square made room for her, Caspian, and Aerre. I couldn't stop the smirk on my face, the satisfaction at seeing her there, just across from me.

"What are you doing here?" I asked.

All eyes were wide and trained on the Lost Princess—especially the guards; they looked nervous, but since Phantom Fangs was with her, they didn't do anything.

Sorissa's beautiful face lit up in a smile. Her dark eyes seemed to produce a light all their own. It was like she had a halo of light following her wherever she went, ensuring she would be the focal point of anyone's attention. I didn't see it so clearly before, but I saw it now, and I couldn't look away. Because she was the right choice. Everything inside of me said so.

"That was amazing," she said.

"What was?" I asked.

"The way you defeated your opponent with one

blow right at the start."

"You saw that?"

"Yes! Not up close, but I saw it."

The way she was beaming at me and the praise made me feel as if I had done something truly remarkable. Little sparks of fire were igniting in various parts of my body, even down to my knuckles. Was this part of her power as the Moonlight Child? It would have made me wary if I hadn't been so taken by her, if I hadn't already switched sides like it was the easiest thing in the whole damn world to do. And maybe it was.

Sorissa took a step forward and then another until she was well inside of the square. I didn't process it until she was almost next to me. The little puffs of dust kicking up from her boots were as small and dainty as she was. That wasn't to say she didn't have any muscles, but she was lean, streamlined. She wasn't dressed like a princess. She wore pants that hugged her legs, making it impossible not to see the definition of her perfect thighs. The shirt she wore was a bit looser. It tucked into the waist of her pants and had short sleeves. This look suited her, but I was surprised. I expected a dress, princess attire. Was this the king's idea or Caspian's?

I glanced past Sorissa to see Caspian standing with his mouth wide open. Aerre looked the same but clearly horrified.

"Sorissa," Caspian said, "the square is only for fight-ers."

"I know," she replied. "Rodrick, spar with me."

Gasps sounded off one after the other until they caught up in a united tone of disbelief. That same disbelief took a second longer for me to register. But, unlike everyone else, it only made my grin bigger.

"I like your spirit, little fighter," I said. I sized her up, looking her head to toe, wondering if she'd really be a match for me or not. I decided not. "We can spar if you like, but you'll lose."

"I used to wrestle bears in the woods," she an-nounced. "Granted, I was using moonlight, but I think I learned a bit about one-on-one combat at least."

I hummed low in my throat. "Spunky werea. Show me your bear-fighting moves then, minus the moonlight. Rules."

"Rodrick!" Caspian exclaimed. "Really?"

"You got a problem with this, Phantom Prince?"

All eyes turned to Caspian. The guards were sweat-ing. The humans were wide-eyed.

"I don't need his permission," Sorissa said.

Eyes were back on the princess.

"Damn it," Caspian muttered. "Whatever. Don't hurt her, Rodrick."

Gasps all around.

Aerre smacked his forehead with the heel of his hand.

"Call the match, Aerre," I said.

"Fuck you very much."

"I'll call it," Caspian stated. "And stop it if it's too much. Seriously, Rodrick. Don't take things too far."

"Yeah, yeah." Hell, what did they take me for? I wasn't going to damage the precious princess. I was going to pin her down and make her submit. A wicked thrill buzzed in my veins at the thought.

Sorissa growled. "I can take care of myself."

"And that's why we had to break into Paws Peak and rescue you," I goaded. "Damsel in distress, more like."

There was fire in her eyes. Her lips were pressed into a firm line. I hit a sore spot, and I didn't feel bad about it. That was how the game worked.

"All the way around the square once. Then the fight begins," I said.

"Circle around," Caspian said reluctantly, starting the match.

Sorissa followed me step by step as we backed away to make our mirrored circle. It was strange how in sync she was with my movements. Yes, every match started with this same thing, but no one ever matched me step for step. My foot hit the ground when hers did and my other raised at the same time. Maybe I had underestimated her. She wasn't going to use moonlight, but that gleam in her eyes was akin to a predator. Werea or not, she was still a werewolf.

"Start."

Sorissa was fast. Her knees bent, and she sprung forward before I had the chance. She was flying through the air and I was slow, grounded, tracking her with my eyes alone. I had never seen anything like it. I wasn't prepared for her legs coming at my neck. She was trying to bring me down with one move, in a delicate twist and curve of her body. She would have if I hadn't ducked in time. She went sailing over my head and landed gracefully behind me. I barely turned around before she was running at me again.

She had spirit, but I had more experience. And I was stronger—discounting moonlight. I was sure of that. So I used it.

Sorissa was forgetting that. She was running at me now, prepared to bulldoze me over with brute force alone, something that apparently worked for her when she was using moonlight. I knocked her hands away and sidestepped, wrapping her up in my arms from behind and pressing her into my bare chest. She didn't give up there. She wiggled and tried to step on my feet, but I stepped back. She almost succeeded in giving me a bloody lip when she jumped up and jerked her head back, dark curls flying, but I was prepared this time. There was no more room for underestimating. I took her down.

I swept her feet out from under her before her skull could crash into my mouth. I didn't intend to be so rough, but she hadn't left me much of a choice. My survival instincts kicked in, that snap-decision clarity. I gripped the back of her head with my hand and forced her face down into the dirt as I sat on top of the back of her luscious thighs. Keeping her pinned was harder than I thought it would be. I had to let go of her head and gather her arms to yank them back and literally hogtie her.

"Gods!" Caspian exclaimed. "I'm calling it. You're done."

I let Sorissa go and stepped off, but she wasn't done. She rolled onto her back and tripped me. I barely caught myself, with my hands to either side of her shoulders and my knees spread to either side of her thighs, rather than crush her.

"Shit," I hissed.

She grinned up at me with dirt on her face. "I'd say never turn your back on an opponent, but I cheated."

"Damn right you did. And you almost crushed yourself in the process."

Then her hands were in my hair, gripping the back of my head and loosening my ponytail. I shuddered. It was an all-encompassing shudder that started from my head and reached all the way down to my toes. She was so close, so warm. If I lowered myself a little more, I would have felt her flush against me. I had to bite back a groan and ignore my throbbing dick. But Sorissa shifted underneath me, hips raised high enough that she hit me just right.

"By the strength of Cor," I gasped. "Enough is enough, little fighter. We're done. I'm going to let you go, and you're not going to attack me again."

"Promise," she said with a smug upturn of her lips.

"Rodrick," Aerre growled from behind me. Next thing I knew, his hands were on my shoulders, yanking me back up to my feet.

"Not my fault," I said quickly. My insides were twisted. I almost felt like I'd be sick. I had betrayed Sorissa and here I was, practically begging to feel her. I had to make things right. I wouldn't give her to the rebels. Not tonight. Not as a prisoner.

I didn't even care that Aerre's hands were still on me, gripping tightly. Caspian was helping Sorissa off the ground. He brushed his thumb against her lips, wiping away a bit of blood. I must have split her lip. It didn't look fat or anything, so it wasn't bad, and it looked like it was already done bleeding.

"I'm fine, Caspian," she said, removing his hand. "You're amazing, Rodrick. You should teach me how to fight like you so I never have to be the damsel in distress again."

The way she looked at me pierced my heart like an arrow. I wanted her to touch me again. And fuck if I didn't need a cold shower right then.

"Well, well, well, if it isn't Phantom Fangs. What the fuck are you guys doing to the princess? Father wouldn't be too happy if he knew."

It was one surprise after another. I held back a growl as I caught sight of two of the king's sons waltzing toward us. The growing crowd parted for them, giving them more than enough room; they all bowed down until they were folded in half. It was basically unheard of to see Caspian's brothers in the Tech Off Zone. I didn't know the princes individually, aside from Caspian, because they all blended together. It was like five different versions of the same stuck-up, spoiled-ass prince.

"How about we show you what a real werewolf can do, Princess?" one of the brothers said all confident like. Cocky bastard.

His lips curved up, baring white teeth. Then blue flared around him. So much blue. Apparently, he didn't figure wasting moonlight like this was an issue since the full moon was tonight.

Caspian shrunk. He froze at Sorissa's side, speechless.

The prince who spoke looked through the crowd of people and grabbed a big man. He was handling him like he had no weight to him, like he was made of paper. "How about you? Want to go a round?" The man's face paled because he couldn't say no to a prince's request.

"Moonlight isn't allowed," I growled. "It gives you an unfair advantage. Where's your honor, Prince of Wolf Bridge?"

This was bad. My hackles were raised. I spoke out when I shouldn't have. This was why I didn't work well as a spy. If I saw something wrong, I stopped it. Luckily for me, up to this point, things like this didn't typically happen in Wolf Bridge. They were "shields" after all. A rebel spy would know that the root of the problem had to be put first, but I was a lowly mercenary and my judgment had been put into question more than once recently.

"Caspian, are you going to let your *bitch* talk to me like that?" The prince's hold on the man tightened to the point it hurt. He was drawing blood with newly extended claws. Fangs were peeking out from his lips, too. The other prince with him chuckled at his side, content to stay on the sidelines and squawk like a bird.

"So this is how you act when your father isn't around to mind you?" Sorissa interjected. She moved toward the prince and his victim. Each step she took was powerful. I swore I could feel vibrations in the ground each time her boots firmly touched the surface. If she had been using moonlight, it might have made sense, but she wasn't.

"Let him go," she ordered.

The prince scoffed and shoved the man to the ground. He shoved him so hard, and with the added strength of moonlight, that I heard something crack. The man cried out and gripped his arm. "I don't need your help," he gritted out. He was glaring daggers at the princess. That set her back. The heaviness in the air and the vibrations in the ground disappeared at the same time.

"You see, Princess? No problem here," the prince said nonchalantly. But I saw the rage in his eyes. Sorissa pissed him off. He would hurt her without his daddy here to tell him no.

"I'll take you on," I spoke up. "Moonlight and all. I won the last round with the princess. Came out on top." I smirked.

That got me the prince's full attention, both of them actually.

"Rodrick," Caspian murmured.

"I won't even use moonlight. But you can use it all you want. I'll take you down without it," I taunted.

That did it. The prince snapped. The blue flames fanned out around him and exploded in a burst of light. He crushed the orange-red rocks beneath him when he dug in his heels and leaped forward. There was no way I could dodge this.

I got the air knocked out of me when he hit me. The impact cracked a couple of my ribs. I bit back the pain and covered my head with my arms and hands curled into fists. He pinned me, and his fists rained down like a hail storm. The blue flames lighting everything around him weren't hot like real flames, but I could feel the energy crackling from them like pinpricks on my skin. He was pummeling me. Each hit left immediate bruises and welts, but his swings were wild and uncalculated because he had given in to rage. That was how I would win. A clear head would always triumph even with a vast difference in strength.

Everything was a blur. My arms ached, and I knew my bones would give if I couldn't act within a few seconds. The prince's fangs extended. He bit my arm. If he had been thinking clearly, he could have just knocked my arms out of the way and bashed my brains in. But this bite was the opportunity I needed, so I wasn't complaining. I moved as quickly as I could, breaking my free arm out of my shield to jab a pressure point in his neck. That made him stop, left him gasping for an instant, which was long enough for me to knee him in the goods. I flung him off of me and rolled onto my feet.

My arms were throbbing. They were black and blue, but aside from my ribs, nothing was broken. I'd live. Maybe. The prince was back on his feet, coming for me again. Another blur of blue streaked in my peripheral vision. Caspian was in front of me. He caught his brother and threw him down into the dirt. The impact left a perfect impression of his brother's body. He was buried a foot deep.

"Enough," Caspian commanded. His calm voice chilled me to the bone. It wasn't often the Phantom Prince used his power, but when he did, he was a force to be reckoned with.

"Shit," the prince who was standing on the sidelines muttered as he helped his brother in the ground, who wasn't glowing blue anymore. It was like the moonlight got knocked out of him.

"What the fuck, Caspian?" the brother he just beat the shit out of spat blood onto the dirt when his brother hauled him to his feet. He was shaking and couldn't stand on his own.

"You took things too far, Alexander. We're done. Henry, take him back to the castle."

"You sure you want me to do that, Caspian?" Henry replied. "What if I tell Dad about how your bitch doesn't fucking know his place? He'll kill him this time like he should have killed him before. But no. You wanted him on your squad."

"This isn't about Rodrick, and you know it."

"I expect a punishment, Caspian," Alexander growled, "or Henry and I break him for good. Also, we'll be taking the princess back to the castle with us."

Sorissa opened her mouth to say something, but Caspian cut her off. "The king gave me and my team orders to take Sorissa back to the castle in time to prepare for the Full Moon Banquet. She is under our care, and he hasn't called to say any differently. Wouldn't he be interested to know about the wound you inflicted on a human who did absolutely nothing to you."

The man with a broken arm trembled in fear alongside a woman placing his arm in a sling. The guards watched everything passively, eyes flickering this way and that. I couldn't tell what the stupid bastards were thinking. Who would they back up?

"We'll get you back for this, shithead," Alexander announced.

Aerre was standing silently behind me. He was wearing the same unreadable expression as the guards, and that pissed me off.

Finally, the bozo princes turned to leave. Everyone stayed frozen in silence until they were well out of sight.

Sorissa moved first. She went to the man with a broken arm.

"Are you all right?" she asked, reaching out her hand.

He recoiled. "You've done enough. Please. Gods, forgive me, Princess." He started groveling.

"I-I'm sorry," Sorissa said. Her lips were quivering as she took a step back.

I came up behind her and she turned. She moved forward until she was close enough for her eyelashes to tickle my chest. I thought she'd cry, but she didn't. She just shook.

"I'm sorry, Rodrick," she said, wrapping her arms carefully around my waist.

I didn't know what she had to be sorry for. So I wrapped my arms loosely around her in return. I had to keep it light even though I wanted to squeeze her tightly. Lightly touching her already aggravated those broken ribs, bruises, and welts. Gods, but being close to her felt good. Her skin on mine especially felt good.

The portacomm clasped to Caspian's belt let out an annoying beep. He answered it without saying a word. He only listened. I doubted Alexander and Henry had gotten to the castle already, but they probably had called and cried to their daddy by now. I was certain Caspian was getting an earful from the king, but I was too worn out to use what I had left of my nearly empty moonlight reserves to listen in. It was too bad I didn't have enough to heal my wounds.

After a few minutes, Caspian clipped the porta-comm back onto his belt and announced, "We're taking Sorissa back to the castle. Well, Rodrick, *you're* taking her back. You'll escort her all the way to her room. Aerre and I will be going to the throne room to speak to the king."

Nobody spoke. Sorissa pulled away from me. Where I thought I'd see tears, there was fire. I wondered what she was thinking as she lined up behind Caspian, ready for him to start leading the way. Aerre moved next. Then I followed, after pulling on my shirt and boots. We were on our way to the castle. I should have been worried, but I wasn't. I was confident this whole thing would blow over. And I was eager for tonight.

I wouldn't give Sorissa up, but I would meet Jobe as planned. Sorissa stuck her neck out for a *human*. She wanted to help a *human*. I would explain how she was different from anyone else. If the rebels agreed to treat her right, and I'd make sure they kept that agreement, I'd tell her the truth. Maybe she'd choose to join them. Maybe she'd be the key to fixing everything. They would have to see what I saw even though she was a werea. Even though she was, by blood, one of the monsters...

I realized it was wishful thinking. The rebels would never accept her. But she was different. She brought out a side of Caspian I had never seen. He outright went against his brothers. He never did that. He bowed his head and always took their shit. In the past, Caspian chose black. He was too worried to cause conflict to ever choose white, but this time he did.

My time as a spy was over. My time as a rebel might have been over too, but I was okay with that. I knew I was where I was supposed to be. Sorissa opened my eyes. It seemed the legend of the Lost Princess of Howling Sky wasn't just a legend after all. She was much more.

CHAPTER 23

SORISSA

I DIDN'T like this. I didn't like that we were coming up to the castle and that each of us was quiet in our solemnness. I didn't want to cause any more trouble for Phantom Fangs than I already had. Rodrick's wounds looked terrible. He didn't say a thing about them. He didn't act like they hurt, but I knew they must have. I was optimistic he'd be able to heal himself after the full moon tonight at least. And I was relieved Caspian stepped in to save the day because I had been useless. I had never felt as inadequate as I did right this moment. I didn't know how to properly thank the "Phantom Prince," so I caught his hand in mine and squeezed.

"Thank you," I said.

He squeezed back. He looked haggard, like he had

the weight of the world on his shoulders. I realized maybe he did.

"You were amazing back there," I continued. Then I looked back at Rodrick and did my best to grin. "You too. I don't know how you managed to fend off moonlight without using moonlight or magic to do it. I've never seen anything like it."

Rodrick smirked his reply.

"I like that about you, Sorissa," Caspian said as he squeezed my hand a little tighter. "You do what your heart tells you to do in the moment. Rodrick's like that, too. That's probably why you both get along so well." He let my hand go.

"I feel like I get along with all of you," I said.

Caspian's lips tugged up at the corners. He walked up to a door that led into the castle. Then we were inside of familiar tan walls. The dark blue carpet muffled the sound of our footfalls, and we passed by guards without a word. I glimpsed the Heart, an area I still hadn't properly seen yet. I hoped to glimpse Todd, so I could talk to him, so he would know. So he could stand by his team. But he was nowhere to be seen. I hated the distance he seemed to put between himself and the rest of Phantom Fangs. And me. I hadn't seen him at all since Phantom Fangs brought me to Wolf Bridge yesterday. I wanted him here.

We had to pass the throne room before we could get to my designated room inside of the castle. I was secretly hoping Caspian wouldn't split us up like he said he would. I didn't know if I should push if he decided to go through with it, though. As we moved, I stared at my boots. I wondered if what happened was my fault, but I also knew I would have done it again if the situation were to repeat. That human did nothing wrong. Those princes wanted to hand out needless suffering to flaunt their power. The thought made my stomach twist and boil.

I lifted my head when I knew we were getting close. I expected the double doors barring the throne room from the rest of the castle to be closed, but they were opened wide, beckoning us inside. I took a step forward, but Aerre stopped me. He looked at me with lake-blue eyes and shook his head.

"Rodrick, take Sorissa to her room," Caspian said. "Aerre, with me."

Rodrick put his hand on my shoulder. He wasn't holding me back per se, but I had the feeling that was what the action was intended for. I was rooted in place as I watched Caspian and Aerre drift away from us, backs to us. I looked past them to see what they were getting into. I saw the two princes who had caused this whole mess in the first place. They were sitting at the base of the throne, looking smug next to their father. He, at least, didn't seem to share their enthusiasm. But it didn't stop the growl building in my throat at the thought of Phantom Fangs being threatened.

Rodrick's grip on my shoulder tightened, and he steered me away from the throne room. "Let's go. Nothing we can do right now. It'll just make a bigger mess."

I stifled that growl, but the energy had to go somewhere. It went to my fists, shaking at my sides, as I followed Rodrick back through tan halls and upstairs. The guards at their posts never looked at us. They stared straight ahead like statues. I wondered what they thought. Then I saw a guard I recognized: Koren. His gaze wavered for just a moment. It was enough for me to see his concern. And it made me feel better. Because Koren was kind even though he wasn't Phantom Fangs. Trace was kind even though she wasn't Phantom Fangs. We weren't alone in this castle.

And then I wondered why I thought of myself and Phantom Fangs as "we." I didn't wonder for long because it felt right. It was an idea that had been planted the day before and was already taking root. I wanted Phantom Fangs to be my home.

"Why do Caspian's brothers treat him like that?" I asked. "Where is the respect? Babaga was very adamant about respect. Respect for the woods, the animals, her—"

Rodrick bellowed, "*Babaga* gave you away to

maneaters, Sorissa. Or have you forgotten that part?"

My jaw snapped shut and tears threatened to bead in my eyes, but I held them back.

"People use each other," Rodrick murmured. "Humans, werewolves, and vampires too because that's just the way the world is."

"What about love and compassion?"

"Myths."

"You don't mean that. Look what you endured for that man. You challenged those two princes. I may not be from here, but I saw what you did. You got hurt because you had compassion for that man. Maybe me too. You followed my lead. Then Caspian did. Aerre... I think Aerre wanted to."

Rodrick laughed and shook his head as we reached the hall my room was in.

"My point is you're all different from everyone else here. Even before you challenged Alexander. None of you fit in. You're like me," I insisted.

Rodrick opened the door to my room, placed his hand on my back, and urged me inside. Then he shut the door behind us. He left those electrical lights off, leaving only the natural light coming in from the windows and the bubble-glass doors leading out to the balcony. It was light, but it allowed shadows, and they twisted across Rodrick's face in a way that made me think he must have been angry. I instinctively backed away when he took a step toward me.

"You are bold, little fighter," he said, taking another step forward. "I'll give you that, but you could get yourself into a lot of trouble talking like this out in the open where anyone could be listening."

My back hit a wall. "I'm only speaking the truth. I'm only saying what I know, think, feel, and believe in. Am I not supposed to do any of those things? Am I supposed to be a doll, a puppet, that does exactly what it's told?"

Rodrick grinned. He placed his hands on the wall to either side of me, pinning me and reminding me just how large he was. His shoulders were strong and broad. His muscles were firm like sculpted rock. I looked over his tattoos and watched a vein bulging in his arm, and my heart ached at the sight of black and blue skin. So many bruises. An unfair fight. And still, he had somehow held his own. This werewolf... this tethered, human turned werewolf, was truly remarkable.

I shuddered when he leaned down, and his lips and short beard grazed my ear. "That's what makes you unbelievably sexy," he whispered.

Heat crawled up my skin. His lips and beard were barely touching my ear, but the warmth of his body encompassing mine made me wonder what it would feel like to have him pressed against me, without the space.

Without the brawling. Gentle touches.

Rodrick must have read my mind because he moved slowly, brushing his lips against my ear to my cheek. It was all dry and warm until he pressed his lips firmly to my skin. Wet, soft lips. My eyes fluttered, and my body buzzed. I was about to reach out and cradle the back of his head, to bring him closer still, but he moved back before I could. He stood up straight in front of me, no longer pinning me to the wall.

"What was that?" I asked. My voice sounded small and far away. I was drifting in a dreamy haze.

"A promise," he replied with a lazy smile. The left side of his mouth always curved up more than the right. He had a distinct lop-sided grin. It was contagious and made me want to smile back. It made my heart beat a little faster.

"A promise?" I repeated.

"Next time I kiss you, it'll be on the lips." He gently took my chin in his hand and ran the rough pad of his thumb over my slightly parted lips.

I was seeing him through the dark frame of half-lidded eyes. It blocked out everything but him. No one had ever had my attention so exclusively. "I'm ready," I said.

Rodrick answered with a low growl that made me shiver. "Not now." He traced my lips with his thumb one more time. "That would be very against the rules, Sorissa.

So is saying your name. I shouldn't push my luck too far all at once. That kiss I left on your cheek will have to do for now. But remember it and remember what I said. Because I'll remember what you said."

He let my chin go. I chased his touch like it was an automatic reflex, eager to feel his warm skin again. I took his hand, wishing he'd touch my face again, wishing he'd brush my lips again. His lips. I wanted that kiss *now*.

"I have to go, little fighter. Stay in your room until someone comes for you, likely your maid. I wouldn't plan on seeing us again until the Full Moon Banquet." He gave my hand a rough squeeze before tearing away from my grasp. "Caspian will take care of things, so don't worry about that either, or you'll cause him more trouble. Got it?"

"Got it," I murmured.

I stood stupidly still, my mind floating in clouds. It wasn't until I heard the door click shut that I came back to my senses. It was like being half asleep and being startled awake by a loud noise, adrenaline pumping through my veins to sharpen my mind and body in case of danger.

I sighed and slid back against the wall until I was seated firmly on the dark blue carpet. Life used to be so simple. Yesterday, it became a huge and complicated web, and I was just starting to learn its intricacies, following individual silver threads. But there were four silver threads that shined the brightest. Caspian, Aerre, Rodrick, Todd... How did they fit into everything? How did I? Could I locate my own thread and unravel the web?

As if to answer that question, I spotted my mother's journal where I had left it on the nightstand last night. I supposed it was an option. It was an account of my history after all.

I stood, grabbed the journal, and sunk into the cloud bed. It immediately tried to swallow me up, so I gave in and lay back, sinking farther into a fluffy embrace. It was almost suffocating, but I ignored it. I held my mother's journal above me and ran my hand across the purple cover. Then I traced the gilded letters. I brought the journal down onto my chest and spread my arms out wide. I closed my eyes and saw only Phantom Fangs. I didn't want answers from a journal. I wanted to spend more time with them, to learn with them.

But I really didn't want to cause any more trouble. Though Phantom Fangs deserved no punishment, I was certain the king would side with his chosen sons. I wondered why Caspian had been cast out.

I lifted the journal, flipped a few pages, and found the next entry I had yet to read.

The 3rd Month of Winter, Day 63. 2525.

My beautiful daughter, Moonlight Child blessed by Lureine, Princess Sorissa va Lupin of Howling Sky, I thought it would be prudent to give you a bit of history. Like everyone, I will start with the Gods.

There are three Gods: Lureine, Cor, and Yessma. You'll find arguments about everything, but this statement has fewer disputes than most things. Take my words over any others you might hear, Sorissa. I have your best interests at heart, and I would never lie to you.

The most powerful of the Gods is Lureine. He is the God who created us. Werewolves. We are superior. We were made to rule this world. It would have been so had the other Gods not created their own species, their own people, and started the Prime War. Prime was born in war.

Vampires are our sworn enemies. There is no use for them. We would slaughter them all at once if they weren't so powerful and cunning. They are the biggest obstacle in this war, and it won't end until they are exterminated.

Humans are plucky little creatures. They can be a nuisance, but they are a valuable resource if free will is beaten out of them. They become nice and docile, hard workers, and quite the delicacy. Howling Sky has an abundance of them. We breed them for different jobs. Some are bred to be strong laborers, others are bred for meat—

I closed the journal with a resounding smack. The sound was hollow. Cold washed over my skin and I shuddered, gripping my arms and rubbing them for warmth. I couldn't stomach it. I couldn't read any more of this journal, of this werea who claimed to be my mother. I couldn't think of vampires or humans that way. I knew little of vampires since I had only briefly met a few imprisoned in Paws Peak, but I had their fairytales in my head. I knew they weren't mindless monsters. They were creative, free souls with dreams of their own. That was true for humans and werewolves too—even if I didn't understand the majority of werewolves and humans I had met. I had met Phantom Fangs, and I knew I couldn't lump all werewolves together. That meant I couldn't lump all vampires together, humans either. Koren. Trace.

But it made me sick. It made me sick to think *my* mother could say those things. She was talking about Aerre, his mother, and sister. She was talking about Rodrick. There was nothing in this journal that would help me because my mother and I didn't see eye to eye. She praised werewolves like they could do no wrong while I had plenty of complaints concerning plenty of were-wolves, my mother among them.

I was a carnivore, but I had never once thought about eating a human. The thought made my stomach churn, and I really thought I would be sick.

I had to get rid of this journal. I had to burn it, to let it die with the rest of Howling Sky in whatever caused its demise. It seemed to me the High Kingdom was better left a distant memory.

I hadn't planned on leaving my room. I was going to do what Rodrick said. But I rationalized it because I wouldn't leave the castle. I just needed to find somewhere I could dispose of this journal. It couldn't sit in my room anymore. I never wanted to see it again.

I opened my door and walked out into the hall. I ducked my way around guards, watching and waiting for them to move like I had when I snuck out last night. I wasn't sure it mattered if there were technocraft eyeballs in places I couldn't see, but it made me feel better. I didn't know where I was going. I was being fueled by pure emotion. I was certain I could find technocraft, maybe in the Heart, that would turn this journal to dust, because ripping it to shreds just wasn't good enough. I wanted ashes.

CHAPTER 24

TODD

*T*HE HEART was bright and warm. It was contained inside of a cylindrical glass energy chamber and, by extension, a bubble-glass shell. The shell reached all the way to the top of the castle tower, illuminating each floor with a light that never went out thanks to the electricity the energy chamber collected and recharged the lightning stone with during thunderstorms. The bubble-glass shell wasn't breached unless work on the Heart needed to be done—unless you were me. I wore tinted goggles to protect my eyes as I sat on the ground next to the energy chamber's console. Sometimes I was programming. Sometimes I was building. Sometimes both.

This was the one place I was allowed true isolation. It was the only place I took off my beanie because no one could see my red hair. When I was in Wolf Bridge, the Heart was off limits to everyone but me. At the moment, I was working on tech inhibitors because I was stuck on how to make a tech field span all the way to Paws Peak. Just because the Heart had basically unlimited power didn't mean I always knew how to utilize it. That meant I had to work on plan B: Phantom Fangs infiltrating Paws Peak once again in order to assassinate Prince Charles. The two-day time limit was making plan A impossible.

I wondered why I spoke up and told everyone I could do it. I could. Eventually. I fought for plan A because I wanted everything to go smoothly, without a hitch. Infiltrating Paws Peak the way we had the first time just wasn't a good idea. They'd be much more alert. Maybe they'd expect it. But we'd do it if we had to.

I was angry. I couldn't stand the thought of Prince Charles with his teeth and claws buried in the Lost Princess.

My cheeks burned at the memory of her hands touching my face, my skin. I wiped away the sweat that had beaded on my forehead. It was too warm near the energy chamber, but only just. It was bearable and a little sweat never interfered with my work, so I dealt with it.

The Lost Princess wouldn't leave me alone, though. I tried to get lost in my work, but my thoughts kept drifting back to her. I purposefully avoided her since

Phantom Fangs delivered her to the king, but it wasn't so easy to keep my thoughts from her. She made my heart palpitate, my cheeks red... Nervous. She made me nervous.

I had never had any interest in women before like most werewolves seemed to. It was apparently quite common for werewolves to at least find women attractive. In Wolf Bridge especially. The only wereas here were either too old and already mated or too young for mates until we brought back the princess. She was the perfect age for mating and the first werea I had met who was almost my age. She was only two years younger, eighteen while I was twenty. Apparently, I was only attracted to females of my own species. I had the sinking feeling that statement wasn't entirely true, though.

It was the Moonlight Child "blessed by Lureine." I didn't believe in any gods, not even the universally recognized Gods. I didn't believe in magic. Everything could be explained, but I couldn't explain this. And that made me uncomfortable.

Werewolves typically lived to three hundred. A werea was usually fertile up to two hundred and fifty. In all that time, the elder wereas had been breeding with their mates and had only produced the few young wereas in Wolf Bridge. It was amazing werewolves managed to hang on with how slowly we could reproduce now. The fact that wereas could produce multiple cubs in a relatively short amount of time was the reason why, but it was still slow. It was hard for werewolves to find mates before, but since the world became so small, it became even harder. Most werewolves would never have a mate. That was just biology, but werewolves wouldn't go extinct—as long as our wereas weren't killed off like the vampyres.

Phantom Fangs killed the last vampyre. Others may have doubted it, but we didn't. That male had no reason to lie. He hated his own species almost as much as werewolves and humans did. I wasn't good with emotions, but even I could see he wasn't lying.

Vampires as a species were still holding on because of the possibility that even one among them might be pregnant with a new vampyre. If a new vampyre grew to adulthood, they would multiply like rats. To ensure their destruction, werewolves would have to hunt them all down eventually. I would have been focusing on how to infiltrate Crimson Caves right now if not for the Lost Princess.

But the Lost Princess caught everyone's attention. She took precedence. Both Wolf Bridge and Paws Peak wanted to claim her because of her age and sex. It would have been the case for any werea her age, but not to this degree. Tonight was the Full Moon Banquet. It was obvious the princess had used up all her moonlight reserves. Everyone was anxious to see what would happen on this full moon when she recharged. If the stories were true, she could hold more moonlight than anyone. That made her the most powerful breeder in our history. It also, quite possibly, made her dangerous. Ensuring she was claimed by a werewolf would make her loyal to whichever kingdom he belonged to.

I could think of many scenarios, of many ways this night would end. It seemed to me that the primary thing on the minds of both kings was to seal the princess with the Mate Claim. They wanted power, but I doubted they had given much thought to the possibility of her own great power, outside of being the ultimate breeder. King George of Paws Peak wanted her sealed right away while King Philip of Wolf Bridge was trying to win her over first, to make her feel as if Wolf Bridge was her home. Maybe Philip was making a fatal mistake, underestimating the Lost Princess because she was a werea.

I didn't get into politics. I didn't usually think about them this much either. Tech was what I did. It was what I knew. It was what I had control over. I wished my brain would let the princess go already. She had nothing to do with me.

Heat spread through my face when I remembered

her touch *again*. My heart beat just a little faster when I saw her face light up as I talked about tech. The werewolves who were passionate about tech didn't even react like that, not that I ever spent much time with them. No, it was something else. It felt like she was looking at *me* with those lit-up eyes. She cared about what *I* had to say. Maybe she found the tech fascinating, but she didn't see me as the "tech guy," like tech was my only function. She saw past that even though I hadn't given her a reason to, just like I had never given anyone else a reason to.

My chest ached. My entire body ached, and it wasn't from sitting hunched over on the reflective surface of a hard floor. I ached for the princess. If I had been delusional, I would have wished her to be my mate. It was crazy because it wasn't all biology talking. It wasn't all because of this driving need for sex that was normal in a werewolf when confronted with an unmated werea. It was a yearning for kinship, something foreign to me. And the irrational notion that she might actually care for me. For the first time in my life, I longed for a connection I had never had with another living being.

I decided it had to be because of biology after all. The need to mate encompassed all of these feelings, chemicals firing off in my brain. It was more than just a sex drive.

It was a nuisance.

I stopped soldering the computer chips I was working on, donned my beanie, and stepped outside of the Heart to the wide, empty space that made up the base of the tower. I leaned back against the bubble-glass shell. Then I shed my tinted goggles and squeezed my eyes shut. I wanted to rub the pressure away, but I knew doing that would make it worse, so I restrained myself.

"Princess, please return to your room."

"I need to burn this!"

I opened my eyes to see the guards at the archway leading out into the rest of the castle. The Lost Princess was trying to push past them.

"Well, there's no way to burn it in here," one of the guards said uneasily.

I pushed off the glass, about to retreat back inside of the Heart when the Princess called, "Todd!" Shivers crawled up and down my spine. Slowly, I turned to face her. One of the guards was holding her back. Her dark eyes were wide open, staring at me. I wondered what that expression meant. Her brow was furrowed, but her lips were curved upward. I didn't think this look passed for happy. But I wanted to know.

"I'll take care of her," I said. "Let her go."

The guards let her pass, and she ran for me. She was holding her mother's journal. Was that the thing she wanted to "burn"? She was crinkling the pages and digging her nails into it like it was a piece of garbage.

I felt uneasy when she didn't slow her pace. I thought about moving out of the way, but she sped up and bulldozed into me. Since I was unprepared, my back hit the bubble-glass shell behind me. My arms went around her instinctively.

"I'm so happy to see you," she said.

I gently pushed her away from me even though that was the last thing I wanted to do. She was so soft and comfortably warm, not borderline too hot like the Heart. That ache in my body got worse, particularly in my aroused dick. What a nuisance.

I glanced up at the guards who just passively watched whatever that whole exchange was.

"Can you help me?" she asked. Then she stepped around me and pressed her hand to the bubble-glass surface. "Is this the Heart?"

"Its shell."

"It really is bright. Can I see inside?"

"If you wear these." I pulled a spare pair of tinted goggles from my utility belt. She took them. Shrugging, I replaced my own goggles over my eyes and instructed the princess to do the same. "Don't take them off," I said. "You'll burn up your retinas. And be careful where you step. I'm working."

"Got it."

I pressed my finger to an inconspicuous piece of glass and my fingerprint was scanned. The glass slid open and shut again once I did the same thing from the inside. To the untrained eye, the shell didn't look like it could be opened at all. That was how seamlessly the glass slid into place. It was one of my many designs.

When I looked back at the princess, her goggles were pressed against the cylinder holding the Heart. The lightning stone sparked at its base, sending off little electrical sparks that bounced through the chamber. The glass making up the energy chamber was also tinted, but the goggles were extra protection. Maybe they weren't strictly needed, but they were for long periods of time. The Heart was unbelievably powerful when charged this high. It wasn't easy to contain, but Wolf Bridge practically had endless power because of it.

"It's beautiful," the princess whispered.

I said, "Sure."

I stared at the back of her head, marveling at the thick curls of her hair. I wanted to reach out and feel them, to twirl them in my fingers. I tried not to look guilty when she turned to face me. Apparently, she had her fill of gawking at the Heart.

"Is there any way I can burn this?" she asked, holding up her mother's journal.

"Why?"

"I don't want it. It should have gone with the rest of Howling Sky, whatever happened to it."

"It burned to the ground."

"See? It's the perfect solution."

I shrugged. If she didn't want to know her history, that was none of my business. In a way, I could relate. My parents escaped Howling Sky before it burned to the ground. We lived outside any kingdoms and wandered for a time. Then my parents were killed by vampires, and I was left on my own when I was eight years old. I didn't remember them all that well. And all I remembered of Howling Sky was fire reaching up past the clouds.

I plucked a lighter from my utility belt and lit the flame. "I can burn it if you want."

"I want to do it," the princess said.

"Fine, over there, on the floor where nothing else can burn."

I showed her how to use the lighter and left her to it while I resumed working on my tech inhibitors. It was quiet for a long time, and it wasn't until the journal was good and burned that the princess moved. She stomped on it with her boot, crushing black pages into fine pieces and reducing them to dust. The leather cover was much more stubborn, but it was good and ruined by the time she seemed to be satisfied. No one would ever know High

Queen Alana's last words aside from whatever the Lost Princess had read. It seemed somehow fitting.

I just finished piecing together a tech inhibitor and checked my work. Solid. As usual. In theory. I hadn't ever made a tech inhibitor before. The idea was to cut off electricity since there was no telling when or where I'd need to use one and tuning a tech inhibitor to a specific kingdom's system seemed like a roundabout way to go about it. The root of what powered every system was electricity.

I took an old pactputer I didn't use much anymore, turned it on, and then tossed the tech inhibitor onto it. It grew metal legs with sharp tips that dug into the device, eating electrical pulses. The screen blinked out. I couldn't get it to turn back on until I removed the inhibitor. Another success. However, inhibiting something as big as the spires back in Paws Peak wouldn't be quite so easy. I'd need stronger inhibitors or a concentration of them, and even then, it'd be best to be inside of the spire, at the control panel.

"What are you doing?" the princess asked.

"Working," I murmured. Something had to be said about my mental fortitude. How I managed to work with the princess so close was an accomplishment.

She sat down on the floor next to me, brushing her arm against mine. She rolled up her already short sleeves after a while because of the heat that couldn't be completely filtered out even with the excellent ventilation system. And now she was taking off her boots. When she settled back in place, touching her bare arm against mine, I shuddered. It was skin on skin. My tank top left my arms exposed. Why did she insist on being so close?

I blamed biology.

"Are you ready to return to your room?" I asked. The guards or the king himself could have called me. There was a comm system inside of the Heart, but they hadn't. It seemed no one was too worried about her not being in her room. I was certain the guards reported she was with me. That only meant the king really was doing his best to win her over, to prove she had freedom here, freedom she didn't have back in Paws Peak.

"No, I'll stay with you," she said. "Can I help?"

I didn't say anything. I didn't know what to say.

"Do you want me to leave?"

"N-no."

I flinched when she reached out for me. She brushed her hand against my forehead. "You won't be so hot and sweaty if you take your beanie off," she said quietly. "Why don't you? I made you upset before."

"I wasn't upset."

"You were uncomfortable. I think your red hair is beautiful."

I shook my head. "The color of maneaters."

"Maneaters have a color?"

"All the redheaded werewolves left after the Hellfire Strike were maneaters, and they lived in Howling Sky."

Her pretty lips curved downward. A tiny drop of sweat was beaded on her upper lip. I couldn't stop staring at it or thinking about how I wanted to lick it off. Her pinkish-red lips looked soft, tasty even.

"So we're both from Howling Sky," she said.

"Yep."

"Maneater blood."

"Yep."

"Why do you hide, though? No one in Wolf Bridge has faulted me for that."

"I don't hide, and that's because you're the Moonlight Child." I paused. "I just don't like werewolves or humans staring."

"I really do think it's a beautiful color. If it's just the two of us in here, do you mind?"

She wasn't going to let it go. So I took off my beanie and ran my hand through my messy hair. It was nice to escape some of the uncomfortable heat.

She reached up and ran her hand through my hair

too, giggling. It was probably sticking up in odd places, I supposed.

"It's like fire," she said.

"You're staring," I replied.

"I'm not a human or a werewolf. I'm exempt from your list. As everyone keeps reminding me, I'm a *werea*. Apparently, I have my own category."

"I guess that's kind of true."

"So, what are you working on?"

"Tech inhibitors for infiltrating Paws Peak to assassinate Prince Charles."

The princess frowned. I wondered why. "Can I help?" she asked again.

I supposed she could help me just fine if I showed her what to do. I was just assembling for the most part anyway, so I nodded. That made the frown go away. I showed the princess what I was doing and explained it to her. She caught on quickly and asked me more questions about tech, about the electrical lights in the castle, about monitors, about computers that read thumbprints and opened doors. She had a lot she was curious about, genuinely curious about. I liked how inquisitive she was. By the time we had assembled several more tech inhibitors, I felt like she knew more about tech than a lot of the werewolves living in Wolf Bridge. And she still wanted to know more.

"You want to shut down the entire system in Paws Peak," she said.

"Plan B. Plan A is seizing control of their system from here, using a humongous tech field cast out by the Heart. I'm just preparing for more than one scenario," I answered.

"Why take control?"

"To assimilate Paws Peak. King Philip doesn't want to destroy them. There aren't many werewolves left. He wants a complete and utter surrender."

"This isn't just about Charles."

"The king believes in efficiency."

"So do you."

"Yes. The goal to assimilate Paws Peak is how we found out about you in the first place," I informed. "It was all by chance. The right place doing the right thing at the right time."

She smiled. "I'm glad you did."

"If I can make a tech field that spans from Wolf Bridge to Paws Peak, I'll be able to hack them from here. But I'm not too close to cracking that problem yet."

"So it isn't an assassination. Plan A or plan B."

I paused to consider the weight of that statement. Caspian issued this mission on his own, infiltrating Paws Peak again specifically, and the king complied—but he didn't offer his assistance. The king didn't know about plan A. As far as I knew, this was a mission for Phantom Fangs alone just like retrieving the princess had been. Retrieving the princess made sense. We weren't supposed to be seen. But we were. We caused an uproar and Paws Peak would be expecting an attack now. Infiltrating a second time would be a lot more dangerous. The king had to know that.

I never worried about these kinds of details because it was Caspian's job. I was in charge of tech. As long as my tech did what it needed to do, I was good. It was the only thing I focused on. But now I wondered. I wondered if the king really wanted to assimilate Paws Peak or if it was said for show, because sending an army with Phantom Fangs would have made the most sense.

Politics were always so convoluted with layer upon layer of deceit. How anyone could find any truth in them was beyond me.

"I don't know what the king has planned. I just know what my task is," I finally replied.

"Are you going alone?" she whispered, eyes wide.

"Probably."

"Maybe you shouldn't go back to Paws Peak."

"It's the only way to get rid of the incomplete Mate Claim. Killing Prince Charles, that is."

"What if I don't want a mate at all, Todd? What if I'm fine like this? I'm not hurt. The incomplete Mate Claim doesn't have to go away. If I ever did choose a mate, it would probably go away anyway, right? That's what Caspian said." She growled. "Why is everyone outside of the woods fighting anyway? It's stupid."

The comm system sounded off, a persistent low beep and a blinking red light showing there was an incoming call. I got off the floor and grabbed the receiver.

"The princess is to return to her room. Her maid is on the way to prepare her for the Full Moon Banquet."

"Understood," I replied and replaced the receiver.

The princess stood up from the floor and stretched out her stiff muscles. She did an exaggerated side stretch, causing her shirt to ride up. A patch of bronze skin drew my eyes. The dip of her pelvis leading to her sex made my brain short-circuit. I wanted to grab her waist, slide my hands down her hips, finger the band of her pants. I wanted to know if the rest of her was as soft as her arms.

"I have to go back?" she asked.

I swallowed. "Yes."

"You can keep working. I know the way."

"I'll escort you."

"Afraid I won't go?"

I stared at the ground, but I forced my eyes back up to her dark ones. They were almost red. A deep red. I wondered if that was because of the tint in the goggles. My gaze wavered. I wanted to look away. Caspian told me eye contact was important, which sucked because it was easier to look away. "I want to take you."

She gave me a big smile and walked up to me, taking my hand in hers. "Okay, Todd. Walk me back to my room."

My fingers were limp in her hand because I didn't know what I was supposed to do. She laced her fingers through mine, holding our hands in place. I closed my eyes for a moment. I wanted to think only about her hand touching mine. I wanted to take in the sensation because it was different from anything I had felt before. And I wanted more. Much more.

"I want to touch," I murmured.

She laughed. "I'm holding your hand. We are touching."

I opened my eyes and reached out my free hand. I hesitated instead of moving her shirt up just high enough to grab her hip like I wanted to. The princess was very good at maintaining eye contact. Her fire-hot gaze made me sheepish. And I remembered she was off limits.

I shook my head and said, "Never mind."

The princess let go of my hand, grabbed my beanie, and reached up to pull it onto my head. She pressed into me when she did, making it impossible not to feel her breasts squish against my chest. I lost my breath. *Soft. Soft. Soft. So beautiful.*

"Now I want to keep your hair to myself," she said.

"Fine with me," I replied.

She looped her arms around my neck. I gave in and grabbed both of her hips, moving her shirt up just high enough to touch warm skin moist with sweat. I had to close my eyes again. My dick was half hard, and I wanted to roll my hips forward. I didn't. I let her go and unraveled her arms from around my neck.

Damn biology.

"Let's go, Princess" I said.

"Todd." She made a clicking sound behind her teeth. "Call me Sorissa."

"Okay." I shrugged. "Sorissa." I liked the way her name felt coming off my tongue.

"Promise to teach me more about tech later. I still have a lot of questions."

"Sure."

"Promise."

"I promise."

She nodded, smiling again.

I realized then I would probably do anything she asked me to. I had never enjoyed being with anyone. Living things were complicated and most of them barely dealt with me and my tech. I didn't mind Phantom Fangs. But Sorissa liked tech, and she seemed to like me.

I needed Sorissa. The thought of going back to my

tech alone, shut away in the Heart, made me want to scream. The thought of being away from her made my chest hurt.

CHAPTER 25

SORISSA

I WAS disappointed when the door to my room was in sight and Todd took me inside. I didn't want to get all dressed up again. I didn't really care to go to the Full Moon Banquet, but at least Phantom Fangs would be there.

"Princess." Trace was practically folded over in a bow.

"Hi, Trace," I said warmly. "I guess you're getting me ready for the banquet."

"Yes, and the king provided you the most beautiful dress." She straightened up and tentatively smiled at me. The smile wavered when she saw Todd was with me. I thought it was funny. Were smiles outlawed in certain situations?

"Are you going to stay?" I asked him.

"N-no," he spat out. "I'll see you at the banquet." His pale face flushed. I hadn't seen that look on him while I was alone in the Heart with him. When it was just the two of us, he didn't seem as nervous.

He went to the door but hesitated. I walked up behind him and wrapped my arms around him. He tensed, then relaxed. He was nice to touch. Nice to hug. I liked that he softened for me. When I touched him, all the tension seemed to leave his body.

I closed my eyes and breathed him in, committing his smell to memory. I savored the little bit of saltiness caused by his perspiration. I hoped he'd teach me more about tech soon. At least I knew what many things were called now and the basics of how it all worked. It made me feel like less of an outsider, and I thought it was all fascinating. I still liked Babaga's word for it, though. Technocraft. It may not have been *magic*, but it was magical.

"Thanks for letting me stay and for teaching me," I said. "Don't forget you promised."

"I won't," he replied. His hands dropped to mine, clasped around his waist. He gently pried my fingers loose. "I have to go."

Reluctantly, I stepped back. Todd was out the door a moment later. I stared longingly at the wood for a few painful seconds. I liked Trace well enough, but I wanted Todd to come back. I wanted to understand more, like why he was so quiet. Why he didn't seem to enjoy being around anyone. I liked to think I was the exception. And he made my body buzz. All of Phantom Fangs. Only Phantom Fangs. I didn't know if it was "normal" for a *werea* to claim things, but I wanted to claim them.

When I turned around. Trace was staring at me.

"What?" I asked.

"Nothing," she replied too quickly. "Do you want to see the dress?"

"Sure."

She led me to the closet where a new dress was hung in the center on full display. It was a long, elegant dress. It would trail well past my toes. The skirt was formfitting with a little added volume. The back swooped low, exposed. The bodice, while not overly lacy, was designed with intricate stitching to give a different look and texture from the rest. It was beaded with little clear crystals. The fabric itself was a pearly white. It changed colors depending on the light.

"As long as I don't have to wear a corset," I said. "It is beautiful, though."

"No corset needed, Princess. If you wouldn't mind, shall we move to the bathroom and get you showered? There isn't time for a bath I'm afraid."

"It would be nice to get the sweat off my skin."

In no time, I was undressed and in the shower, water cascading down over my body. The shower was located in the corner of the bathroom, and the curtains obscuring me from view seemed to be optional. Trace was female, but even she didn't seem entirely comfortable with nudity. Maybe because I was the "Lost Princess."

"I like your brother," I called. "He's nice."

There was a brief silence before Trace replied, "He is."

"Do you ever see him?"

"Maybe in glances from time to time."

"But you haven't talked to him since he became tethered," I said, filling in the void of what she didn't say.

"Yes." Her voice was quiet, suddenly timid.

"Will you be at the Full Moon Banquet? You can talk to him there. I'll help you hunt him down."

"The banquet is for werewolves alone, Princess. Humans can't absorb moonlight."

"And?"

"And it isn't done."

"Koren will be there, right?" I said thoughtfully.

Something clattered onto the bathroom tiles. "Please, Princess!" There was panic in Trace's voice now. She pulled back the shower curtain. Her blue eyes shimmered, threatening tears.

"I won't tell anyone." I tucked a strand of blond hair that had drifted out of her ponytail behind her ear. "I found Aerre the other night, watching over you and your mother. I just think it's unfair."

Trace's pink lips trembled as she nodded and pulled the curtain back into place.

"I like Aerre," I said.

"He's a wonderful little brother," Trace agreed.

"I'll tell him to talk to you instead of hiding like a coward."

"It's hardly cowardice. He's doing it to keep us safe. Just like he always has."

"He can sneak in at night. No one will see."

"He won't take the chance. It's not done, Princess. Werewolves and humans… there are rules."

"Maybe it's time for rules to be broken. How else will you and Koren ever be together?"

Trace came back with a towel and tugged me out of the shower, shutting off the steady flow of water in the process. She fussed over me, patting down my skin like I was a cub unable to do it myself.

"Please be careful, Princess," she warned. "I want to be with Koren. I don't want to hide, but we can't be rash. Nobody likes change, and everyone has a hard time accepting it. You could get into a lot of trouble if you spoke to the king the way you speak to me. I think you have a good heart, but you're the Lost Princess." She sighed. "Maybe I've just said more to you than I should. You need to be careful, though. For your own sake. I'm not just telling you this to try and save my own skin."

"Maybe nobody likes change, but change happens anyway. It needs to happen. How can you be with Koren, how can you talk to your brother again without fear unless there's change? Something like this isn't going to happen gradually." I was getting fired up. I was practically growling my every word. "There's too big of a difference between werewolves and humans, even though the king, or somebody, claims the werewolves in Wolf Bridge are shields. What do they do for humans? They don't eat them? Well, that's great. What about the man I saw who got his arm broken by 'Prince Alexander'?"

Trace stared at me with wide blue eyes. She ushered me from the bathroom after tying the towel around me and sat me down on a chair in front of the vanity mirror. She pulled out the hairdryer and worked through my sopping hair.

After a moment, she shut it off so she wouldn't have to speak above the noise. "I want big changes too, but it's easier to put it off and hide in the shadows. I think there is room for change. I was telling my mother that last night."

"I heard," I said.

"As much as I want and believe that, I know this kind of change, a human and a werewolf together openly, in love, as mates, as a married couple, wouldn't come easily. We're all part of a fine thread that could snap under the slightest pressure. I want things to change for the better, but they could just as easily change for the worse. Talking to my mother last night reminded me why I haven't done anything yet. I don't want to see anyone I love die. Consider that, Princess."

CHAPTER 26

SORISSA

*T*HE DAY was fading away and night would soon set in. The last rays of sunlight came in through the bubble-glass doors leading to the balcony. Trace and I hadn't said much of anything after what she told me to consider.

By the time Trace was finished with me, I looked like a proper princess, similar to the ones in fairytale illustrations. She didn't overdo my makeup, so I still looked like me. I wasn't wearing a corset. The dress fit snugly on my figure. I looked in the mirror and considered all of this as well as everything Trace said. I had a choice. I could take all of this lying down, or I could fight for the kind of world I wanted to see outside of my woods. Did either path lead me to Phantom Fangs or were they out of my reach? Was it selfish to want change? How could it be when I would be sticking up for the persecuted? How had the world even come to this point?

Thoughts swirled around and around in my head like a whirlwind, and I didn't know if they would ever stop. I was tempted to stick my hand out in the wind and grab hold of the first solution flying by that I could catch.

My door burst open without a single knock and three boisterous and brightly dressed werewolves let themselves inside. It was half of the Princes of Wolf Bridge. I was relieved to see that the two causing trouble at the square weren't among them, but I was disappointed to see Caspian wasn't either. Trace bowed low to the ground, and she didn't move from that position.

"Ravishing," one prince exclaimed as he drank me in with his dark eyes.

Another prince walked forward and offered me his arm. "We're here to escort you to the Full Moon Banquet. It's time to begin."

"Too bad Alexander and Henry had to get themselves into trouble. We get dibs on the princess."

I hated how they talked about me as if I wasn't standing right in front of them. I bit my tongue so I wouldn't lash out reflexively. I also took the prince's arm. That was good enough for them. They walked me out of the room and continued their chatter, none of it meant for me to join—not that I had any desire to anyway. Trace was still bent over when the door clicked shut.

The three princes walked me through the castle and out a door I had never been through. It led outside to a series of neatly trimmed gardens. The grass was cut short and each blade was fine. I was certain it would feel soft underfoot. There were walkways made of the same orange-red stones as the streets outside of the castle. There were decorative fountains of wolves, a stream, a bridge, trees, blooming flowers… It was quite beautiful, especially when the sunlight caught on the fountains and reflective water one last time before the sun disappeared from the sky and dusk painted everything a deep purple.

A large table was set up in the middle of a courtyard near a pond holding pink waterlilies that were just starting to bloom. The courtyard had the highest concentration of werewolves. Most of them were in the process of getting seated as humans carried trays of succulent meats from the castle. The smell permeated the air and made my mouth water.

I supposed that meant Trace could have come if she were a server. I thought it was a shame she hadn't. I spotted Koren among the other werewolves. He seemed a little tense tonight. He wasn't wearing that dreamy smile he had on when he had escorted me to the throne room.

My skin prickled and the fine hairs on my body

stood on end as the full moon slowly appeared. My body was already thrumming with the promise of power, with the tiniest hint of restoration. It was too early in the night for me to get much out of the full moon at the moment, but I could feel it. The moonlight. It was like drops of liquid splashing intermittently down into my core and rippling out across my body, all the way to my fingertips and toes. Each time a drop fell, goosebumps covered my skin. I wanted to undress, to expose every inch of my skin to the moon so I could take in as much moonlight as possible. I didn't because of a few things: the alignment wasn't perfect yet, I remembered Caspian's lecture about modesty, and because Trace took a long time getting me ready.

I reclaimed my hand from the prince guiding me when I spotted Phantom Fangs. They were all together, standing at a spot near the long table, about to take a seat. The sight of them all together made me smile and my chest swell. I was about to run for them, but Philip barred my way.

"A pleasure to have you, Princess Sorissa," he said. He even gave me a tiny bow, which I thought odd. The King of Paws Peak never would have done that. I couldn't figure out the King of Wolf Bridge. His sons reminded me of the royalty in Paws Peak, but Philip had his own code of conduct—or something.

He took my hand and kissed the back of it. His lips were soft, but his beard was coarse. He looked up at me with eyes that were almost identical to Caspian's. But there was a void in his eyes. The sapphire flakes danced in Caspian's eyes. In Philip's eyes, they were frozen into place.

"Please take your seat next to me and my sons," Philip said. I let him lead me to the head of the table, the side nearest the castle. His sons sat at either side of him and me. Alexander and Henry were already there and seated—farthest away from me.

I sat quietly and awkwardly, surrounded by royalty I didn't understand, while Philip looked out at all of the werewolves gathering and taking their seats. I stared longingly at Phantom Fangs. They weren't clear on the other end of the table, but they were several werewolves away from me. As if they could feel the weight of my gaze, they all turned to look at me. This time the shiver that racked my body wasn't because of the moonlight I was passively intaking.

When everyone was seated, Philip stood and said, "Your attention, please." All chatter died, and he was given everyone's undivided attention. "The Lost Princess of Howling Sky lives, and she is with us tonight." The king held out his hand to me. I took a steadying breath and reminded myself to do as I was told for now. I let him help me from my chair and stood in front of countless werewolves at their king's side. The bite I had mostly forgotten about began to itch just then for some reason, like having so many werewolf eyes looking upon me was in violation of whatever half-claim Charles tried to put on me. On the other hand, I finally did see a handful of other wereas. None of them were my age, but I wasn't completely alone.

"Princess Sorissa is home, here, in Wolf Bridge. We saved her from imprisonment in Paws Peak, and next we will free her from the shackles forced upon her by Prince Charles."

I reflexively touched that bite between my neck and right shoulder. I tried to rub away the sting, but it made me wince.

"Tomorrow, Phantom Fangs will free our princess by assassinating Prince Charles ve Paz of Paws Peak. Lureine willing, Paws Peak will soon be ours after that. King George will see they are powerless against us when Phantom Fangs infiltrates them a second time. That, or they will call us to battle. We will win. One way or another, we will force a surrender. Soon werewolves will no longer fight against one another. It's time to put an end to the Prime War."

The night was filled with howls, cheers, and clapping. I stood silently. I wondered if Philip really thought

Phantom Fangs would get out of Paws Peak unscathed for a second time. I believed in their abilities. I saw what they could do. But Philip wanted to "assimilate" Paws Peak. Supposedly. It would be safer for Phantom Fangs if he sent his army with them instead of waiting to see what happened with Prince Charles. Did he really think Paws Peak would surrender after something like that? Wouldn't it just make them angrier? Wouldn't it just give them time to prepare an attack of their own?

Philip raised a glass of dark red liquid. "To our princess and Phantom Fangs' success."

More howls, cheers, and clapping followed. These werewolves were praising Phantom Fangs, but I also noticed there was a gap in the seats from either side of the four members, effectively isolating them from everyone else even though the table was full and two werewolves were probably sitting on top of two others in order to leave those seats empty. Wolf Bridge considered Phantom Fangs their champions, their secret weapon, but they wanted nothing to do with them?

"I have a gift for Phantom Fangs," I said, but nobody heard me. I closed my eyes and used the few drops of moonlight I had absorbed from the ever-growing presence of the full moon. I coated my vocal cords in the soft blue light I could see in my mind's eye and said it again. "I HAVE A GIFT FOR PHANTOM FANGS." I didn't shout, but my voice rang loud and clear, powerful, like it had come straight from the mouth of a god. I released my active moonlight, allowing my reserves to once again grow passively deep inside of my being.

The silence that followed was full of tension. Philip and the princes hesitated. I didn't wait for their permission. I moved away from my chair and walked down the table. Each member of Phantom Fangs was standing by the time I got to them. They were wearing fancy clothes like everyone else, and I decided I liked that look on them. Their facial expressions were quite different, though. Rodrick looked like he was trying to hide a smirk. Aerre's blue eyes were wide with concern, reminding me of his sister. Todd's face was almost as red as his hair, and he stared at the ground. Caspian stood at attention like a soldier awaiting a command.

"Thank you," I said. "Each of you are brave protectors, warriors. But you haven't forgotten your kindness. You haven't forsaken your compassion." I paused and spoke my next words quietly. "I want you all safe, and I don't want you to go. But if I can't stop you, I want to at least give you this."

I went to Rodrick first. I was glad to see his wounds had been treated; he should be able to heal the rest of the way once his moonlight reserves were filled tonight. He was much taller than I was—and I wasn't short. I beckoned him closer. He leaned down in compliance. It felt right to start with him. He was the one who gave me the idea after all, and he owed me. I placed my hands on either side of his face, burying my fingers in his short beard as I pressed my lips to his. The kiss he had given me on my cheek felt so nice. It seemed like a perfect way to express my fondness for them. It turned out, lips on lips was much better. A low growl rumbled in Rodrick's throat, and he swallowed a moan of my own. I wanted to linger, to lick, to bite, but I didn't have time for it. Besides, this was payback for him teasing me before.

I smirked when I pulled away and he tried to follow me. I went to Todd. He was shaking his head, eyes darting every which way. I wrapped my arms around his neck, coaxing him down slowly. The tension faded. His arms loosened up a little, and he grabbed my waist. I kissed him too. Softly, So softly. His lips parted, and he tasted like an assortment of spices crackling on my tongue. I didn't want to stop this kiss either, but I had two more werewolves to kiss, and I wanted to do that too. I *needed* to do that too. And I couldn't let anyone stop me. That meant everything was being cut short. I didn't know when the crowd's shock would wear off. Todd reluctantly let me go.

Aerre's mouth was hanging slightly ajar. When I

stepped up to him, he took a step back and said, "No." I wasn't sure what to do. If he didn't want me to kiss him, I wasn't going to force it, but Caspian nudged Aerre with his elbow and nodded to that obnoxious bite of mine. It was glowing, bright and blue with moonlight. I wasn't actively controlling my moonlight, but now that Caspian pointed it out, I could feel it active inside of me, little drops of luminous blues fading and replenishing at the same time as the moon's alignment drew closer. It was nothing, hardly any moonlight because the alignment wasn't perfect yet, but it was still there. Still powerful.

"Aerre?" I asked, feeling suddenly shy.

He closed his eyes. When he opened them again, the blue was so bright I wondered if he was using moonlight too. He leaned down and let me kiss him. His lips were soft against mine, humming with energy, but he didn't make a move—except for when he pressed his lips a little bit more firmly into mine. He was the one to move away. His chest was bouncing up and down with heavy breaths like he had just run a marathon. The blue light streaming from my bite grew more intense. I could almost feel it burning against my skin. Moonlight was pouring more steadily into my body now. It wasn't time for the moon to align yet, but things were moving quicker, like what we were doing drew the moon in.

"Caspian," I said. "I met you first."

"And yet I'm last," he said quietly, but his smile was radiant. "Hardly fair."

"Kiss me already."

And he did. He kissed me like no one else was here. I had all but forgotten about everyone but Phantom Fangs. I was lost inside of each kiss, but this one was the most intense. Caspian was prepared. He grabbed the back of my neck, angled my face just so, and kissed me hard and with a vigor none of the others had because I didn't give them a chance to warm up. He sucked on my bottom lip. I was helpless and let out a just as helpless whimper as my entire body burned brightly. My sex tingled, and I pressed as firmly into this Phantom Prince as I could. I wanted his skin on my skin. For just a moment, I felt his hardness.

Caspian broke away from our kiss—against my delirious wishes—and looked right at my bite. The moonlight flared and then disappeared with a spark and a *pop*. Only smooth bronze skin remained like I had never been bitten in the first place.

"It's gone," he said, amazed. "It's really gone."

The sounds of all the other werewolves was a white noise slowly becoming clear. Gasps sounded off when moonlight burst around me and Phantom Fangs. It was a bright blue almost too bright to look at. My moonlight reserves had never filled so quickly. And then the moonlight flare was gone, leaving only the trickling flow of moonlight coming down from the full moon that wasn't perfectly aligned yet. It was like it had popped into alignment for that one moment, and then it phased back to where it should have been.

A restless energy crawled beneath my skin. When I looked at Phantom Fangs, they seemed brighter somehow, like they were marks on my vision that would never disappear. The energy in my body was pulling me toward them. Like magnets. No, more than that. They felt like an extension of my own body. I knew what they were going to do before they did it. I swore I could hear whispered thoughts not my own swimming around in the back of my head. They had familiar voices, the voices of the werewolves standing in front of me.

"It can't be," Philip said. A vein was bulging in his forehead. His teeth were clenched. "The Mate Claim made on the full moon. Legends of such a thing... But a werea making a claim?" He was struggling for words. "Four mates?! Two tethered?!" His vein looked like it was going to pop out of his head.

Alarms ripped through the air.

Fire lit up the east wall.

A deafening explosion followed.

And the world descended into chaos.

CHAPTER 27

CASPIAN

"*P*ROTECT SORISSA!" I ordered. My team formed a circle around her, and each one of us stood ready to shield her from anything that might come. Werewolves around us were all growling with their hackles raised. Some of them were exuding moonlight and shifting. Others were grabbing weapons. Others were circling the king and my brothers. Wolf Bridge was under siege, but it hadn't reached the gardens yet.

"What's happening, Todd?" I demanded.

He was paler than usual, staring at his inteliband. It was a good thing he insisted on being connected to the Heart, and the system, at all times. I didn't have mine. Neither did Aerre or Rodrick—not that any of us had the same access or knowledge Todd had anyway.

"Part of the east wall. Someone blew a hole in it."

"I pretty much knew that already. Why didn't we see it coming?"

"Someone breached my system? The Heart is okay. Things look normal. I don't know! It was a big-ass bomb. We're under attack," Todd barked hysterically.

"It's because of *you*!" Aerre growled and turned toward Rodrick. "You were in contact with your agitators. You snuck out. You've been stealing tech, haven't you? You told them to come here tonight. You gave them information that allowed them to blow up our wall like it was nothing!"

He was hysterical too. I felt my own heart racing as if I were the one accusing Rodrick. I also swore I felt Rodrick's own reaction, a stutter, a pinch of guilt? I was hyperaware of everything, and it didn't have anything to do with the adrenaline pumping through my veins—even though it heightened my awareness too. I felt like my thoughts were being invaded, my body. The susurrus of unfamiliar thoughts crowded the back of my mind like a high-pressure air leak. It was like having extrasensory perception, but I couldn't make sense of it. Not yet.

"What are you doing?!" Aerre cried.

I looked behind me to see Sorissa stripping. I expected her to just tear out of the expensive dress, knowing her, but she slipped through it seamlessly instead. I turned forward again, averting my gaze and watching for any enemies sneaking into the gardens. Gods, but I was weak. And I wasn't the only one.

I peeked over my shoulder, matching the others on my team. Sorissa's eyes were closed. Her arms were held slightly away from her sides, palms open to the moon. Her chest was open like her heart was the focal point of receiving moonlight. Her perfect breasts were perky, nipples hard from chilly air. Her bronze skin started to glow blue with moonlight. Like flames, the energy rose up, and her hair danced in the embers. She was the most beautiful thing I had ever seen. Nothing compared. Absolutely nothing.

"Aerre's right," Rodrick said suddenly. "I have been in contact with the rebels. I stole tech. I told them about the Lost Princess. I was supposed to bring Sorissa to them tonight."

"I fucking knew it!" Aerre shouted.

"I wasn't going to follow through! I couldn't. They would hurt her." Rodrick shook his head. "No, this isn't the work of human rebels. I can promise you that. This wasn't the plan. It's something else." I couldn't explain it, but he *felt* sincere.

"I'm shifting," Sorissa said, her eyes snapping open with a burst of moonlight. I had never seen such a dense concentration of energy, not even from the Heart itself.

I looked forward and tried to speak. "Sorissa—"

I didn't get a chance to finish. The crackling of bones reshaping cut me off. I looked behind me again to see that Sorissa had called upon her moonlight form. I had seen it only once before. But this was different. We had to widen our circle. She was a huge black wolf with slick fur. Her eyes were almost white with moonlight. I couldn't fathom how much of it was inside of her. Never had I seen such transfixing eyes. Such power. They hadn't looked like that before when she shifted. Before they were dull, a result of having hardly any moonlight to spare. These eyes contained a power that might have touched the Gods. If she had been the enemy, I might have cowered with fear, my tail tucked in between my legs. Instead, I was struck dumb, lost in awe.

"Rodrick is telling the truth."

I flinched as Sorissa's voice sounded in my head. It was as if she had spoken directly into my ear. But that was impossible. We couldn't speak in our moonlight forms. I wondered if I was hallucinating at first, but I saw the confused looks on my team's faces. I wasn't the only one who heard it.

"I can feel it. Rodrick is telling the truth."

"How are you doing that?" I asked. "How are you speaking directly into our minds like they're linked to each other?"

"I don't know."

"Heads up," Todd announced, drawing the small handgun he and the rest of us kept on our person at all times. "They're here. It's Paws Peak, not rebels after all."

Werewolves all in moonlight form sped through the gardens, emerging from bushes and flowers, jumping through trees. They filled the night like yellow-eyed demons. They bared their teeth and their growls mixed with our own, polluting the air and drowning out the blaring alarms.

It all happened so fast. I had barely drawn my gun and a maelstrom-level gust of wind almost blew me over. A blur of black and blue streaked across my vision. A howl filled the night, louder than everything else. And it was all Sorissa.

She moved faster than any werewolf I had ever seen. I had to activate my own moonlight and really concentrate it in my eyes to even keep up with her. She was like lightning. When she struck, the ground trembled. She was mowing down werewolves like it was nothing, catching them in her jaws, tossing them to the side. This kind of strength... No one knew this was what the Lost Princess would be capable of. Everyone said she would be the perfect breeder for a new generation of werewolves, but no one thought she would be more powerful than any werewolf, than many werewolves combined. She wasn't like any werea I had ever seen or heard of. She was a monster. A beautiful, captivating monster.

Paws Peak thought tonight would be the perfect night to wage a war on Wolf Bridge after the long stand-still in order to reclaim the Lost Princess. But they were wrong. She didn't belong to them. She didn't belong to anyone.

I thought I saw something lurking in the shadows, but an enemy werewolf in moonlight form leaped at me from my right, drawing my attention away. I dropped to the ground and held my gun ready as the wolf overshot me, flying harmlessly over my head. I fired when he was about to land, hitting him square in the chest. He let out a pained whimper and dropped dead. I had hit his heart, and there was no recovering from that. Unless, maybe, you were Sorissa.

"Caspian?"

"I'm fine."

I took a quick look to make sure I had tabs on Sorissa and Phantom Fangs. They were all engaged, fighting valiantly. Phantom Fangs delivered quick killing blows. I noticed Sorissa hadn't killed a single werewolf, but she beat them bloody and broke bones.

"Sorissa, take them out!" I growled. "This isn't the time to be charitable."

"Like you have room to talk!" Aerre shouted at me as a werewolf barreled into him with snapping jaws. Aerre managed to shoot his soft underbelly and shoved the big wolf off of him as he fired a kill shot.

Then I spotted Prince Charles in his base form. He had his firearm aimed for Sorissa, and she wasn't moving at the moment because she was laying into another werewolf. He would be able to hit her, but I wouldn't let that happen. I raised my gun and fired before Prince Charles could decide if he had lined up his sights or not. The bullet I fired ripped through both of his wrists and his gun fell with a thunk onto the grass below.

I fired again immediately. This time, I hit him in the chest. The armor he was wearing saved him, though the impact sent him to the ground. He curled up in a gasping, wheezing ball. I marched over to him and pressed my boot down on his windpipe.

"You made a mistake," I said. Then I put a bullet in his brain. I flinched. Barely. But I still flinched.

I watched as his eyes rolled up into the back of his head and blood oozed from the wound. He wouldn't be getting back up. A blow to the brain was as effective as one to the heart. He was dead. No amount of moonlight would save him. Why had he even come? He didn't know what the hell he was doing.

Paws Peak was retreating—the werewolves who

could anyway. It was all over so quickly, within the span of a couple minutes, but they had taken heavy losses. I took out two werewolves. Sorissa probably went through thirty or more on her own. But everyone in the gardens did their part. Wolf Bridge took losses, but it was nothing compared to what Paws Peak just endured. They had utterly failed. This was a half-assed and ill-prepared attempt probably led by Prince Charles himself. I had a strong hunch King George hadn't approved this. He would have been better prepared. And I wondered what that meant.

The blue flames that blazed all around Sorissa had died down. They were almost snuffed out. I had no idea how much moonlight she went through to accomplish what she just did, but it was a lot, and she was running on empty. Todd rushed over to her as she shifted back, midnight-black fur receding in place of bronze skin. There wasn't a mark on her, but she was exhausted. She grasped Todd, and he held her in place. I tried not to burn at the thought of his hand on her bare back, near her firm ass, her breasts and thighs pressed into him. I shook my head. Now wasn't the time for that.

And something caught my eye. Something in the shadows, the same thing I had spotted earlier. This time, I noticed it too late. Something sharp cut my throat, and warm blood sprayed down my neck, soaking my chest, my clothes. My carotid artery was severed clean. I was choking.

"Caspian!" Sorissa screamed.

My brain was going fuzzy, but I managed to fire up my moonlight reserves, concentrating it all on healing. Surviving a serious wound like this took every ounce of moonlight I had. I was lucky my reserves had just been filled. Without it, I would have been dead.

When I regained clarity, I realized someone was re-straining me. The sharp object was at my throat, a gleaming knife. It barely pressed against my skin and it cut through, but this time it was just meant as a warning, nothing more than a superficial wound. A scratch.

Blood-red nails stuck out against ashy skin that held the cold, metal knife steady. A female said, "Stand down or I kill him." Then I felt fangs and a hot tongue licking away some blood that had dripped down my arm. She would have gone for my neck if she had been taller.

"You picked the wrong werewolf to take hostage, vampire," I informed. "I'm expendable." I would have ripped out of her hold, but vampires were stronger on average than humans and even werewolves at night—un-less moonlight was involved. And I was out of moonlight. The tiny trickle coming in from the moon wasn't enough.

I silently cursed when I realized vampires were eve-rywhere. They had used the werewolves from Paws Peak as cover to get into place. They left their caves during daylight to set this up. They must have been hiding away in their sunlight-resistant vehicles, just waiting for the right moment. Prince Charles gave them the perfect opportunity. Did they know he was going to attack tonight? They were certainly prepared. They must have done something to Todd's system. Paws Peak wouldn't have been capable of that. I didn't think anyone was. I was so wrong. The vampires had the high ground and heavy-duty revolver guns raised and ready to blow this place to bits. The gardens were at their mercy. With this, the royalty in Wolf Bridge would be annihilated along with a great portion of the guard and all of our wereas. Wolf Bridge could fall tonight. Just like that.

That was the thing about war and simply existing: it was unpredictable. It could go on for years or end in the span of a single breath.

"Stop," Sorissa demanded. "What do you want?" It was the king's place to talk, but, just like Sorissa had stolen the show during the short-lived fight, she took the king's place now. Nobody made a move.

"I want you, werea. Moonlight Child blessed by Lureine," the vampire replied. "Give yourself up, and I won't kill a single werewolf."

"Bullshit," I growled.

She pressed the knife harder against my throat, cutting just a little deeper. "Silence, Phantom Prince."

All Phantom Fangs' eyes were on me. Aerre's face was twisted in pain. I looked at him first because I felt that pain like a throbbing wound in my chest. I wondered if he was hurt, but I didn't see anything serious if he was. Rodrick's veins were popping in his arms, his muscles coiled tight, ready to spring forward. I could feel his rage. Todd's lips were curled into a ferocious snarl. I could feel his despair. Then there was Sorissa. She had tears in her eyes. I was pretty sure my heart would physically break from the weight of them all. Right here, right now, my entire world consisted of a single werea and three werewolves. They didn't believe I was expendable at all, not like my brothers. Not like my father. I could feel it. I knew it was true.

"I'll do it," Sorissa said as a tear fell down her cheek and left a streak of moonlight. "Keep your word, and I'll do it. If you don't, I'll hunt down and kill every last one of you myself. Don't think I won't."

"No need for threats," the vampire replied. "I know what you're capable of. I watched the whole thing. I will keep my word."

"Sorissa!" I pleaded and ignored the vampire cutting into my throat a little deeper. "What are you thinking?"

Todd let her go. She walked toward me and the

vampire, tall and proud, chin raised. Her bronze skin looked silver in the night, a perfect complement to the moon. The Moonlight Child. Most beautiful creature ever born.

"Todd, stop her!" I demanded.

"I-I can't." I noticed his pale hands shaking. I felt the resistance against a much more powerful resolve. Sorissa was holding him back like an alpha who had given a command. But she hadn't spoken a word. And she didn't have to. She bound us together after she kissed each one of us. It was like the king was trying to say before. We were connected. We belonged to her now.

"Don't do this, Sorissa," I implored. I had been reduced to begging. I wanted to fight the vampire anyway, do my best to escape her grasp despite the likelihood of her killing me as a result, but I was hit with the same overbearing wall of resolve that Todd was. That all of us were. I couldn't move. All I could do was clench my hands into shaking fists. Sorissa hadn't left us any room for debate.

"They'll kill you!" I screamed as she kept advancing without even a hint of hesitation.

She stopped when she was standing right in front of me. For some inexplicable reason, the vampire standing behind me let me go. I wanted to move, but I was frozen in place by Sorissa's iron will.

"I'd like to see them try," she said. Then she reached her hands up and placed them on my cheeks. I saw a flash of residual moonlight in her dark eyes when she blinked. "Goodbye for now, Phantom Fangs. Until I see you again."

"Sorissa." I choked back a sob that came from a puncture in my heart. The hole grew wider, a manifestation of my own grief as well as my teammates'. It was too much to bear. It was worse than any physical wound. Useless tears escaped my eyes as if trying to relieve some of the pain. "Please."

"Thank you, Princess." The vampire stepped forward, put her hand on the princess's shoulder, and threw something on the ground. It exploded into smoke that made me cough and my eyes burn. It was ridiculously condensed. That one little device filled all of the gardens in smoke as thick as paste. I couldn't see a thing.

For several minutes the smoke stayed thick, and I was still stuck in place. I heard other werewolves scampering around, trying to locate the princess and the vampires, but none of them got very far. The vampires had used their great speed to escape the smoke before it even touched them. Most of the werewolves here still had little to no moonlight other than the growing trickle from a still unaligned full moon. I kept waiting for the killing blow to come, but there was nothing. The vampires had a chance to kill all of us, and they didn't take it. They didn't kill a single werewolf.

But they had Sorissa. And I had no doubt they would kill her.

My lips trembled, and I ground my teeth. I squeezed my eyes shut. Then I dropped to the ground. I pounded my fists against the ripped-up earth, and I howled out Phantom Fangs' collective agony.

CHAPTER 28

TODD

*T*HAT SMOKESCREEN the vampires made was a nuisance. It lasted for several minutes before it dissipated into the air enough for us to see and move freely again. By then, the princess was long gone. My lips burned with the fresh memory of her kiss. My first kiss, and it couldn't have been any sweeter. I had no idea what I had been missing, but it wasn't the kiss itself that I had been missing. It was the princess. And now she was gone.

I wanted to chase after her right away and rip her out of the vampires' grasp, but the vampires had a big enough head start that we'd only be chasing them all the way back to Crimson Caves. We wouldn't catch up before then. We'd die if we acted recklessly, and that wouldn't help the princess. But neither would waiting. I needed to come up with a plan quickly. I couldn't let her die, especially not when she was starting to feel as necessary as the air I breathed. My chest felt like it was bleeding open without her here, like a piece of me had been ripped away with her.

Caspian hadn't gotten up from the crumpled position I found him in after the smoke cleared. He was shaking, staring at the dirt. Rodrick was breaking things. Aerre was pacing. I had never had an easy time reading my team, but I understood them perfectly now. Their pain blended with my own. Sorissa had tied me to these three just like she had tied me to herself.

It wasn't jarring like I might have thought something like this would be. In fact, it probably made things easier for me. There were four living things in this world that meant something to me. Now I could understand them. I thought maybe I even cared about them. More than anything. I knew, at least, that I wanted to keep them safe. Phantom Fangs meant something to me. It always had even when I used tech as an excuse for my actions. Sorissa came in and made it all clear. *Sorissa.*

My brain cycled through several plans, and I kept the gears turning as I stood statue still. King Philip hadn't bothered to say anything to us. He was talking to his guards, trying to get things back in order. Everyone was purposefully avoiding Phantom Fangs. I understood we had become bigger outcasts than ever before after what the princess did. I wasn't sure exactly what her kisses entailed or how it worked, but I'd figure that out later. I knew it didn't involve the king's plans for the Lost Princess.

The king shot glances our way as he continued damage control. It looked like he was debating about when to come over. He was no doubt formulating his own plans. I'd come up with a plan first. I made tech inhibitors. I'd be able to use them with any kind of system as long as I could get close since they turned off electrical currents. The princess had helped me assemble enough of them that we might be able to do something about Crimson Caves, but the real problem came with the caves.

The Crimson Caves were nearly impenetrable with motion-sensing gun turrets that could blow anyone to pieces. It would be impossible to sneak in undetected unless I could somehow hack into their system, but that would be much harder to do than it was with Paws Peak, and that was only partly because a tech field wouldn't work unless I was inside of the caves. There was a reason we were gathering intel on Paws Peak when we overheard talk of the Lost Princess. I was still new at this infiltrating business. Two months in Phantom Fangs didn't make me an expert.

"Todd, what are you thinking?" Aerre asked and

stopped pacing.

"Anyone who needs to should restore their moonlight reserves when the full moon is aligned, but brute strength alone isn't going to get the princess back. I've got a plan." I said that, but I wasn't confident I'd come up with anything good in time. I didn't have the time or the intel to properly prepare. I think the others sensed that, but they didn't say anything. Apparently, the four of us would try anything if it meant saving Sorissa's life. And we couldn't afford to wait.

There was one other possibility, though. Since the full moon wasn't aligned, that meant Sorissa would get another chance to recharge. Maybe she would get away on her own. Maybe not. The vampires saw what she could do. They must have been confident they could contain it or prevent it now that she was spent. I absentmindedly bit my lower lip.

Finally, the king decided to break away from the other werewolves to scold us outcasts. He went up to Caspian specifically. He raised him from the ground by the bloody collar of his formal shirt and growled in his face. "What have you done?" he demanded.

Caspian wouldn't meet his gaze even though he told me over and over how important eye contact was.

"The bloodsuckers will either try to use her as some

kind of bargaining chip or experiment on her and eventually kill her. We were going to end this, Caspian, the war, but your team failed. You were distracted by a werea you knew you couldn't have. Nothing good comes of her being tied to you. You're a suicide squad. You agreed to be expendable, to do everything it took to keep Wolf Bridge safe, to end the Prime War, but you've damned us all."

I had never seen Caspian avoid eye contact like this. I had never seen him so despondent, and I had certainly never felt it stemming from him. I didn't like it. I walked forward and announced, "We have a plan. We'll get the princess back. We're bound to her somehow, right? I can feel her presence just under my skin even though she's getting farther away with each passing second." I paused. I wondered if this worked the same as having planted a tracker on her. There was no way we could miss her if that was the case, even if the vampires tried to give us the slip. This connection should have made me uneasy, but all I could think about was saving the princess. I didn't even care about the mechanics of it, not right now. Not unless understanding would help us save her. The cogs in my head continued spinning.

"Todd, do you really have a plan?" Caspian rasped. For the first time since the princess was taken, he seemed coherent. He was staring at me intensely with his dark eyes. The intensity was worse because I could feel it crawling inside of me.

"Yes," I lied.

The king let him go, and Caspian stayed standing on his own. Then the king said, "Don't leave until after the full moon is aligned. I will have soldiers prepared to leave with you. Phantom Fangs is our secret weapon, but the vampires will be expecting you. You won't get the princess on your own, plan or not. We can't let the vampires have her. You'll need all the help you can get, but I can't spare much. Paws Peak will likely launch another attack soon. Prince Charles is dead, and King George won't take that lightly." He walked away after that.

I was shocked. Phantom Fangs never had support before. It was always just the four of us, but this was apparently big enough of a problem for the king to get involved. I was glad he did because now we had a real chance at saving the princess's life. It'd turn into a bloody battle more than likely, but I'd be able to use my tech under adequate cover. Maybe that would be enough. We'd recover the princess. It would work. Somehow, it would work. Because it had to.

"It's reckless," I told Phantom Fangs.

"Reckless is what we do," Rodrick replied, taking an angry swing at the air with his right fist. "And we always come out on top."

"I can't believe I'm saying this, but Rodrick is right," Aerre agreed.

Caspian looked up at the moon. "Rodrick, use your moonlight to heal your wounds right now so you can re-charge again when the moon is aligned." Then he looked at each one of us. The moon was captured in his eyes, shining brightly. "Let's save our princess."

Claim the princess,
rule the world.

PHANTOM FANGS

THE LOST PRINCESS OF HOWLING SKY PROLOGUE

KESTRA PINGREE

BONUS SHORT STORY

BONUS SHORT STORY
PHANTOM FANGS

CHAPTER 1

CASPIAN

WITH A flick of my hand, I signaled my squad to get into position. Aerre and Rodrick moved ahead and out of sight. Their job was to perch in a couple of the giant trees making up this thicket. The height would be advantageous for them to watch unseen; they would also have an easy time sniping the maneaters if the situation called for it.

Todd and I dashed out from our cover of trees and bushes a moment later. Winter was almost over and green leaves were beginning to sprout on mostly bare branches, defying the frigid air for the promise of spring. We plowed through detritus before reaching the small clearing where the enemy's roader was parked. The vehicle was too big and bulky to go any farther, so the Paws Peak scouts were stuck on foot for the rest of their patrol, easy targets for Aerre and Rodrick. That worked out well for us.

I looked back to make sure I couldn't see any of the four towering black spires through the tree-branch canopy. I thought we'd be in trouble because of the lack of leaves, but the branches twisted together and choked out the sky with or without leaves. I didn't have anything to worry about. The roader was deep enough inside of this thicket there was no way Paws Peak could see us. We couldn't see them from in here either.

"Get to work," I said, keeping my voice low. "Let me know as soon as you plant those bugs and let's get out of here." Today wasn't about engaging maneaters in a fight. This was pure research. And recon.

"On it," Todd replied. He was busy at work, sticking ladybug-sized tech on the roader and some of the gear it carried in its short cargo bed.

The commsbud in my ear let off the tiniest hint of static before stabilizing as Aerre's voice came through. "Pay attention, Caspian. The maneaters are coming back around."

"Don't shoot unless you absolutely have to," I reminded.

"Heard you the first time," Rodrick said, joining in on the conversation relayed through our commsbuds.

I closed my eyes for a couple seconds, concentrating

as I looked inward to the pool of moonlight waiting undisturbed within me; I always pictured it in the base of my stomach, deep blue like a lake. I visualized a drop of water from above disrupting the still surface. It sent out a ripple of light, restoring the dormant energy to its true power as my body buzzed. When I opened my eyes again, a flare of light blue, almost like flames, sparked across my black skin. I sped forward with silent steps as my combat boots barely touched the ground, leaving Todd behind. I came to an immediate halt as soon as my enhanced eyesight zeroed in on the maneaters who were now deep within the thicket.

Crouching down to keep myself hidden, I focused the moonlight in my eyes, observing. I would be able to read into the scouts' tiniest movements like this without having to waste much of my moonlight reserves. Good breeding made me one of the most powerful werewolves in the world—though that wasn't saying much, considering how small the world had become. If the Paws Peak scouts headed back too soon, it was my job to distract them without giving us away, to keep them from their roader until Todd could finish his setup.

It didn't look like that would be a problem either. The Paws Peak scouts, three werewolves in total, were hyper-focused on the trivial gossip they were exchanging. I hadn't met many wereas in my life since females of my species were rare, even before adding war to the equation, but these careless maneaters and their constant jabbering reminded me of the old wereas back in Wolf Bridge who had nothing better to do than talk.

"I'm done," Todd commented, his voice warbling through the commsbud.

"Easiest damn mission we ever did," Rodrick replied and let out a hardy guffaw that made my commsbud screech and me flinch.

"Shut up, you oaf," Aerre growled. "The scouts aren't that far away."

"Yeah, and you see how fucking observant they are."

Rodrick did have a point though. The scouts were carrying on with their conversation, oblivious to the world around them.

"Regroup," I said. "And Aerre, don't call names. Rodrick isn't an oaf."

I tucked my remaining moonlight reserves deep into the recesses of my body; I pictured that still blue lake at the base of my stomach before I had messed with it. I needed to conserve what I had so it lasted until I could recharge on the next full moon.

"Okay, *Mom*. Rodrick isn't an oaf. He's an agitator spy and outsmarting all of us," Aerre growled again, causing the commsbud in my ear to crackle. It must have had a short. I didn't remember it being so grating on my ear before. I made a mental note to ask Todd about it once we got back to camp.

"Aerre," I warned, "enough."

I popped the commsbud out of my ear. It was almost as small as those bugs Todd just planted and looked like a polished gray pebble. I pressed its smooth metallic body lightly between the pads of my thumb and index finger and made my way back to camp. Todd beat me there and was already messing with the branches and camouflage tarp hiding our roader to unearth the keyboard for his pactputer.

After he pulled out his pactputer, a few-centimeters-thick rectangular computer small enough to hold in one hand, from his backpack and attached a keyboard, I approached him. "Think you could take a look at my commsbud sometime? I think it's shorting out."

Todd held his left hand open, palm up, as he typed away with his other hand. His skin was pale like he never saw the light of day—which wasn't true. He didn't tan. He only freckled. We were on opposite spectrums.

I gave him my commsbud and he pocketed it. Then he continued typing away and tapping the pactputer's touchscreen without missing a beat. Todd was the youngest of us, twenty years old, three years younger than me. He was inexperienced in combat, not to say he was incapable, but he was the weakest of us in that regard. His technical know-how more than made up for that, though. He was the reason why we were here, in a thicket outside of the wall surrounding Paws Peak, the last werewolf kingdom aside from Wolf Bridge. You'd think being the last we could have found some kind of common ground, but Paws Peak was full of maneaters and Wolf Bridge prided itself as shields. Paws Peak ate humans, we protected them. But that wasn't entirely accurate either.

"Get a reading on those bugs? They connect?" I asked.

"Yeah, but this isn't anything new. The scouts' roader isn't out of range of anything I've tested before. The real test for my tech field tweaks will be when they head back. If the bugs stay connected when they get inside the walls, I'll just have to figure out how to strengthen my field to reach out to foreign tech and I'll probably be able to hack into the spires and the entire Paws Peak system."

"Impressive."

Todd's pactputer was our central hub when it came to the technical parts of our missions. It held everything together. It connected our commsbuds, allowing us to communicate. It uploaded and synced information to our intelibands, somehow bulky and still slick metal bracelets with their own little touchscreens. We had them covered in rubber so they'd be less abrasive since we wore them so often. They were one of Todd's newer inventions and utilized actual holograms. The holograms themselves weren't interactive, but we could spin a 3D map using the touchscreen. We often ghosted through missions with the powerful information we could have at our disposal. It was thanks to Todd we earned the name *Phantom Fangs*.

Todd scratched at the black beanie on his head, revealing stray strands of his fire-red hair. He quickly tucked the strands back under the fabric when he noticed. He never acted like he cared about anything outside of his tech world, but I had been around him long enough to know he was self-conscious about how he looked. I had a theory about that. Redheaded werewolves like him didn't exist anymore. He was the last, and he was from a line of maneaters. Todd never talked about it because getting him to talk about anything other than tech was like pulling teeth, but I didn't think I was wrong.

Rustling brush and a string of heated retorts signaled Aerre and Rodrick's arrival back to camp. Those two never stopped. Rodrick was big and imposing with tattoos and white scars that stuck out against his brown skin, but that brawler look wasn't what got to Aerre, the blond pretty-boy type with skin that tanned easily in the sun. No one would have ever mistaken any of the four Phantom Fangs members to be related. My skin was almost as dark as coal. Basically, none of us looked anything alike.

Even when Aerre and Rodrick stopped verbally harassing each other, they continued with their scathing looks—meaning Aerre. Rodrick rarely took the bait. Aerre really needed to let this spy thing go.

Phantom Fangs was formed about two months ago. Aerre and Rodrick had plenty of time to get past their differences, but Aerre wouldn't try. He and Rodrick came from different backgrounds, from a different place, but they also had something major in common: neither of them were actual werewolves. They were tethered. Humans changed by a werewolf, by me. Thinking back on it made my stomach churn, but they chose *me*. They chose *this*. In that, they were exactly the same.

Our squad was good. Amazing even. We may have been new players in the Prime War, but we made our name infamous on our very first mission. We had been marked in history for as long as our history would last because we killed the last male vampire. We knew it was true when the vampires fell back, reluctant to get caught in any more squabbles. That wasn't how vampires played. They were running scared when they used to be big players in the Prime War.

The Prime War was timeless, probably as old as the beginning of this world: Prime. It all came back to werewolves, vampires, and humans. The cycle of killing between and among these three species was the world's history, and it almost resulted in its end when the Hellfire Strike happened. War was done a little more carefully now that the planet itself had suffered such grievous wounds from the Prime War. Tech was even banned for a time, leaving us somewhere between medieval and modern, but it didn't stop the war. However, I could see an end. I could also see the hazy beginnings of a world I wanted.

I was twenty-three, surrounded by war my entire life. Nothing new. But, the more I saw, the more I wished it would end, the more I wished the world could change. That was the start of the path that led me to form Phantom Fangs. All that was left was to have patience. I wanted peace and to rebuild a world that was broken almost beyond repair, but the time had to be right. The Prime War finally had to end. That or the entire world would finally end. But I never dwelt on the worst-case scenario. Giving up wasn't an option. I had a squad and an entire kingdom to protect. Already, I was on my way to accomplishing *something* because Phantom Fangs had influence despite my father's attempts to keep me out of politics.

Sometimes, I forgot I was, by blood, a Prince of Wolf Bridge.

"The scouts are heading back inside the walls already," Todd informed as he pressed a finger to his ear. He must have been listening to whatever audio his bugs were transmitting through his commsbud. "They're in their roader, moving fast. Signal's still strong."

Aerre found it in him to turn off his aggression for once. We all joined him in a neutral silence, waiting for Todd to divulge more information. He was staring at his screen, monitoring a tiny moving blip that consisted of the four bugs he planted. If they moved away from each other, they would become their own blips. Some of the screen had charted area, but once they entered the walls, the blip floated along a dark grid space.

"Still working?" I asked.

"I'm in," Todd confirmed. "I'll continue monitoring and recording their conversations while I work on my tech field. Maybe some of the stuff I bugged will get taken out of the roader and we'll have multiple intel feeds."

"It'll probably be a whole lot of nothing," Rodrick muttered and leaned against a thick oak trunk. "This will be thrilling."

"Interesting conversations would just be a bonus," I said. "Todd's goal is to hack into the spires."

Rodrick grunted. "Yeah, yeah. Research mission, all

about Todd, I know."

Aerre settled onto a rock on the opposite end of camp, as far away from Rodrick as he could get. He cradled his gun and began polishing it obsessively. He puffed a long strand of blond hair out of his face that had escaped the braids hugging the sides of his head. That was another thing Aerre and Rodrick had in common: long hair. Why couldn't they try to find something in common? I did it easily enough—even if the hair observation was stupid.

I grabbed a protein bar from the roader for a quick pick-me-up snack and settled down onto the grass. It wasn't as good as fresh meat, but this was all we had. Eventually, I worked my way onto my back. I closed my eyes and let my mind wander.

My squad was dysfunctional yet effective. I picked Aerre, Todd, and Rodrick for a reason. Because of their differences. Our differences.

There was a world I wanted to see. I didn't know the details yet, but they were slowly becoming clearer.

CHAPTER 2

RODRICK

*T*ODD'S LITTLE tech project was taking way too fucking long. I thought for sure we'd be out of this stupid thicket and on our way back through and down the mountains to Wolf Bridge within a few hours, but no. We wasted the entire day outside of an enemy kingdom's wall, and now it was hours into the night. Part of the day, I was allowed to hunt for our meals. It kept me from losing my damn mind at least. But it didn't solve my problem.

I was supposed to meet with Jobe tonight, outside of Wolf Bridge. That wasn't going to happen, obviously. We had already spent days outside of this wall, waiting for Paws Peak to send out a scout, or someone from inside, we could quietly ambush to test Todd's stupid bugs and tech field. Apparently, all this time wasted wasn't actually *wasted* because Todd's research-experiment-thing was working. It just wasn't working as fast as I wanted. He was glued to his pactputer, doing Gods knew what, working his techy magic to find some way into Paws Peak so Wolf Bridge would achieve "High Kingdom" status.

We'd see about that. This was the kind of information I needed to pass along to the rebels.

I zipped up my coat when a cold wind blew past. We didn't get to use a fire for our camp since the smoke, and maybe even the light, would have drawn Paws Peak's attention. It was a good thing werewolves and tethered alike could digest raw meat without a problem.

Todd was hunkered down inside of the roader, mostly obscuring himself and the light from his devices with the camouflage tarp. His teeth were chattering and his pale face looked blue—whether from the pactputer screen or cold, who knew—but he made no move to grab a damn coat. Caspian noticed as well and draped a blanket around Todd's shoulders. He didn't embellish it, no tucking in of the edges and swaddling Todd up like a kid or any shit like that. If he had, I would have had to call him out on finally transforming into a full-blown mother hen. His dark eyes flickered over to me like he knew exactly what I was thinking. I smirked in response and thoughtfully tugged at my short beard.

"How much longer?" I asked. Huh, turned out I was the kid here.

"As long as it takes," Caspian replied with the perfect I'm-apparently-the-only-adult-here tone. "We went to the trouble of doing this, so we're giving Todd as much time as he needs."

"Yeah, all right," I muttered.

Jobe would have to wait or leave and then try to meet with me again the next chance he got. There wasn't anything I could do about it. It was unfortunate I couldn't find a way to cure my boredom, though. Lying around and sleeping only worked so long before my body and mind rebelled, and they were in full-on rebellion mode.

I turned to a big oak tree and unsheathed my knife from my combat belt. I absentmindedly shaved away at the spongy green moss bulging from its bark at first. Then I started cutting deep into the trunk, chipping away at the wood. I wasn't really into defacing trees for no damn reason, but there was this restlessness itching its way just underneath my skin. Without a task to accomplish, I was reduced to this state of purposelessness until I could get back on task. I didn't like waiting, but I'd do it for my purpose, the greater good, the white against the black. Still, I was a better warrior than a spy, and I was better use as a spy than a dead man.

"You'll ruin your knife if you keep chipping away at it like that. It's not an axe, dipshit, and that trunk is thicker than you are." Aerre commented, the condescending tone of his voice was omnipresent. Also, he was *still* slaving away, polishing every damn one of our weapons he could get his anxious hands on. He didn't do well with sitting around either. No, it wasn't that. He didn't deal with being away from Wolf Bridge for an extended period of time. A couple days away and he started with these tics.

In most cases, I found it best to ignore Aerre. Getting caught in an endless loop of quips with him was just that: endless. But I didn't have anything better to do right now.

"I know you're just jealous," I said and flexed my right arm to show off my bicep. As far as muscle mass went, I beat everyone here. Ironically, that didn't make me the strongest. It made me strongest when moonlight wasn't involved, but when it was, the winner in physical strength went to Caspian. It sounded like a bad deal, but moonlight had its limits. Our hierarchy wasn't as unfair as it seemed at a glance—unless you factored in the part about me being tethered to the Phantom Prince.

"Why don't you tell us the real reason why you're cutting through that poor, defenseless tree?" Aerre suggested. "It's because you can't contact your agitator buddies out here, isn't it? How long have you been in contact with them? Ever since Caspian changed you into a tethered and let you join this team? How do you do it? Do you sneak out?"

Caspian let out a heavy sigh. "Not this again."

Aerre jabbed a finger in his direction. It was such a severe gesture I almost wondered if Caspian could feel it from across the camp. "*You* need to stop brushing this off like it's some kind of non-issue. Why do you act like you trust him? He's a monster, and you never should have made him part of this squad in the first place! He's an enemy of Wolf Bridge. He's agitator scum, from the same line of misled humans who almost burned the whole fucking world to ash!"

Whoa, he's really going for it tonight, I thought to myself.

And I was right. He got up from his seat on that damn rock he claimed and stormed over to me with clenched fists. That kind of aggression meant one thing to me. I sheathed my knife and readied my stance. As soon as he was within range, I punched him square in the jaw with deadly precision. He didn't see it coming and went down easy. Maybe I misread his body language. Maybe he wasn't coming over here for a round of fisticuffs at all. I should have known. He probably just wanted to yell and spit in my face, though it would have been more hilarious than anything since he would have had to get on his tiptoes to do it.

"Aerre," Caspian growled, "to me." His dark eyes lit up in that blazing blue glow that meant he was using moonlight and his rank as Aerre's maker in order to command absolute obedience.

Aerre rose from the ground the same way I would have imagined a corpse popping out of its grave. He stumbled over to Caspian before straightening out. His head was slightly bowed in submission and his eyes mirrored that intense blue in the eyes of his alpha—our alpha. Then Caspian turned his gaze on me. My muscles seized up the same instant. It was like my body was crumpling inside of itself or being forced to straighten after being crumpled. It was a painful sensation however I tried to spin it.

"Explain yourself," he ordered.

"Thought he was going to swing at me. Made the first move," I replied. My tongue was heavy and my words clipped.

"Fine." The blue in Caspian's eyes subsided, leaving only the dark brown of his natural eye color behind.

My lungs begged for air and I sucked in a huge breath of cold. It froze my insides and made me cough.

"I don't want you two anywhere near each other for the rest of the night," Caspian said.

That was fine with me. I turned my back on my fucking squad and went back to dulling the blade of my knife against that thick-ass oak.

Amazingly, I didn't hate Aerre, but I sure as hell didn't understand him. It wasn't like he belonged to this *werewolf* squad any more than I did. If his head was screwed on straight, he would have been part of the rebels too. But he chose to side with werewolves. He chose black, I chose white, and that was all there was to it.

CHAPTER 3

AERRE

I GINGERLY rubbed my jaw and winced as I sat back on the rock that was getting on very bad terms with my ass. Rodrick really went for it. That was the first time he actually laid a hand on me—or a fist in this case. Usually, he shot me his annoying grins or flat-out ignored me despite everything I did to try to rile him up and prove my point. All in all, I considered the punch an accomplishment. I figured it was one step closer to revealing the agitator's true colors. He took the first swing. *He* did it. There was a reason I didn't start any fist fights with the brute, and those reasons didn't include the fact that the tattooed and scarred tethered was a boulder in the form of a man.

My jaw had a welt on it, though.

"Here. It'll help the swelling."

I looked over my shoulder to see Caspian holding one of our water flasks. It was plenty cold out here already, but the object called out to me, and I took it. The instant the nearly freezing metal hit my jaw, I winced again. Then relief slowly washed through my system as I steeled myself to endure the discomfort—after wrapping the flask up in my scarf to make the cold less intense. When I looked over my shoulder again, Caspian was still standing there.

"Go away," I said.

He looked down at me, hands hidden in the pockets of his coat. "A squad, a team, doesn't work unless we trust each other."

I rolled my eyes. I liked it better when Caspian was the annoying werewolf kid trying to become my "best friend." He didn't give lectures back then. Lectures didn't suit him.

I glanced at the misfits in our "team." There was Rodrick, who wasn't really part of this team because he was an agitator. Once an agitator, always an agitator. There was Todd with his head buried so deep in tech he never came up for air. There was Caspian, the Phantom Prince, basically shunned by his own species when it came to his birthright. Then, of course, there was me, tethered and hater of werewolves, serving werewolves more than willingly, serving Caspian. We were a bad mix in terms of camaraderie, but when it came to getting things done, we were the best of the best. That was the thing that kept this team together. We all had a goal here, and that goal included acing our missions. For now. But I was determined to keep it that way.

"We seem to be doing just fine," I commented. Then I lowered my voice to make sure only Caspian would hear my next words. "And we'll continue to do just fine because that's what keeps my mother and sister safe. I'll *make* you see the problem with Rodrick soon enough."

"I'm sitting," Caspian replied. I couldn't figure out why he said it. It was almost like he was asking if that was okay with me, but he also wasn't asking. He plopped right down on the grass next to my rock.

"You know I'm indebted to you for everything you did," I said quietly. "I won't sabotage Phantom Fangs. My goal is to keep it running." I gritted my teeth. "So yeah, maybe I've been a little out of line, but it's hard being away from Wolf Bridge for this long. It wouldn't be if *he* was dead."

"I know," Caspian murmured, "but Zecke hasn't gone near your sister since then. It's been years. The king wasn't pleased. I know that's not enough, but I truly don't believe Zecke will try anything again. King Philip ve

Casst's words tend to be taken seriously."

"But he's still breathing. I know you're not that naive and you're just trying to make me feel better, but you, Prince Caspian ve Casst, know better than that."

"You're right. I'm sorry. I should have put the mongrel down when I had the chance."

"You still could. You'd be pardoned. The king must put one of his sons, even the Phantom Prince, above a lowly guard, but we're all too comfortable with what's familiar. That's why Phantom Fangs will never be anything but the king's dark horse."

Caspian went silent. He stared at the grass in front of him for a full minute before standing up. He clapped me on the shoulder. "I think it's about time to call it a night."

I watched his back as he walked away. It was dark as dark out here, but I managed to see everything I needed to in the form of their basic shapes. If I really needed to see, I could delve into my moonlight reserves, but turning in for the night was probably the best thing to do right now.

I never used the word "friend" when referring to Caspian. I didn't know what Caspian was to me. Was he a friend, my alpha, my prince? I did know I trusted him as much as I could bring myself to trust anyone outside of my mother and sister. Maybe I even trusted him as much because I knew him before this. I knew him when he was this five-year-old cub sneaking out of the castle and following me around at seven years old because he was so determined to become my "best friend." He was unlike any werewolf I had ever known, but I did my best to ignore him since werewolves and humans couldn't be friends. Since werewolves couldn't be trusted. I was convinced Prince Caspian ve Casst was trying to lead me into some kind of trap. It didn't help that Howling Sky went up in flames not long before. But he wasn't. He was just being Caspian. At one point, I recognized that, and we did become friends, hidden friends since no one would have approved.

Maybe I was starting to see werewolves differently, as more than terrifying masters I would be wise not to anger. I saw Caspian differently after a while. Because he treated me differently. Then I was reminded why werewolves couldn't be trusted at the age of seventeen. I was reminded of the kind of beasts they were when *that* bastard did the unspeakable.

My sister was always a beauty, but she only grew more beautiful as she became a woman. Zecke, a guard stationed in the Human Zone, or the politically correct Tech Off Zone, of Wolf Bridge had his eye on my sister for some time. He wasn't allowed to touch her, but he wanted to. Humans, werewolves, and vampires were all different species that couldn't interbreed. There were no human-werewolf hybrids or anything like that, but that didn't mean sex wasn't apparently pleasurable between the different species. We looked similar enough, were built similar enough, that there were many cases like my sister's.

Wolf Bridge claimed to be shields as of thirteen years ago. It would have been noble, perhaps, but they were never *maneaters* to begin with. Maneaters did whatever they wanted to their humans because they were meat. If they wanted to rape their food and then eat it, they did. Zecke didn't eat my sister, but he did rape her. He hurt her and scarred her forever.

I wanted him dead. I lost it when I found out what happened right along with Caspian. I would have gotten my whole family killed trying to kill Zecke if Caspian hadn't been there. Caspian took the diplomatic approach, spoke with the king, and managed to get Zecke exiled from the Tech Off Zone. I realized Caspian saved our lives. I realized humans weren't equal to werewolves even among shields, and Caspian did the only thing he knew how to protect us from Zecke and myself. But it did nothing to ease the hatred festering inside of me. And yet, I couldn't kill Zecke or my mother and sister would pay the price. So I bowed down to the werewolves. I became their dog, Caspian's tethered, to keep my family okay.

I wished I could do more, but being a part of Phantom Fangs and watching over them at night to make sure Zecke never returned was the extent of my capabilities. I couldn't truly save them because I didn't have that kind of power, and I never would as an individual. But Caspian did, or he would. I risked everything on that, on the belief I had in a werewolf who might be my "friend."

CHAPTER 4

TODD

CREATING MY own remote access point into any of the four spires was proving to be more difficult than I had anticipated since no one in this world used a universal tech field. Every piece of tech from a different area was built on the same principles, but anything wireless was all floating on different wavelengths. I liked a challenge, but I was getting tired, frustrated tired. I had the suicidal notion of storming into Paws Peak and knocking on a spire door so I could tap into their system locally. The technical side of hacking their system would be easy then, but dangerous physically. No, I needed to improve my tech field. I could beat this challenge, and it would give us the tactical advantage. Not that I cared about that. I only wanted to improve my tech.

I rubbed my eyes with the back of my hand, a bad idea. My eyelids felt like sandpaper. I was tired. And jumpy. I nearly jumped out of my skin when the driver door of the roader I was camped in swung open.

"Time to give it a rest, don't you think?" Caspian asked as he rested against the open door.

"I'm almost done," I muttered. I glued my eyes back onto my pactputer's screen and searched through my lines of code to see what I was missing.

"You'll do better after you've had some sleep."

Maybe he was right. "Fine. I recorded a bunch of chatter by the way."

"You did? Why didn't you say anything? I thought the bugs were sitting quietly on their parked roader. Were they taken to different areas inside of the city?"

"Yes."

"Should have had Aerre and Rodrick actively listening in on that stuff. It would have given those two nutcases something to do."

"I didn't think about that. That would have been an efficient use of time…"

Caspian shook his head and had this sort of humorous smile on his face. At least, I thought it was meant to be humorous. I wasn't good at reading into someone's body language. "Todd, you're the smartest guy I know, but you can be unbelievably dense sometimes."

"I've been letting the recordings play as background noise through my commsbud while I work," I said, feeling attacked "Most of it is just senseless chatter. Rodrick and Aerre would have gotten bored anyway."

"That wasn't a jab or a threat, Todd. No need to get defensive. But we are a *team*. I think you forget that sometimes. It's okay to rely on us once in a while…"

Caspian was still talking. I was staring at his mouth as if that would help me read his words while simultaneously tuning him out. I had just finished telling him about how there was nothing interesting in the chatter I was picking up, but one line suddenly became very interesting. I turned to my pactputer and singled out a specific feed, the one where I heard the words "the Lost Princess of Howling Sky."

"Shut up," I said, interrupting Caspian's monologue.

He raised a dark eyebrow at me, but he listened. I ripped out the commsbud from my ear and turned up the sound on my pactputer. The thin slits on its sides were homes for decent speakers.

"Think King George lost his mind?" a male's voice came through. "Sounds far-fetched."

"He's the fucking king of Paws Peak, dumbass. He hasn't lost his mind. You remember the story as well as I do. Everyone does," another male replied. "And now we know the Lost Princess survived."

"Aerre, Rodrick, get your asses over here!" Caspian yelled.

One more male chimed into the conversation being played through my pactputer as Aerre and Rodrick joined us at the roader. "Yeah, but to think she's been living with that witch for the last, what, eighteen years? That's crazy. The Witch Woods are the only thing untouched in the badlands. It's unnatural. I think I liked it better when the Lost Princess was just a legend."

"Are you insane? This changes everything. A werea, *the* werea, eighteen years old, perfect for mating, is alive. She's perfect for Prince Charles. Paws Peak has won the war."

"I don't see how a single werea of mating age changes everything."

"Gods, why do I have to spell out every single fucking thing? She changes everything because she's the Moonlight Child blessed by Lureine. Did you forget that?"

"But she's an individual, not an army. And a *werea*."

"What he said."

"That *werea*, if the legends are true, which they must fucking be, is like the embodiment of moonlight. Who knows what kind of power she has?"

"Still sounds weird to me."

"Fuck what you think. We set out for the badlands

and those damn Witch Woods on the last day of winter. We need to be there bright and early on the first day of spring to pick up our new princess."

"Prince Charles and King George don't want to do it themselves?"

"Well, there's still the chance of it not panning out, isn't there, my little dummies? Of course the fucking king and his favorite son aren't going!"

Everything went silent after that explosive ending to what had to be the craziest conversation I had been privy to in my entire life. The Lost Princess was real? The witch herself contacted the King of Paws Peak? How? Did she use tech? I had so many questions and no answers to any of them.

"Is this for real?" Aerre was the one who broke the silence.

"There's only one way to find out," Rodrick replied.

"Do you know what this means?" Caspian asked.

"Paws Peak will probably become the High Kingdom and rule the world?" Rodrick said with a tone that had to mean sarcasm.

Caspian brushed his response off. "We have to get the princess first."

"What if it's not real?" Aerre asked. "What if it's a trap?"

"We'll have to risk it. If it is real, if *she* is real, this will be the most important thing Phantom Fangs ever does."

Aerre bared his teeth and growled. "The most important thing we can do is throw a werea at a werewolf's feet and force her to become a breeder?"

Caspian frowned.

"You know that's what would happen. Fighting for that, racing to get this girl just so she can live as a piece of property for the rest of her life doesn't sound like you."

"That's not my goal," Caspian defended. "We have to get her first and bring her back to Wolf Bridge, where we can protect her. That's our territory. And you're wrong, Aerre. King Philip won't act rashly. He'll do his best to win her over, yes, but it won't come down to force. He'll want her on his side because *she* wants to be there."

"Yeah, because King Philip is a rat."

I could tell they'd be arguing like this for a while, so I tuned it out. All of it. I tried to get back to modifying my tech field. But I soon found out I couldn't ignore it. I couldn't ignore the Lost Princess. I didn't want to think about things outside of tech. I didn't know how to relate to things that were alive. I wasn't sure I related to anything, but I could understand tech. I didn't understand much of anything else.

But the Lost Princess of Howling Sky held my attention. I knew the legend as well as anyone else. It was impossible not to when Howling Sky was the High Kingdom, literally on top of the world, during a time when tech was practically outlawed worldwide because of the Hellfire Strike. They were physically the most powerful werewolves in existence and had a very special child almost eighteen years ago—eighteen on the first day of spring—just to be blown to hell by vampires who hadn't completely shunned tech. If the Moonlight Child survived that attack, she must have been like a god, because she was a newborn cub when it happened. I didn't believe in any gods. I didn't believe in anything that couldn't be explained with science because everything could be, including a werewolf's ability to absorb moonlight during a full moon in order to store that energy for later use. It wasn't magic.

If the rumors were true and the Lost Princess was the Moonlight Child full of untapped power, the Prime War was going to come back in full force. Everyone would want her for one reason or another. Things would get uglier. Many more would die. The Lost Princess would probably put an end to the world once and for all.

I wondered if I hated her for that.

CHAPTER 5

SORISSA

*M*Y POWERFUL black paws padded against the forest floor, but the impact hardly registered. This kind of speed, with no resistance, was like skating on the lake when it was frozen over—except it was much faster, with even more force behind it. This was something I could only achieve in my moonlight form, and I got faster each time I tried it. I was so pleased with my progress I wanted to throw back my head and howl to announce an early victory. However, I didn't give in to the urge because I needed to focus.

Today, I would escape.

I could see the light, the cracks between the thinning trees showing a hint of the world outside of the woods. This time, I'd beat Babaga. This time, I'd be fast enough.

I was inches away from the light, the door to my freedom, when the woods spun around me. My sensitive ears popped and everything went black for an instant before it all came rushing back and I skidded to a dirt-spraying stop as I dug in my claws. The trees were bigger here. The light was gone. I was back in the center of the woods all within the span of a few stomach-churning seconds. I growled in frustration. Then I threw back my head to howl, not in victory, but in a challenge. Babaga twisted into the space in front of me with the same warp magic she used to transport me here.

I let go of my moonlight form in shimmering sparks of blues and shifted back. My midnight-black fur receded, leaving mostly the long curly hair cascading down from my head to keep me warm against the cold. I stood straight on two legs while the witch standing before me was hunched over. It was freezing in this form, my naked skin broke out in goosebumps, and my breasts ached a little, but I didn't care. I stomped up to the witch so there was only a small space between us. I looked down at her, feeling a false sense of superiority for simply being taller.

"If you faced me fairly, I would have won by now," I challenged.

"Our strength isn't of the same make, my sweet Sorissa, and these woods belong to me," she replied.

"I just want to go outside, Babaga."

"We've been over this. Over it and over it again."

"But there's a world out there! Isn't there? You've told me just enough to get me curious, you've made me read their fairytales, so when do I get to *see* it? If you didn't want me to try this so often, you shouldn't have fed my curiosity. I don't want to leave forever. This is my home. You're my home. You know that, right? You could make it my eighteenth birthday present. It's only a week away."

Babaga took off her shawl and wrapped it around my shivering frame. Then she did something unexpected. She hugged me. Babaga wasn't affectionate. She had hugged me before, but those were rare occasions.

"Babaga?" I asked as I wrapped my arms around her in return. I thought this whole thing, trying to leave and stopping me from leaving, had become a game between us, like Babaga would honor my request if I finally bested her, but now I wasn't so sure. Was she really that worried about me leaving the woods?

"One day, you might best me, but today isn't that day," she said and pushed me away.

Any doubts I had floated away like they never existed. I just tired her out today. That meant I was getting closer. Maybe she'd even give me that birthday present.

"It's time for supper," Babaga announced. "Come home and get dressed so you don't catch pneumonia."

"Coming."

I looked at the trees surrounding me, from every angle, a complete rotation, to see if I could find another crack of light from in between the trunks and branches. Nothing. I missed that opportunity. It didn't matter. I would get out of these woods one day, because there was a world waiting for me. I could feel it on the breath of the wind, hear it in its haunting howls.

But I didn't know just how much would change.

I didn't know how broken the world outside was. I didn't know my own legend. I didn't know about the four werewolves in my future or how my love for them would change everything.

PRIME
WORLD GUIDE

Prime: the world.

> *The Prime War:* the world war that has existed since the beginning of time.

Gods

> *Lureine:* the werewolf god.
>
> *Yessma:* the vampire goddess.
>
> *Cor:* the human god.

The three species

Werewolves

> *Base form:* a werewolf's human-like body.
>
> *Moonlight form:* a werewolf's wolf-like body.
>
> *Wereas:* female werewolves.
>
> *Cubs:* werewolf children.
>
> *The Mate Claim:* the bind that seals a werea to a werewolf.
>
> *Maneaters:* werewolves who feed on humans.
>
> *Shields:* werewolves who protect humans.

Vampires

> *Vampyres:* male vampires.

Scamps: vampire children.

Bloodsuckers: a derogatory term used by all other species.

Humans

Rebels: humans who still fight.

> *Agitators:* a derogatory term for rebels used by shields and complacents.

Complacents: a derogatory term used by rebels for humans who don't fight.

Tethered: humans turned werewolf.

Thralls: humans turned vampire.

Meat: a derogatory term used by maneaters.

Blood: a derogatory term used by vampires.

Glory Valley: the last human kingdom, responsible for the Hellfire Strike, and consequently destroyed by the kingdoms that remained.

The Hellfire Strike: an attack launched by Glory Valley that used planet-destroying tech. It defaced and changed Prime forever.

Goodlands: the small amount of land left untouched by the Hellfire Strike.

Badlands: the large amount of land destroyed by the Hellfire Strike.

The Tech Ban: worldwide prohibition of tech after the devastation caused by the Hellfire Strike.

The Reintroduction of Tech: tech comes back after a time, starting over from the remains of old tech and from scratch.

The High Kingdom: the kingdom that "rules the world."

> **The High King:** the king of kings.
>
> **The High Queen:** the queen of queens.
>
> **Howling Sky:** the once most-powerful werewolf kingdom and the High Kingdom that ruled after the Hellfire Strike.
>
>> **The Fall of Howling Sky:** when Howling Sky was destroyed by Crimson Caves.
>>
>> **The Moonlight Child/the Lost Princess of Howling Sky:** a werea cub blessed and chosen by Lureine. She was presumed lost after the Fall of Howling Sky.

The standing powers

> **Paws Peak:** a werewolf kingdom that was always in competition with Howling Sky.
>
> **Wolf Bridge:** a werewolf kingdom that has stayed mostly neutral in terms of werewolf politics.

Crimson Caves: the last vampire kingdom and the one responsible for the Fall of Howling Sky.

Freedom: the home of the surviving descendants of Glory Valley, and the base of operations for the rebels.

Tech: technology.

The Heart: the source of power for all of Wolf Bridge.

Roaders: werewolf-made off-road vehicles intended for rough terrain.

Gliders: vampire-made vehicles, sleek and powerful.

Pactputers: portable computers.

Tech fields: hotspots that allow communications with the tech inside.

Intelibands: intelligence bands, portable intelligence devices.

Commsbuds: communications buds, hands-free communicators.

Portacomms: portable communicators.

Moonlight: the substance that gives werewolves their power, but it can typically only be absorbed on a full moon.

Lunalite: a mineral that amplifies moonlight and is found only at the bottom of Lake Luminous.

Lightning stones: stones that store and release electricity.

Suffress Mushrooms: mushrooms that can be used as an inhibitor of the mind and senses. Scentless and tasteless. Poisonous if ingested.

Hardskull Cattle: big herd animals with skulls as hard as metal. The bulls are very aggressive and have a six-foot-long horn on their heads.

Garstraude: a werewolf hero from old fairytales, wielder of a hardskull-horn sword and defender of the weak.

Witches: rare beings born with unexplainable power.

Witch Woods: a forest well inside of the badlands, but it is untouched.

> **_The Witch of Witch Woods:_** the only known witch left. She will grant you anything should you navigate her woods and give up what you value most.

Phantom Fangs: a secretive squad of four unconventional werewolves stationed in Wolf Bridge, responsible for killing the last vampyre.

Find out what happens next in *Saving the Werewolves*.

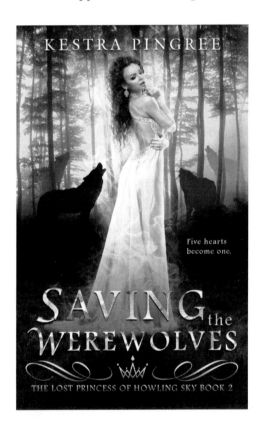

BOOKS BY KESTRA PINGREE

Marked by the Moon

Her True Wolf

Her Brave Wolf

Her Fierce Wolf

Her Wild Wolf

Her Noble Owl

Her Bad Cat

The Lost Princess of Howling Sky

Phantom Fangs

Taken by Werewolves

Saving the Werewolves

Queen of Werewolves

The Holiday Shifter Mates

Halloween Werewolf

Christmas Polar Bear

Valentine's Day Tigers

These Immortal Vows

Demon Snare

Angel Asylum

Desire

Guardian

On the Precipice

The Soul Seer Saga
The Wandering Empath
The Lonely King
The Lost Souls
The Beautifully Cursed
The Lunar Dancer

Novels
Blind to Love

NEWSLETTER

Never miss a new release by signing up for Kestra's newsletter.

kestrapingree.com/subscribe

MESSAGE FROM THE AUTHOR

Thank you for reading *Taken by Werewolves*.

If you enjoyed the ride, please consider leaving a review. Tell your friends too. If you're anything like me, you're already shouting your favorite stories from the rooftops. I commend you.

Your support is what allows me, and so many wonderful authors, to write these stories for you, so thank you.

From the bottom of my heart, thank you.

ABOUT THE AUTHOR

Kestra Pingree is a creative who doesn't know how to stop. They are first and foremost a writer and storyteller with an endless library of books in their head just waiting to be typed. They are also an artist and animator, as well as a singer, songwriter, and voice actor. One day they swear they're going to make their own video game, too.

If it involves creating, they are there.

They can also be seen cuddling their cat, reading, or playing video games.

kestrapingree.com

Made in United States
North Haven, CT
29 August 2023